What others are saying...

"In *His Love Revealed*, author Cynthia Herron welcomes readers back to Ruby, Missouri and pens a happily ever after that's a long time coming ... and well worth the wait. Ida Mae and Chuck's love story shows readers the challenges of falling in love with your best friend and how we can often misinterpret today's events through the lens of who we were years ago. Through it all, Herron never wavers in reminding readers how faith provides us with true hope."
~ **Beth K. Vogt,** *award-winning author of the Thatcher Sister Series*

"A delightful trip to the Ozarks. With **His Love Revealed**, Cynthia Herron has created a lovely Ozarks town where a plucky heroine named Ida Mae embarks on a faith-filled journey of the heart. Herron's lush descriptions bring Ida Mae's world to life in vivid color. The love story between Ida Mae and Chuck was charming and had me rooting for their happily ever after. I thoroughly enjoyed it."

~ **Belle Calhoune,** *Publisher's Weekly best-selling author of Her Alaskan Cowboy*

His Love Revealed

The Welcome to Ruby Series

Her Hope Discovered Book One
His Love Revealed Book Two

His Love Revealed

The Welcome to Ruby Series

By

Cynthia Herron

His Love Revealed
Published by Mountain Brook Ink
White Salmon, WA U.S.A.

The website addresses shown in this book are not intended in any way to be or imply an endorsement on the part of Mountain Brook Ink, nor do we vouch for their content.

This story is a work of fiction. All characters and events are the product of the author's imagination. Any resemblance to any person, living or dead, is coincidental.

Scripture quotations are taken from the King James Version of the Bible. Public domain.
ISBN 978-1-943959-91-4

The Team: Miralee Ferrell, Alyssa Roat, Cindy Jackson
Cover Design: Indie Cover Design, Lynnette Bonner Designer

The Author is represented by and this book is published in association with the literary agency of WordServe Literary Group., Ltd, www.wordserveliterary.com.

Mountain Brook Ink is an inspirational publisher offering fiction you can believe in.
Printed in the United States of America

Dedication

For Mama and Daddy, the stewards of my heart.

"For our light affliction, which is but for a moment, worketh for us a far more exceeding and eternal weight of glory; While we look not at the things which are seen, but at the things which are not seen: for the things which are seen are temporal; but the things which are not seen are eternal."

2 Corinthians 4:17-18 (KJV)

Acknowledgments

Just like earthly seasons, from time to time, each of us encounters metaphorical change that correlates with man's calendar. Some seasons burst with color and promise. Other seasons cloud perspective and skew hidden blessings. As I wrote *His Love Revealed*, I experienced some of both.

My deepest gratitude goes to my Heavenly Father who redeemed something good from the original mishmash of words on pages. God, you took my raw, unvarnished ramblings and crafted a worthy, powerful story.

Thank you, beloved family, for your patience and understanding as I camped out in my office for days on end pounding the keyboard when words wouldn't wait. Your belief in me is unmatched.

To my prayer warriors Julia, Wanda, and Vickie— your intercession centered me and made me press forward. Thank you for your faithfulness.

Heartfelt appreciation to my agent Sarah Freese and to the WordServe Literary team. Your encouragement and discernment are a blessing.

A huge thank you to my editors Miralee Ferrell and Anna Zogg who nudged me past my comfort zone. Thanks for shepherding this project and enabling me to bring it to fruition. In addition, to the MBI team, I so appreciate your wisdom and knowledge as we continue this journey together.

As always, there are many others who cheered me on

and supported me from behind the scenes as I wrote this story. I'm forever grateful for your wisdom, guidance, and perspective.

And to you, dear reader, *thank you*. Breathing life into this small Ozarks town and her vast array of quirky, lovable characters is a privilege and a delight. I love what I do, and I'm humbled by your genuine interest in the series that holds my heartstrings. I look forward to bringing you my next story from the beloved community where no one is a stranger.

Chapter One

September in the Missouri Ozarks...

It's the time of year when earth yawns and new colors emerge, replacing summer greens and once-vibrant blossoms. Though the metamorphosis is subtle, change tiptoes upon the horizon as leaves grow restless and weary with the shifting season. Fall is on her way.

Ida Mae scrutinized the menu. What to keep? What to replace? The sheer dilemma sparked myriad emotions. If life had treated her differently, the decision would be a no-brainer. Out with the old, in with the new. The trouble with that? Old had grown comfortable. Expected. Easy. *Risk-free.* But...tiresome with room for improvement. The Come and Get It Diner needed a revamp. Truth be told, so did she. At almost forty, Ida Mae recognized stagnation when she saw it, and the inevitable almost overwhelmed her. How was she supposed to think? The sad songs the radio DJ insisted on playing tonight only fueled her pity party.

One right after another. Woeful ballads referencing love, loss, heartache, and pain. The words and melodies could demotivate even the cheeriest Pollyanna. Finally, the gloomy chorus ended, and a soothing, female voice coaxed listeners to shift gears, take charge, and follow their dreams.

"I made a mistake, but it didn't define me," the voice

continued. "Maybe you know what I'm talking about. Maybe you've been there. All of us have things that kick us to the curb, tie us down, and threaten to smother us. Well, tonight, my friend, I'm here to tell you that's your yesterday, not your forever. Past blunders don't predict future successes. For a moment, think about this. What have you allowed to suck you dry and steal your oxygen? What do you need to let go of in order to move forward? What are you willing to do about it? Catch your breath. I'll wait."

Ida Mae's skin prickled. Her spine tingled. Had the radio announcer read her thoughts? The dubbed-in cry of a seagull mingled with ocean waves crashing upon the shore in the perfectly timed call for self-reflection.

Thirty seconds later, her tone soft and compassionate, the DJ emphasized her point. "It's time. Time to rise up and resuscitate new dreams. Time to step out of your forest and move toward higher, brighter things. I believe in you. Will you do it?" More ocean waves followed the announcer's heartfelt entreaty. Then, her trademark sign-off. "This is Simply Serena. Always your cheerleader. Forever your friend."

Piano music soared in the background, blending with the seashore sound effects, until it reached a moving crescendo and seamlessly merged with the cued advertisement for a prominent greeting card chain. From there, the mood evolved as the next thirty second spot featured an adoption and genetic testing service. "When you want to know more, we're here for you…"

The blood rushed to Ida Mae's toes and the room spun. Blessedly, she remained upright in the booth. Why that commercial? What were the odds?

She forced herself to take a deep breath. Then, she exhaled. In, out. In, out. Ida Mae repeated the exercise a few times until her nerves calmed. Gradually, her equilibrium returned to normal.

She slapped down the menu. Picked it up again. Melancholy, raw and peculiar, snuggled up beside her, yet she refused to give it ownership. *Get hold of yourself, honey. It's a menu, not a Monet. Change never hurt anyone. It's time. You can do this.* She knew she could. After all, she'd faced harder decisions. She chewed on that truth and washed it down with a swig of tepid soda pop. There. Better already.

Pen poised, she started with the crowd-pleasers. For instance, the difference between Mack's Monster Meatloaf and Miss Sugar's Pucker-Up-Buttercup Gooseberry Pie was about five hundred calories and four dollars and ninety-eight cents. The entrée boasted a savory slab of the world's best meatloaf flanked by a creamy mound of mashed potatoes and gravy, garden green beans seasoned with salt pork and onion, and two light-as-a-feather, melt-in-your-mouth angel biscuits brushed with homemade butter. The dessert, on the other hand—Miss Sugar's gooseberry pie—dropped you at heaven's portals and let you linger a while. Both selections had their merits. Both warmed bellies and coaxed a grin. Ida Mae marked them as keepers.

Down the menu she went, crossing off items that had worn out their welcome and circling those that pleased patrons' palates. The task seemed silly, but the black X's noted progress.

"Let me guess."

Ida Mae jumped. Hadn't Chuck left an hour ago?

He slid into the seat across from her, the booth barely accommodating his tall, strapping frame. "Sorry to startle you. Tic-Tac-Toe?"

"I wish, but no." Her heart eased back into normal rhythm. Well, almost. The guy still had an uncanny knack for tugging her heartstrings. She'd reconciled the fact that anything more than friendship was a fantasy, but that didn't make it easy. She'd loved Charles—"Chuck"—Farrow since they were kids, and most likely, that would never change. Unfortunately, he didn't return the sentiment. If he had, they'd be married by now...with a passel of kids and a two-story house with a white picket fence. Maybe a dog or two.

"Art therapy then?"

"Nope."

"Hey, I've got it!" He snapped his fingers. "Reordering the menu. Shifting entrées around, right?" His voice resonated enthusiasm. For the past year, he'd suggested that Ida Mae update the menu. Give it a revamp.

"You could say that. I'm eliminating some items and adding others. I want to change a few things before sending the final copy to the printer."

"Oh. Mind if I have a look?"

"Be my guest." She scooted the pink and green laminated menu across the table and watched his eyes scan the X's.

"Heddy's Hog Jowl. Fiona's Frito Pie. Dab o' Dander's Deer Steak. Hmm..." Chuck rubbed his chin, as he ticked off a couple more. "*Whoa.* This." He pointed to Chuck's Very Cherry Cheesecake. "Say it isn't so. You're *not* crossing off my beloved creation? As the Come and Get It's top chef, I cry 'mutiny!'"

"You're my only chef…er…cook, and I say phooey." An unladylike snort rose up within her. How did he do it? Even on her low day, he still had the ability to tickle her funny bone. Abandoned at ten by a no-account daddy, it was anyone's guess how Chuck Farrow grew into such a good-natured ham. A mighty attractive one, at that. Not only a comedian and easy on the eyes, add smart, sensitive, hard-working, and honorable too. Why, oh why, did he have to possess the one trait she couldn't abide? Commitment-shy. It grated on her. "You said we needed to think cutting-edge. Well, I'm thinking and I'm cutting."

Green eyes sparkled beneath sandy-colored hair—thick, unruly shocks of it. The tiny scar above his left cheek—the one from a decades' old playground mishap—shifted slightly as his expression brightened. Within seconds, the corners of his mouth lifted, expanding the grin into a full-fledged smile. Never mind the bib apron, grease-stained and a little ragged around the edges. Chuck Farrow wore unkempt well. Always had.

"Why today, may I ask?"

It shouldn't take a load of bricks to fall on the guy's head. It wasn't every day a girl stared thirty-nine in the face with only a diner—albeit a real fine one—to show for it.

"Why not today? I've done the same thing here, the same way, for ten years. You've said so plenty of times." September's chill wafted through an opened window adding a poignant pause to the moment. Scents of stale, musty earth and burning leaves drew Ida Mae to another time, another place, but she tamped down those memories. Nine-thirty and bone-tired, all she wanted now was a bubble bath and bed.

"Aw, girl. I know what you need." Chuck reached over and tapped her hand. "Come with me."

"Come with you where? I've been here fourteen hours." Ida Mae pointed to the pink pig wall clock. "Are you nuts?"

"No, ma'am." He unfolded himself from the booth and stood, offering his hand. "It'll only take a minute."

"Now, stand up and close your eyes."

"Whatever for?"

For the love of Pete, Ida Mae Hoscutt could certainly try a man's patience. "It's a secret. Just do it, okay?"

She heaved a sigh, blonde tendrils swaying in the wake of it. "Look, it's been a long day. I'm in no mood for secrets or charades."

"Come on, Ida Mae. It's not like you to be such a grouch. Besides, the diner's closed the next two days. You can nap after church tomorrow, and all day on Monday, if you want. Please?"

"Oh, forevermore." Still, she stood and closed her pretty blue eyes.

"Okay, keep 'em closed 'til I say when. Here—hold on to me." He rather liked that part. As her employee, he didn't dare cross the line. As her friend and someone who wished it were more, he longed to hold her hand a tad longer. Not the time or place for that now. Maybe one day. A guy could dream. Wait. It was more than a dream. Wasn't that why he hatched this hairbrained plan for today to begin with—to kickstart a new beginning? Certainly, he'd never tried this before. But this time, this year, was different.

He and Ida Mae weren't getting any younger. Might

as well do something completely out of character. Something fun and crazy to start the ball rolling. Slowly, Chuck led Ida Mae to a table for four in the middle of the diner. "Stay put. Don't open your eyes yet."

"Why on earth not?"

Uh-oh. Her voice had an edge to it. He recognized that tone. Better work fast. "Trust me, all right?"

He turned and gave a thumbs-up signal to Horace Sapp, county deputy and beloved local, and through the back door of the diner, the giant fellow lumbered...with half the town of Ruby, Missouri trailing in after him. What a sight to behold!

Everyone gathered close, forming a circle around Ida Mae as Miss Sugar Perkins, party planner extraordinaire, wheeled in a cart filled with sheet cakes and paper plates.

"What's going on? I hear mischief."

"No worries. You can open your eyes now." Before he joined the others in a rousing rendition of "Happy Birthday," he couldn't help but state the obvious. "Admit it. You thought no one remembered. And since this is the first time I've ever thrown you a surprise party, I hoped you wouldn't figure out my secret."

Chapter Two

Oh. My. Word.

Tears pooled in Ida Mae's eyes and dampened her lashes. Rarely at a loss for words, she stood silent for a moment. How had they pulled this off? And this was Chuck's idea? The love and admiration in her friends' faces tugged her heart and tied it in knots. Loud and a bit off-key, about seventy or so folks joined in unison as the well-wishers belted out their rendition of the birthday song with heartfelt sincerity.

"You sneaks. What am I going to do with the lot of you?"

"Offer us some birthday cake?" Chuck reached in his back pocket and handed her a white handkerchief. "No worries. It's my spare—and it's clean."

"Good to know." She met his gaze and laughed. Dabbing the moisture from her eyes, they exchanged a knowing glance. The last time he'd passed her his hanky they'd stood side by side in a packed pew down at the church.

Chuck had assumed the tears she'd shed were for the happy bride and groom, and they were. Sort of. But there was another reason too. How could he possibly know or understand that the moisture that leaked from her eyes had anything to do with him? Emotion held in check far too long nearly bubbled over that day—the day of Sam and Charla Packard's beautiful spring wedding.

The day it slammed her full force in the gut that, likely, she would always be an old maid. Since Chuck hadn't popped the question by now, obviously his sentiments didn't mirror hers.

Oh, he liked her all right. After all, they'd known each other since they were kids. Attended school together. Worked side-by-side at the diner together for the past ten years. Shared laughs. Hopes. Dreams. Heartaches. Even a secret or two. But intimacy? Anything beyond the evolution of their history? Wasn't happening. The choice she made twenty-one years ago clinched it. And the sooner she wrapped her mind around that, the better.

Ida Mae blushed down to her bones when she recalled the many subtle and not-so-subtle attempts to woo Chuck Farrow. Though she'd stopped referring to him as "my Chuckie," half the town of Ruby still paired them as a couple, and innuendoes however well-intentioned, continued to hound them. How utterly humiliating!

Unrequited love was a terrible thing. Unfortunately, she wore the emotion well. No. Strike that. She *knew* the emotion well. Big difference.

"Don't stand there like a dazed jackrabbit." Horace Sapp ambled forward, laughter punctuating his words. "Let's get down to business!"

"Yeah. I second that." Chuck rubbed his palms together and nodded toward the elaborately frosted sheet cakes. "Does the birthday girl want to do the honors, or does she need help?"

How like him to inject a dose of levity at a time like this. Of course, he couldn't know the depth of this infernal ache. How could he? Most people enjoyed birthday celebrations. They didn't tick them off as yet another year marked by loss. Another reminder of dreams dashed.

"Chuck Farrow, what do you mean 'Does the birthday girl want to do the honors?' Honorees don't cut and serve their own cake." Ida Mae's best friend of the last three decades skewered him with her gaze. "I'll slice. You serve." Sugar slapped his belly with a stack of paper plates. "Here."

"Ow!" Chuck feigned an injured midsection. "And while we're at, step on up, Horace. You can help him."

"Why, Miss Sugar, I'd be downright delighted." Deputy Sapp advanced with all the grace of a moose on ice. What he lacked in finesse, he made up for in heart. "Who says big guys can't waitress? I got da moves!" To prove it, he struck the infamous John Travolta pose, minus the white suit.

"Careful, hot stuff," his wife Hattie called. "If you bust those buttons on your shirt again, you'll have to work shirtless tomorrow. I'm not mending any more clothes tonight."

Ida Mae tamped down the laughter that rose up within her. She dabbed once more at her lashes and crumpled the hanky within her palm. Oh, heavens. How could she not love this crew of good folks who'd turned out just because today was her birthday? They didn't have to be here. On a lazy, fall Saturday night, they could be out toasting s'mores and gathering with family. Instead, here they were—huddled together like kids at Christmas as if Santa himself stood in their midst.

A speech seemed in order, yet the words stuck in her

throat. How did one thank her friends for such a grand surprise? They'd rescued a day gone south, buoyed by grins and good wishes.

"You guys..." she paused and swallowed, "are the best. The absolute best."

The crowd cheered. Nothing else was necessary. They understood. Not everything, naturally, but they grasped her sentiment. That their presence here tonight mattered more to her than mere words could possibly convey.

Sugar began cutting the birthday cake and Chuck presented Ida Mae with the very first slice. "Twenty-nine looks awesome on you. Happy birthday."

He meant well, but the compliment stung. Twenty-nine. *If only.* It took everything in her to return his smile. To look him in the eye and nod. "Thank you."

In another lifetime, she might have shared more. Now wasn't the time or place for decades-old truths or secrets exposed. Ida Mae accepted the paper plate, their fingers brushing in the process. A smile played at the corners of Chuck's mouth, though he offered no further words. Only that disarming grin and silent vibes. Vibes that she used to mistake for something more than "like."

The crowd milled about, savoring birthday cake and laughter. So many wonderful folks—some, lifetime friends, and others, new Ruby, Missouri transplants— here in one room to share kind thoughts and affection. Their sentiments somewhat eased the sting of yet another passing year. Lord love 'em.

Her eyes scanned the colorful, loveable group. Mom and Dad, arms entwined, listened with rapt interest to one of the old-timers' infamous fish stories. Sam and Charla Packard and little girlies in tow, along with dear soul Edwin Ramsey, navigated with plates in hand toward the booths to visit with Pastor Bill and Sister Sharon. Nora and Ned—that would be *the* Nora and Ned Brewster, owners of Ruby's only General Market—seated themselves at a table beside Jerry and Ann Marshall, Zeke Ledbetter, and Delia Scroggins. Melinda Brewer, whom newcomers often confused with Nora and Ned's kin because of similarity in last name, tried her best not to look ruffled as Sunset Meadows' handsome, young new hire swaggered by and flashed a grin.

Jake and Billie Gail Brewer's daughter could feign disinterest all she wanted. A body would have to be three bricks shy of a full load not to recognize the sparks that flew between Melinda and The Meadows' social services director, Matt Enders. *Oh, young love.* What Ida Mae wouldn't give to erase twenty years and make wrongs right.

Other folks filtered into the diner, the crowd now numbering seventy-plus people. Maximum capacity for the Come and Get It was ninety. They had room for more.

She stabbed a bite of birthday cake, the heady scent of cherries and chocolate teasing her nostrils and causing her to salivate. Combined with the inch-thick buttercream frosting, this small slice of heaven surely held five-hundred calories or more.

"Hey, doll. Don't even think about it." Sugar plunked a maraschino cherry onto Ida Mae's paper plate. "No calorie-counting tonight. This is a birthday, not a funeral. 'Course if it were, then I'd be serving my Funeral Taters. So, there's that."

She couldn't help but laugh. Sugar's sense of humor

often rivaled hers. Had since they were nine—roughly about the same time Chuck Farrow appeared on Ida Mae's radar. "Thanks. That makes me feel tons better."

Sugar quirked an eyebrow. "Seriously? You're concerned about a few calories?"

"No, not really." Ida Mae lowered her voice a notch. Though Chuck busied himself with other things, he needn't overhear this conversation. "But in high school, I struggled with my weight, remember? And then when I passed thirty-five, everything shot straight to my hips and middle—not to mention, bust. And you know I've always been kind of on the full-figured side anyway. It's tough to own a diner and not nibble."

"You're beautiful, my friend. Believe it. But if it makes you feel any better, this birthday cake is healthier than it looks."

"Oh, honey. I'm sorry." The last thing Ida Mae wanted to do was offend Sugar. "I know it's divine." To prove it, she scarfed down the bite on her fork and smacked her lips. The ooey-gooey goodness tap-danced on her tongue and awakened her senses. *Wow.* Numerous flavors burst in her mouth. "What do you call this one?"

"That good, huh?" Sugar laughed and leaned in close. "Sinner's Delight. Want to add it to your menu? I'll share the recipe."

"You read my mind. Might have to rename it, nevertheless. What do you think about Operation Paradise?"

"I like mine better."

"We'll think on it." They shared a giggle, reminiscent of the old days. Ida Mae hugged her friend, careful not to dump the remaining plate of cake down Sugar's back. "Gotta mingle. I'm the star of this show."

"That you are. Don't ever forget it." Sugar returned the hug and then resumed her cake cutting.

Ida Mae wandered between tables and booths, welcoming guests and extending thanks. Those parked at the counter saluted her with their punch cups. Dander Evans sloshed the drink down the front of his plaid flannel in an awkward attempt to raise his cup along with the rest. Graceful wasn't exactly the guy's middle name, though it was a complete and utter wonder that hunting and barbering seemed to be his God-given gifts with the latter occasionally earning him a little ribbing from those in the community. Why any parent would name their kid "Dander" in this century made one think all sorts of things and most of them uncomplimentary at best. In his mama and daddy's defense, however, who knew Dander would grow up to be a barber, and a right fine one at that?

Names didn't necessarily define the person. A lot of fine folks here in the Ozarks had some real doozies. Take "Ida Mae," for instance. Maybe a popular name seventy or so years ago, but by the time she came along, the name had long since worn out its welcome. Regarding her namesake, Great Grandma Ida, if she were alive, might be thrilled. Nonetheless, to this day, Ida Mae longed for something classy or even ordinary. Why, she didn't know, other than the fact that tonight her young body had aged another year and it housed a very old soul. A common name inherent to her generation, might remind her she wasn't a relic, but instead, a twenty-first century woman with a lot of living left to do.

Gracious. If turning thirty-nine unleashed this much emotion, what would forty bring? Ida Mae inhaled, then prolonged the release of air from her lungs in an effort to re-center her thoughts.

"Too much excitement?"

The deep timbre of Chuck's voice washed over her, temporarily suspending space and time. A witty comment or quick comeback, as was her nature, lay dormant and unyielding. She couldn't muster the strength to sum up in a few appropriately-timed words what tonight—specifically, this birthday—was. Too much of something, all right.

"Ida Mae?"

Tears she'd held at bay threatened to spill forth. They clouded her vision and gathered on her lower lashes. Once again, she wiped them away with the borrowed hanky.

"Hey…" Chuck lowered his voice a notch and cocked his head to one side. His eyes searched hers for a moment. "Those aren't happy tears like earlier, are they?"

She attempted a smile. "Of course, they are. You know me. I'm a sentimental gal."

"You're right. I do know you and you're a terrible liar. All day, you seemed off-kilter. Want to talk about it? I can follow you home when this shindig winds down."

"Which doesn't look like that'll be for a while, but no, I'm fine."

"Uh-huh." Someone fired up the jukebox, the refurbished and much-beloved diner centerpiece, and those sitting jumped to their feet. Chuck yanked off his chef's apron and tossed it on a nearby table. He slid the paper plate from Ida Mae's fingers, parked it next to the apron, and grabbed her hand. "Perfect. Let's go."

"Huh? You're crazy." She shook her head and tried to extricate her palm from his. "Need I remind you that my feet are killing me and dancing's the last thing on my mind?"

"Don't believe you. Since when?" And then he took her in his arms and twirled her around to the upbeat tempo that filled the room.

Folks would have to be senile or dead if they didn't at least tap a foot to this one. Kenny Loggins' "Footloose" could cause even an ice cube to thaw and catch fire. Despite her grumbling, Ida Mae matched him move for move. He immediately sensed the shift in her disposition and her lightheartedness triggered fond recollections.

Paired as dance partners for a school production when they were nine laid the foundation for future endeavors. Because they seemed to have a knack for dancing, as well as entertaining, teachers often selected Chuck and Ida Mae for holiday shows and special events, and everyone in Ruby gobbled it up. When it came to performing, the chemistry between them sizzled, and other kids were only too glad they weren't the ones under the spotlights.

Tonight, emotion fueled by memories electrified the packed room. Men scooted tables and chairs out of the way as Chuck swung Ida Mae back and forth to the upbeat tempo of the oldie but goodie classic. The crowd cheered and many joined in as he played showman to the hilt. A few teenagers whipped out their cell phones to catch the antics on video.

"Didn't know you still had it in you!" Ida Mae shook her blonde head, causing her shoulder-length curls to tumble wild and free over her shoulders, and she laughed.

"Haven't you heard? Almost-forties are the new twenties. It's stuff like this that keeps us in shape."

He spun her around again and she giggled like the schoolgirl he remembered. Oh, how he'd always loved the sound of her laughter! When she'd left town for a while after their high school graduation, the absence of that sound pricked holes in his heart. He'd missed his friend—his childhood buddy and confidante. When she returned to Ruby four months later, Ida Mae seemed different. A few pounds heavier than her normally curvaceous frame, less inclined to laugh, and not near as chatty. She never offered an explanation either, other than some drummed up nonsense about leaving to "find herself."

Even now, twenty-one years later, her sudden departure still stung. They rarely spoke of it, and as years passed, Ida Mae settled into her perky, bubbly self. Except today...today there was the slightest hint of something not quite right. It was more than birthday blues or work exhaustion. PMS maybe? Nah. That didn't seem to trouble Ida Mae like it did some women. Not that he wouldn't understand if it did. After all, he did have a mother and sister, and he was no dummy. Chuck often whipped up a batch of brownies or another special treat to deliver to Voni and Jim and the kids when Voni felt low.

Ida Mae's laughter echoed throughout the diner. Too soon, the song reached its climactic finale and the partygoers clapped and high-fived each other. Chuck bowed. Ida Mae curtsied. Guests slugged back punch and helped themselves to a second round. Someone propped open the front and back doors to facilitate a cool draft, causing the cow bell at the diner entrance to ring. Betsy's fat, pink teats chimed together as if begging for an encore.

"See? You gotta admit that was fun."

Ida Mae punched his shoulder. "Yeah. Like old times, right?"

"Except now we're not as limber."

"Speak for yourself. I may not be able to turn a cartwheel anymore, but I can certainly shake my groove thing."

He had to agree there. That she could. He best not let his mind wander any further than that.

More revelry and fun ensued with a few of the old-timers reliving favorite moments at the Come and Get It. Born-and-bred local Edwin Ramsey snorted and slapped his knee as he shared the memory of a tour bus chock-full of big city sightseers rolling into town. When the sharp-dressed, high-toned ensemble trooped through the door, Ida Mae extended a warm welcome like she always did to visitors and locals alike. As was customary, she personalized the greeting for everyone—especially wide-eyed tourists with a penchant for adventure.

"Good afternoon, my hungry, little jackalopes." Edwin raised his voice a notch and mimicked Ida Mae's Ozarkian twang. "Right fine day for a tour of our awesome community. Where're you from?"

"The Windy City." Horace played the part of the stodgy, older guy in his yellow and blue plaid designer duds. "We understand the Come and Get It is a must when visiting the Ozarks."

"You understand correctly. Help yourselves to a seat wherever you like, and I'll rustle up menus and ice waters." Edwin nailed the exaggerated pause. "And no worries, friends, if you have to go, the outhouses in back are in swell shape. Ladies to the left, gents to the right."

Horace gulped like Mister Designer Duds had. "You're kidding."

Chuck remembered that day with vivid clarity. The regulars grinned and continued eating, despite the travelers' wagging tongues and whispers. A full minute lapsed before Ida Mae came clean. "Don't get your shorts in a tangle, Al. Just our Ozarkian humor."

"Al's" mouth twitched, then he laughed full throttle and extended a palm. "Actually, name's Pembrooke. Adam Pembrooke. We're with Pembrooke's Tour and Travel."

"Delighted to make your acquaintance, Mister Pembrooke. The Come and Get It family welcomes you."

Despite the travelers' initial guardedness, it hadn't taken long for them to warm up to Ida Mae's zany wit and downhome charm. By the time the tour group said their goodbyes, the diner dubbed Pembrooke and crew honorary Ruby citizens.

In addition to the fun, albeit wacky, atmosphere, the real claim to fame was the Come and Get It's awesome home cooking, and Ida Mae herself. Since the Hoscutts transferred ownership ten years ago to their daughter, business had mushroomed. Ida Mae took a great thing and made it even better. And with the menu revamp in progress, maybe this birthday was the motivation she needed to kickstart a whole new era.

As the celebration wound down, Chuck grabbed a trash cart and gathered paper plates, napkins, and cups, and deposited them in the waste container along with plastic forks and spent party favors. Sugar wiped down tables, and men returned them to their rightful positions. Everyone pitched in, and they reordered the diner in a snap.

When the last person filed out the front door, Chuck set the lock, flipped the sign to "Closed," and drew the blinds. He turned to Ida Mae. "Bet you never had a surprise party like that."

"Can't say that I have. How'd you pull it off without someone revealing the secret?"

"Oh, I have my ways." Should he tell her? Yep. He should. "I threatened to put laxative in the culprit's next meal here if that happened and I found out who blabbed."

"Ha! You would've too." She snapped a napkin dispenser lid in place and scooted it into proper position at the counter. "I think we're done here. Ready?"

"Yeah. We'll set the security system on our way out." The keypad was at the back entrance where the diner staff always came and went. "How about I give you a lift home? We can drive down tomorrow for your car."

"Thanks, that's a nice offer, but I'm not too fragile to navigate the four blocks home. I can stay awake that long, anyway."

"I know you can. Consider it an additional birthday perk. Part of the star treatment and all." He liked pampering her, true, but he also saw no need in her driving alone at eleven-thirty. While Ruby boasted a relatively crime-free score card, it wasn't necessary Ida Mae drive at this hour if she didn't have to.

She appeared to give it some thought. "Star treatment, huh? A girl could get used to this." She tried, unsuccessfully, to stifle a yawn, and Chuck placed a hand under her elbow, guiding her along. All they had to do was turn off the lights.

He pushed open the swinging doors at the kitchen and they made their way past stainless steel countertops, commercial appliances, and an array of pots and pans, gleaming and sanitized. Everything was as it should be except one thing. Ida Mae's fingers paused at the light switch.

"What's that?" She tipped her head to the right and scrunched her eyebrows. In the not-too-far distance, something whirred and clicked. A few seconds later, a familiar melody floated through the diner.

The very distinct Righteous Brothers tune grew louder and there was no mistaking its source. The music came from the jukebox.

Chapter Three

"Unchained Melody." Their song. Well, if they'd had a song, this would be it. Ida Mae doubted he even remembered that this blast from the past was the first slow song she and Chuck danced to at their high school prom during their junior year. They'd been closer in those days. Almost on the verge of something more than friends. And then, for whatever reason, Chuck pulled away. His rejection smarted, but ever the unflappable social butterfly, Ida Mae bounced back and resolved to move forward. If only she'd used better judgment.

"Hmm. That happened last week to Pastor Bill. He slipped in his change and the record hung. Can't remember the song now, except an hour after he left, the thing played. Crazy machine." Chuck's voice snapped her back to the present. "No worries. It'll play through and reset."

"You sure? Tomorrow's Sunday, and we won't be back until Tuesday. Maybe it has a short and we should unplug it."

"I doubt it. We had it serviced about a month ago." Chuck reached in his pocket and drew out his car keys. "But to ease your mind, wait here. I'll go take care of it." Then, with a glint in his eye, he shoved the keys back in his pocket and grabbed Ida Mae's hand. "Come on."

Once again, Chuck led her through the swinging doors in the direction they'd come, and into the main seating area. As the music swirled around them, he motioned with his other palm. "No sense in wasting a perfectly good song. Shall we?"

Really? This wasn't the type of song friends danced to. It was far too romantic. A song reserved for those in love, not employer and employee. They were friends and that's as far as it went. Chuck's decision, not hers. A boundary she wouldn't compromise. "Footloose" was fun. This, dangerous. She wouldn't risk her heart to him a second time.

She shook her head. "No, thanks. Pull the plug and let's go. I'm so tired, my whole body feels like a limp dishrag."

"Okay. Understood." He recovered quickly and dropped her hand.

Ida Mae's heart constricted as he stepped around her to the jukebox. Wishing they could turn back the clock didn't make it so, but for the briefest moment, she envisioned what life could have been like as Mrs. Chuck Farrow. They might have shared twenty years' worth of dances by now if fate hadn't kicked them in their backsides.

"I can drive myself home. You don't need to worry about me. Really." She forced a smile. He had to be tired too. They'd both been here since before sun-up.

"I know you can, but I wish you'd let me, please. After Sunday service tomorrow, I'll drive you back down and you can get your car then."

His concern moved her. Other than her own parents and her best friend Sugar, no other person quite read her the way Chuck did. She might be an old maid, but terrific friends counted for a lot in today's world. Who needed marriage?

A few moments later, they drove the short distance to

Ida Mae's Craftsman-style bungalow. Chuck pointed at the sky and whistled. "Wow. That's quite a moon. Look how bright it is."

Iron-gray night, lit by moonbeams and stars, stretched overhead for infinite miles. He cut off the ignition, and for a while, they lingered in silence. Out of the corner of her eye, Ida Mae watched him flex and relax his fingers against the steering wheel. Those hands had turned many a pan and whipped up many a meal during the last ten years at the Come and Get It. The kitchen was Chuck's happy zone. Though he enjoyed mingling with customers, he preferred working behind-the-scenes and thrived when creating homecooked meals and treats. He had a knack for the culinary arts, and the personal spin he added to various dishes won favor with the locals.

Occasionally, Ida Mae wondered what else he did in his spare time. Granted, his long work hours mirrored hers, but surely, the guy must do other things on Sunday and Monday—days the diner closed for church and rest. After high school and community college, he worked as an executive chef for a small upscale restaurant in another town. Even now, it seemed incredulous that he traded such an illustrious career when Ida Mae offered him a similar, albeit much less notable, position at the Come and Get It. His salary today certainly couldn't compare to what he'd made a decade ago. Why he'd accepted her offer, one she fully expected him to decline that cold December eve, still boggled her mind. Maybe he did it as a favor.

In school, Chuck excelled in journalism and wrote monthly columns for their school paper. Later, he joked that maybe one day he might combine his skills and pen a cookbook. What ever became of that notion? Maybe he'd ferreted away a potential bestseller. He'd once let it slip that he'd started a manuscript. A dressed down, homespun how-to for the "non-cook" cook. Had he ever finished it?

Chuck merely grinned when Ida Mae asked him about his future goal, but she speculated he'd actively pursued the cookbook or *something*—at the very least, he was working on it. The guy seemed pretty driven regarding this aspect of his life, maintaining, "I have no secrets. Only hopeful inclinations. You'll know when I know."

"Know what and know when?" she'd prompted. "I'll know you've written a cookbook when I see it in the bookstore with your name on it?"

"Ha." Chuck had given a slight laugh. "Right now, I'm tinkering. But wouldn't that be a hoot—me, an author?"

Ida Mae didn't press, though his response tickled her. When Chuck arrived at the diner in the mornings with an old leather binder tucked securely beneath his arm, she silently cheered him on. Encircled by a frayed, elastic band, the accordion-pleated binder fanned out about two inches and bore telltale signs of much wear and tear. When on the clock, Chuck stashed the binder in an office locker. During breaks and at close, he'd whisk it out, tug out its contents—about half a ream of paper and a red pen or two—and mark furiously on the pages. Was this evidence of a lifelong dream? Time would tell.

Maybe, on Chuck's off-days, he simply relaxed. Lord knew he'd earned it. Ida Mae stole another glance at the guy in the driver's seat. He worked like a horse, and the Come and Get It's continued success hinged on Chuck Farrow. She'd be the first to admit it. Ida Mae cooked her fair share and could turn a pan with the best of 'em, yet it was Chuck's expertise and innovativeness that appeased hungry customers and had them drooling for more. Mom and Dad needn't worry, knowing their beloved establishment was taken care of and thriving. Retirement agreed with them. They enjoyed volunteer work, church activities, and hobbies the years running the diner hadn't afforded them.

"I guess I should go in." Ida Mae broke the silence as a yawn escaped her lips. "Thanks for the ride...and the birthday party."

"Hey, you're welcome on both counts. Glad you accepted the ride, and I'm happy you liked the party. Think you'll be up to church in the morning?"

Service didn't start until eleven, so with a good night's sleep, she'd be fine. Physically, anyway. She'd dissect her other emotions after tomorrow's first cup of coffee, but she saw no reason now to share that with Chuck. She needed to get that radio commercial out of her head. The one about adoption services and genetic testing. The one that planted the most insane thought into the deepest recesses of her mind. "Yes, I'll be ready with bells on. You know me."

"I realize I asked earlier. Want to talk about it?"

Wow, smooth. The guy didn't forget a thing. "Talk about what?"

"Whatever it is that's troubling you."

"You're imagining things. We put in long hours today and it's late. That's it. There's no story there."

Chuck turned sideways to face her. Bright white moonlight sliced through the windshield, illuminating his handsome features. "If you don't want to discuss it, say so. Don't lie. We've known each other way too long for that."

Goodness, he didn't mince words. Ida Mae flattened her palms against her lap. Her heart thudded like a runaway train beneath the fabric of her uniform and her mouth went dry. He wanted the truth? Okay. Why not? Nothing to lose now. He hadn't wanted her then. He sure wouldn't want her after she served him a big ol' dose of truth.

"Tomorrow, twenty-one years ago..." She tried to choke out the rest of the words, but they wouldn't come. Nausea roiled in her stomach, and the sudden urge to throw up made her gag.

"Ida Mae?" Chuck touched her arm. "Please, what on earth is it?"

"I'm sorry. I thought I could talk about this, but I can't." She grabbed her handbag and fumbled with the door handle. As she lurched from the vehicle, Chuck bolted from the driver's side and caught her before she toppled, face-first, onto the grass. It took a strong man to hold a gal's head as she lost birthday cake and punch all over her front lawn.

Another heave and that was that. He'd never seen her so sick. He wouldn't have prodded if he'd known whatever "it" was would make her physically ill. Guilt slammed him in the gut and forced the air from his lungs. When words finally came, they seemed painfully inadequate.

"Aw, girl. I didn't mean to push." Chuck handed her

a clean rag he'd seized from the glove box of his car. "It was stupid of me."

"Don't blame yourself. There are some things I can't discuss, that's all." She wiped her mouth, and he helped her stand to her feet. Blonde curls askew, she brushed new fallen leaves from the pink and white dress that served as her diner uniform. "Gosh, yuck. Color me embarrassed."

Things she couldn't discuss. Like what, for instance? Except for that four-month disappearance act right after high school, he'd never known Ida Mae to be secretive. For her to have this sort of reaction when he asked what was troubling her caused alarm bells to clang in his brain. Maybe she truly was ill—like, physically. Worry gnawed at his insides. Granted, she worked 'round the clock, but illness hadn't derailed her. The woman never missed work.

"No need to be embarrassed. I'm really sorry I pressed." He steadied her against the crook of his arm and steered her forward. "Here, let's get you inside."

Ida Mae blew out a breath. "I'm fine now. That is, other than having vomit on my grass and smelling like it too."

Her subtle jab at humor lightened the moment, however, it did little to ease his concern. Two peas in a pod, the two of them. Wasn't that what he always defaulted to—witty banter and jokes—when faced with hard or awkward conversations? In this way, he and Ida Mae were alike. Maybe not so much regarding the secrecy. His life was pretty much an open book. A book...hmm. A half-hearted pun or a fitting analogy?

Anyway, Chuck ticked off the mental narrative.

Deadbeat dad abandoned Mom, Voni, and him when he was ten. Mom worked her tail off at two jobs after that to make ends meet. Chuck dated some in school, but never traveled down the marriage path. Did community college. Studied the culinary arts. Dabbled at a writing project. Before the Come and Get It, he'd acted as executive chef for a small, swanky place in the adjoining county. Enjoyed his niece and nephew. Lived alone and liked it that way. There you had it. Chuck Farrow's uneventful life summed up in sixty seconds. Of course, he omitted a chapter or two. Specifically, the ones titled "Ida Mae Hoscutt."

"Don't stress about the puke. You'll wash. And your lawn will too. According to my weather app, there's an eighty-percent chance for an early morning shower."

"Great to know." She rifled through her purse for her key ring. "Thanks for trying to make me feel better."

"You're welcome. It's true."

She found her keys and extricated herself from Chuck's steadying arm. "I enter around back because that's where my detached garage is."

Yes, he knew that. He parked at the street curb because he didn't want to give any night owls the wrong impression. Parking out here in the open versus pulling into the garage wouldn't call Ida Mae's morals into question. He was dropping her off, not staying the night.

After he saw her inside, he'd head home. Alone. The thought jabbed his subconscious, though he refused to examine why. "Mind if I settle you in first? I'd like to know you're okay before I leave."

"I appreciate that, but I do this every night by myself."

She said it matter-of-fact, yet the words tiptoed across his heart and lay there. *I do this every night by myself.* Chuck didn't know why the words bothered him, but they did. "You don't have to tonight."

Ida Mae rolled her shoulders and she held out the key ring. "Then be my guest."

"Thanks."

Together, they fell into step and followed the short expanse of sidewalk around to the back door. Pale yellow light illuminated the kitchen where Ida Mae usually left a light burning, and when Chuck unlocked and nudged open the back door, the room immediately drew memories. He hadn't visited in a while, but the place was as he remembered. Bright and cheery with splashes of color and scents of cinnamon, the kitchen boasted a happy, down-to-earth aura. From the red and buttercream checkerboard tiled floor to the vintage-era wall art to the sturdy, antique table for four, one had the feeling he'd stepped back in time. Ida Mae always had an affinity for the past. An old soul, yet a free spirit, residing in a young body. Perhaps, all the reading she did about simpler days fueled her fascination with a period she longed to recreate.

Somewhere else, Ida Mae might be perceived as an eccentric. An oddball. Here in Ruby—in their quiet Ozarkian community tucked back in the rolling hills and close-knit hollows—she fit right in. Simple with a hearty mix of unconventional suited almost everyone in Ruby. Admittedly, there was nothing simple about this colorful woman who could charm the stripes off a garden snake.

"See? No boogeyman here. All's as it should be." Ida Mae slung her purse strap over a kitchen chair. She stepped to the sink and moistened a couple paper towels, blotting her forehead and cheeks with the cool, makeshift compress. Her skin tone resumed its normal shade, for which Chuck breathed a sigh of relief.

Nevertheless, he wasn't quite ready to leave. "Mind if I stay a while?"

She stopped blotting. Her fingers tightened around the paper towels. "Look, I'm okay now. Except I need to brush my teeth and I want to shower before bed."

"I can park myself here at the table and you holler if you want me."

She hitched an eyebrow.

"Wait. That came out wrong." Oh, man. He hadn't meant to imply anything inappropriate. "I mean if you get lightheaded or sick again, I'd be here in case you need anything."

"Relax." Ida Mae's mouth curled upward in an effort to reassure him. "I won't lose my birthday refreshments a second time. Been there, done that. All I need is to cleanse my palate, grab a quick shower, and snooze for eight hours, and I'll be good to go."

"You sure? I don't mind staying."

"Stop being such a worrywart. I'm fine. Go home."

She spoke with conviction. However, something in those beautiful blue eyes troubled him. He had no reason to second guess her, other than the fact that when you'd known someone for three decades, you kind of knew her better than, say, an average Joe might. And Ida Mae and Sugar Perkins might be tight, but theirs was a different relationship than his and Ida Mae's. Chuck and Ida Mae shared a bond that few experienced in this lifetime. Not romantically. Though, certainly more than friendship.

Sometimes, he wondered what life would have held for them had he pursued his inclination when they were teens. Still, facts were facts. He wasn't husband material. Then or now. Too many scars. Dad's leaving soured him on marriage and happily-ever-afters.

"Tell you what. I'll go. Shoot me a text in the next hour. Please?"

Ida Mae tried her best to look aggravated. "Sure."

He resisted the urge to say more. Instead, he clamped his mouth shut, nodded, and turned to go. As he strode out into the night, her words echoed after him.

"You're one in a million, Chuck Farrow."

If only that were true. She meant it, though, and her sentiment—however innocent—warmed him. Chuck's battered heart expanded a bit. Without turning around, he raised a hand and waved.

He drove home, haunted by remnants of a birthday fiasco. If only he hadn't urged Ida Mae to talk about whatever it was that hounded her.

Tomorrow, twenty-one years ago... The day after her eighteenth birthday? What in the blazes was that about? Chuck searched his memory. Twenty-one years ago, Ida Mae was a ball-of-fire, seventeen-year-old kid, on the cusp of her eighteenth year. They'd graduated high school in May, and one week later, his friend left Ruby for four months to "have an adventure and find herself." A curious and out-of-character thing for Emory and Selma Hoscutt's daughter, but no one except him really questioned it because, after all, Ida Mae had always been given to wild hare tendencies. There was a vast difference, Chuck concluded, between wild hare and borderline crazy.

During that summer, those heat and humidity-laden days characteristic of the Ozarks, Chuck worked odd jobs around town until community college started in late August. While he prepared for a future, Ida Mae gallivanted off heaven knew where, savoring the last vestiges of her youth just shy of adulthood.

Chuck mourned his friend's absence, and truth be told, resented her for leaving without so much as clue to where she was headed. Her parents, swamped with diner renovations then, shrugged their shoulders and smiled when folks asked them about their girl.

"Oh, you know our Ida Mae," her daddy used to say. "That young lady has the world by the tail…or thinks she does. Wants to live a little before pursuing college."

To which her mama added, "Drew out everything in her bank account to do a bit of traveling. She has the wanderlust, that one."

When she returned late September, two weeks after her eighteenth birthday, Chuck didn't know what surprised him most. The fact Ida Mae decided to help her parents run the Come and Get It rather than enroll in college after all, or the fact that four months had transformed Ida Mae from the perky, vibrant girl he remembered into the quiet, withdrawn young woman he no longer knew.

Chuck flipped on his turn signal and headed east down Marmalade Lane, a few streets over from Ida Mae's. His home, an older brick, nine-hundred square foot affair and nestled beneath a bank of towering maples, distinguished itself from other homes on the block by way of its size and historical connection. Chuck's house was the smallest, yet most notable, among the cluster of meticulously tended residences. Many years prior to him purchasing it, the circa 1950 relic served as parsonage to a preacher or two. If walls could talk, they'd say a lot, he imagined. He understood the place had seen its fair share of witnessing, weddings, and funeral planning. In its heyday, it functioned as a small social hub, a respite to the weak and weary weighed down by life's complexities and disappointments.

There'd been children too, along the way, as evidenced by telltale crayon marks and fingerprint smudges. Now forty and unmarried, Chuck guessed kids weren't in the picture for him. Probably for the best. Not a husband, nor father material. From time to time as he observed yesterday's traces of lives well lived, truth's sting smarted. Nevertheless, better to remain single and pining rather than married and a failure. Good ol' Dad convinced him of that.

Chuck eased his vehicle beneath the carport and switched off the ignition. He sat there, motionless, mulling over things he hadn't in years. Like, for example, his life path. Bachelorhood. Love stirred and love not realized. Ida Mae. The stories her eyes conveyed—ones she refused to share.

Thump! He struck the steering wheel. Why think about that? Frustration mingled with fear skulked up Chuck's spine. The realization hit him with the force of a two-by-four.

Tonight, the story in Ida Mae's eyes mirrored the same one she'd had twenty-one years ago...and silenced.

Chapter Four

Ida Mae stood beneath the shower head, giving her tears free reign. She sobbed so hard that she had to reach out to steady herself against the pink tiled wall. It had been building all day—this heart-wrenching release—and tonight, the dam burst.

Rivulets of water mixed with raw emotion and skimmed down her body. Fleetingly, she wondered if crying ever killed a person. Anything, she guessed, was possible.

A puddle of water accumulated below Ida Mae's feet where the wash cloth lay, and she bent to scoop up the cloth. Another sob rocked her forward. She gulped hard, determined to stop weeping. What would Ruby's upstanding kith and kin say if they could see her now? *Okay. That's funny. They'd hand you a towel, gal, and tell you to cover yourself.*

How she managed to find a sliver of humor in the midst of upset temporarily derailed her tears. Wasn't that what she was known for—her quick wit and sharp tongue? Always joking, forever smiling. Inherent traits she came by honestly. Hoscutt attributes passed down from generation to generation. She could thank Mom and Dad for that and their parents before them.

She supposed it could be worse. Despite most good-natured souls in this community, there were a few stinkers whose attitudes smacked of rotting eggs. They could not care less about giggles and grins or anything remotely funny. Some people wouldn't crack a smile unless it was painted on their face with a permanent marker.

Well, not her. Despite what life doled out, Ida Mae knew how to take it on the chin and rise above the debris. If she could survive loss heaped upon loss with a figurative cherry on top, then she could survive anything. Even days like today, her birthday, and days like tomorrow—her baby's twenty-first.

Ida Mae shut off the water and sniffled. The water gurgled as it drained, paralleling her thoughts. Spent, like her. She had no more tears left. At least not tonight.

She grabbed the bath towel slung over the shower door and dried off quickly. How would she face Chuck tomorrow? She'd acted like a certifiable idiot. He wouldn't forget the unanswered questions or the emotional display afterward, including the pool of vomit that he'd most likely see again when he picked her up for church in the morning. If ever she wished it would rain, she sure hoped it arrived tomorrow in buckets.

Later, in bed, sleep eluded her. On another night, somewhere in the distant past, it was the same but for a far different reason. Ten hours of labor on one's birthday thwarted any attempt at shut eye. Too, knowing the outcome, that soon, she would hand over her newborn to others, never to see her baby again—nipped sleep right in the bud.

Twenty-one years later, Ida Mae remembered every tear, every contraction, every spike on the fetal monitor. The scurry of nurses, the hushed voices in the hospital hallway, the doctor's words of encouragement as she pushed until the early morning hours the next day...until her child's first cries pierced the air. She remembered all that too. Then, when it was over, staff examined the infant and they whisked her precious baby away without her so much as touching that soft, pink skin—her preference because she knew if she held that tiny, beautiful bundle there'd be no turning back.

She'd forever lose herself to those sweet, rosy cheeks and eyes the color of Mom's favorite handmade quilt— baby blue with golden flecks—those eyes, indeed, such a wondrous mystery. Ida Mae wouldn't have done what needed to be done. She wouldn't have given a loving, barren couple the child she so desperately wanted to keep, but certainly, couldn't provide for, and she wouldn't ask that of her parents either.

Also, there were other considerations. Their close-knit community would probably have curtailed questions and welcomed, with open arms and hearts, Ida Mae's wee one into their midst. Would it have been fair to her child though? Sometimes, the most well-meaning tongues could wag faster than a dog's tail. Mom and Dad might have gotten over the initial shock of their daughter's indiscretion, but Ruby, Missouri might not have. Ida Mae hadn't wanted to risk that, but most of all, she hadn't wanted her past to affect her child's future. It would have grieved her heart if story fodder and whispers defined her baby's life.

She did what she thought best. She researched, weighed options, and allowed her child to be placed for adoption.

A few weeks after the baby's birth, medical bills covered by the adoptive parents, Ida Mae drove the five hours back home. Motherhood and a birthday behind her, with an aching heart in tow, she picked up where she left off after high school graduation.

"My gracious, it's good to have you back home, sweetheart!" The happiness in Dad's voice almost made her forget that season in hell's abyss.

When she announced she wanted to work at the diner full-time with the intent of one day taking over the business, it was then that her parents voiced concern.

"That's wonderful, sugar." The unspoken "but" lingered on Mom's tongue. "Your father and I couldn't be prouder, you know that."

Dad didn't beat around the bush. "What about college?"

"I don't need a degree to teach me our family business, Dad. Everything I need to know, I can learn from you and Mom. Right here at the Come and Get It."

"True, sis." Dad placed his palms on her shoulders. "We only want you to be sure. We don't want you to live with regret."

Too late, Dad. I regret that I let Chuck push me away when I sensed that wasn't what he really wanted. I regret dating bad boy Tyler Fenston to spite him. I regret making poor choices. I regret shoving God out of my life and allowing Tyler to take up residence. I regret mistakes and the consequences from them.

"I agree with your father, Ida Mae. To work at the diner out of a sense of misplaced duty will only make you resent it. We wouldn't want that."

Ida Mae shook her head. "No, Mom. I could never resent the Come and Get It. I love it here. Ruby's my home and the customers are like family. All I needed was a little vacation to clear my head. I'm ready to settle down now. Honest."

Not a lie. With the past behind her, Ida Mae planned to move forward with life—obviously without Chuck, and most certainly, without Tyler.

"I'm what you call 'emancipated.' The old man signed the papers, so me being on my own is totally legit. If anyone asks questions, it's all legal." Tyler told her when they first began dating. "Perfect scenario. He runs his fancy car dealership, and I run my own life. No complaints there. He set me up in Ruby to finish school and stay out of trouble. Figured there'd be a lot less of it here than in the city, I suppose."

The smooth talking, beer guzzling, temporary town transplant lasted in Ruby about five months. The same amount of time it took to finish high school, wreak havoc, and make a baby.

Ida Mae gazed at the ceiling, remembering. During those first few months, Fenston fooled everyone with his charm and charisma. Including her. When she initially missed a period, she wasn't too alarmed. When she missed a second one, she knew. And the pregnancy test she'd purchased in another county confirmed it. That she was able to conceal the pregnancy for almost five months with baggy shirts and bigger jeans proved miraculous.

Then again, because she'd never been a svelte girl, the additional weight gain wasn't as noticeable and as she established a plan, she only told one person. Sugar. Leave it to her best friend to poke holes in her rationale.

"Tyler's agreed to this?"

Ida Mae nearly jumped from her chair. "Are you

nuts? I'm not telling him. There's no way he can be a father to this baby. No way I'd want him to. He's such a narcissist, I don't even want to think about him raising a child." Ida Mae twisted the wad of tissues she held in her hand. She trembled as she voiced her next thought. "I'm not telling Mom and Dad or anyone else. Only you. You're the only one who knows, Sugar."

Sugar tilted her auburn head. "Your parents love you. They'd want to know."

"No." Ida Mae squeezed her friend's hand. "Promise me you won't say a word."

Sugar's eyes filled with tears. "How will you explain this? How do you plan to be gone the entire summer without seeing your mom and dad?"

"They know I've always wanted to travel. I'll write. I'll call. I'll come home after…" She couldn't even finish the sentence. As close as she and her parents were, she knew it wouldn't be the same, yet it had to be this way. "They know I have a good head on my shoulders. They trust me." She almost choked on the words.

Ida Mae left town on a sunny, cloudless morning, the day following her high school graduation. Chuck waved as she drove past his mother's home, and Ida Mae plastered on a smile and waved back.

When Sugar phoned that evening, cell reception being spotty then, at first Ida Mae only picked up snippets. *Took a curve too fast. Accident. Killed on impact. Sorry to tell you this way…* She struggled to breathe. Her hands shook. *Not Chuck! Please, God, not him.*

It wasn't. It was Tyler. Her baby's father. A knot of sorrow, and to her shame, relief, formed in her chest. It wouldn't be necessary to list him as the baby's father on the birth certificate, not that she'd planned to anyway.

A sudden, somewhat familiar chime jerked Ida Mae back to the present. Who in the world would text her at this hour? It had to be nearing twelve-thirty. She rolled to the left side of the bed and reached toward the nightstand for her phone. Ida Mae slid her finger across the smooth surface and accessed the text.

Hey, birthday girl. Following up since you didn't. Are you all right?

In tonight's craziness, she'd forgotten her promise. How like him to call her on it. The missive, although brief, conveyed Chuck's concern. She tapped a quick reply.

Yes, thanks. I'm in bed.

I'm worried about you, you know.

She hesitated before responding. What to say? To minimize his unease, she did her best to reassure him.

Don't be. Working through some things from the past. You know me. I bounce back like a rubber ball.

He quickly answered.

Yeah. That's it. I do know you. Something's going on, but I'll try not to push. I'm here, if you'd like to talk.

She tapped again.

Thank you. You're a great friend.

This time, Chuck delayed his reply.

Appreciate that. See you in the morning for church. Afterward, we'll drive over and pick up your car. Does that sound okay?

Sure. Good night.

Good night, girl.

Their exchange was quick and to the point. Texts weren't for small talk or pleasantries, and he used "girl" more as a footnote than a term of affection. Had since they were kids. Ida Mae slid the phone onto the nightstand and curled into the warmth of her covers. Never had the bed seemed so lonely or the night so dark. Where moonlight once danced across her room and lit every corner, now only a vague dribble remained.

The ache in her chest expanded, and she wondered if Chuck ever thought of *what if*. *What if* he'd responded to their obvious connection so many years ago? *What if* he hadn't rebuffed her many attempts to woo him? *What if* he'd opened his heart and accepted her love?

There wouldn't have been Tyler Fenston, for one thing. And she and Chuck might have married and had babies. At least three. Maybe four.

Ugh. Stop it. Don't go there. Ida Mae clutched the covers to her chin, and she closed her eyes. If she could make it through tomorrow like she did every year, this fog would lift. Until her next birthday anyway.

She forced herself to count puppies, not sheep. In another life, besides lots of kids, she'd wanted puppies. She'd also wanted the house and the white picket fence and a man to share it all with. Not any man. The one who lived on Marmalade Lane. The confirmed bachelor who she assumed wanted a woman and children and furry critters to love but thought life had robbed him of his wants and wishes.

Ida Mae dozed off with all these thoughts, and one more, on her mind. Somewhere tomorrow, a child turned twenty-one. Years had come and gone, but the thing that mattered, lingered. It drew Ida Mae in and wrapped her in its sweet embrace.

Hadn't the Lord promised that His love was always the answer?

Morning arrived bearing gray skies and ominous clouds. Within moments, the threat of rain became a reality. It began as a mere smattering of droplets on his front windshield. As Chuck maneuvered his Dodge Charger down the length of his drive, the droplets morphed into a deluge. Ida Mae would get her wish. This should wash away any telltale signs from last night's...events.

He flipped on his windshield wipers and pulled onto the street. The rain poured down in buckets. Normally, he wasn't the type of guy who carried an umbrella, but he'd decided to toss one in the car when he checked his weather radar app this morning. Now he was glad he did. Wouldn't want Ida Mae to get drenched while all dolled up in her Sunday best.

As he passed through the various residential areas, Chuck noted the usual Sunday morning activity. Families, many armed with umbrellas, scurried to their vehicles. Other folks, already in cars, entered the beeline to church. Some dashed out to their front lawn for the Sunday paper in an effort to save it from a premature baptism. As customary, most waved or nodded. Even a thorough dousing couldn't dampen spirits today. Dinner on the grounds revived waterlogged parishioners like hound dogs trailing a squirrel. Of course, Delia Scroggins' country fried chicken and Hattie Sapp's homemade fudge drew people, dogs, and even squirrels to their Sunday-go-to-meetings in a way that Pastor Bill's dandy sermons occasionally didn't.

Pastor Bill knew it and joked about it. "Nothin' wrong with salivating during a sermon. Heightens awareness. God saves souls by feeding sheep. Don't ever knock decent preachin' followed by good fried chicken."

Chuck paused at the four-way stop and thought on that. Pastor Bill could sure make a point. Didn't the Lord often meet physical needs before addressing the spiritual condition? Didn't He know when saints and sinners visited the well, they listened better after a drink? Lots of wisdom there. Wisdom that Chuck filed away for future reference. Didn't have to be a theologian to recognize starvation or thirst.

Why he ventured down that path surprised him. Maybe whatever disturbed Ida Mae bothered him more than he'd like to admit. At the moment, he couldn't think of any physical or spiritual needs of his own that the Lord wasn't meeting.

Strike that. Hadn't he wondered why life went the way it did? Why some people seemed to have blessings heaped upon blessings while others struggled with dashed dreams and unanswered prayers?

Chuck turned left and maintained his train of thought. Deadbeat dads who walked away from loving families. Wives and children forever affected by irresponsible, life-altering decisions. Boys who entered adulthood haunted by ghosts of the past, gun-shy themselves of commitment and potential failure. Private musings, harsh realities.

A thought floated on his subconscious. A woman's arms to wake up to in the morning and cling to at night. What would *that* be like?

He never intended to live a life as a bachelor. It kind

of worked out that way. He could count on one hand the times he'd dated. All great girls, but none of them *the* girl, and definitely, no one he pictured as a lifelong partner. Except for...one.

He didn't consider his time with Ida Mae as "dates." Naturally, good friends spent a lot of time together. They navigated life's sorrows and celebrated life's joys. They balanced perspective through an impartial lens. They loved more than the person, their "friend." They loved that friend's soul, their spiritual essence.

As lifelong partners went, if he were to choose one, it would be someone like Ida Mae. On that front, however, he'd crashed and burned. Boy, did he. Their chance had come and gone. Mixed signals, mostly on his part, had seen to that. Finally, Ida Mae grew exhausted. Who could blame her for responding to the charms of another? But Tyler Fenston? *Why him, Lord?* The couple of months those two dated nearly drove him nuts. Couldn't she see what a player the guy was? Thankfully, it didn't last long.

As tragic as Fenston's car accident was, blessedly, Ida Mae hadn't been in the passenger seat that evening. According to news reports, the only thing in that mangled car besides Tyler were the empty beer cans strewn about the car's interior. By the time Fenston wrecked his vehicle and lost his life, he and Ida Mae were no longer an item, and she'd already hightailed it for parts unknown.

That chapter of their lives remained a mystery. Chuck pondered it and vowed, one day, they'd discuss it.

Snapping back to the present and the state of one's wellbeing, another unknown remained. Something huge pestered that woman. It was more than a birthday. More than menu changes, exhaustion, or September doldrums. Whatever the significance of "twenty-one years ago," today would prove interesting. It would either tell the tale or further cloud the issue.

With his insides in a tangle, he mulled over various possibilities and proceeded on to Ida Mae's place. Somewhere between Peachtree and Elderberry, the rain ceased and the sky parted. A strand of sunlight shone through. Surely, a good sign.

Chuck's mood lifted. The barest hint of a rainbow arced across the western horizon, fading before the colors fully formed. He wished he could bottle up the moment and save it to share with Ida Mae. If anyone deserved a rainbow, or a thousand, that girl did. Everyone adored her.

The shift in Ida Mae's countenance not only baffled Chuck, it scared the daylights out of him. Each year during the fall, her mood nosedived for a day or so. It wasn't anything specific he could pinpoint. She didn't wield anger or meanness or go on a tangent. There wasn't a malicious bone in her body.

The change was subtle. More like a deep-seated sorrow masked in jesting and smiles, yet those who knew her well recognized a chink in her otherwise shiny armor. The mood lasted for only two or three days, then it was back to business as usual.

What did it mean? He wished he knew. And this time...Well, this time there was a marked difference. Throwing up didn't normally accompany the mood shift. This year, this time, something significant threatened to upend. But what?

The lightness in Chuck's chest that he'd experienced only a moment ago, evaporated. *Please grant another rainbow, Lord. And paint it right across the skyline for Ida Mae to see.*

The wobbly entreaty would have to do. An intercessor, he wasn't. Not that he didn't believe in prayer. He wasn't good at it. Eloquence had passed Chuck by. Along with a hundred other things.

He didn't dwell on those other things. Couldn't change any of them anyway. Instead, he eased alongside the curb facing Ida Mae's house and parked. He raked a hand through his hair, wishing he'd visited the barbershop last week. At least he'd shaved, which he did on a daily basis.

Today, since this was dinner on the grounds *and* dress-down Sunday, he wore blue jeans and a casual shirt. Now that the rain had stopped, he wouldn't need the lightweight jacket he'd tossed in the backseat beside the umbrella. Bright, glorious sunshine eked its way past remaining clouds, the golden rays spilling across the dashboard and onto Chuck's lap.

Dress-down Sunday and rain notwithstanding, no doubt Ida Mae would wear something fancier than blue jeans. That woman had a flair for fashion, as well as a deep reverence for tradition.

"God probably doesn't care if we wear blue jeans," she'd stated more than once. "But I wear a waitress uniform five days a week and cute as it may be, it doesn't present the best me. Neither do blue jeans. Makes me feel like I'm sinning in the sanctuary. If I feel like glamming it up on Sunday, why not? It's my own preference, something between God and me."

Chapter Five

The way he stood there with his mouth agape gave Ida Mae pause.

What? Was there jelly on her face? A spider in her hair? Had she missed a button on her blouse?

Mentally, she gave herself a once over, running fingers through her shoulder-length waves. She swiped a hand across her cheek and double-checked her blouse buttons. Nothing seemed amiss. "What's the matter? Too much fiber this morning?"

He clamped his mouth shut and collected himself before he spoke. "You're wearing...blue jeans."

"Yesssss. Dress-down Sunday, right?"

"But you never wear jeans to church, even then."

"Is that all?" Gracious. You'd think she'd stepped off Mars. "Well, I am today. Is that a problem?"

"It's unlike you." Chuck stuffed his hands in his pockets. "How're you feeling? Stomach better?"

Ida Mae stepped back and waved her arm, ushering him inside. "Much, thanks. Sorry about last night." She wasn't about to go any deeper than that. Not before church. In fact, probably never. "Let me grab the pound cake I pulled from the freezer. Good thing I always have pre-made goodies on hand. I'd hate to show up at the church emptyhanded." Anything remotely having to do with cooking or baking hadn't happened last night or this morning.

"If I were you, I wouldn't worry about it. I didn't this time because Voni said she'd make an extra batch of cookies to contribute. But really, you know how these dinners are. There's always more than enough food—even with big, ol' boys like Deputy Sapp having seconds, and occasionally thirds." His voice trailed after her as she made her way to the kitchen.

When she returned with the pound cake container in tow, Chuck's eyes followed her as she gathered her Bible, purse, and sweater. The questions were there. She sensed them.

"Here. Let me carry something." He spoke gently, not with his usual teasing tone. Arms outstretched, he waited.

Funny how awkward pauses inserted themselves between two people who'd known each other almost a lifetime. Was this how it would be today? Polite courtesies and formalities? She didn't want that. She wanted their usual playful banter and easy companionship. She needed that. Today, of all days, she craved routine and solace.

Okay. It would be up to her to break the ice. Ida Mae manufactured a smile and handed him the plastic container. "Careful now. If you jostle that too much on the way to the car, the cake'll fall apart."

His eyes widened. He wrapped both hands around the container and handled it like it was hand-cut crystal. "Wow. I'll be super careful."

She waited until they were almost to the church to say it. "I was kidding."

"Huh?"

"Since when are my pound cakes anything less than

perfection?" She couldn't help but laugh. "You seemed so serious back at the house. I thought levity was in order."

"Ahh. Good one." He shook his head, not quite laughing. "I admit, you had me worried. I thought maybe you'd neglected adding an extra egg or something."

"My feeble attempt at lightening the moment."

"Ida Mae, look. We don't have to discuss whatever is going on with you. As friends, though, I hope you know that it doesn't matter what it is. I want to help." He angled the car in an empty parking space. They sat in silence, the quiet filling the empty void.

She knew he waited. Waited for her to tell him. She'd already decided that could never happen. To this day, there was only one other person in Ruby, besides her, that knew the significance of today, and they never talked about it. Twenty-one years ago, she'd sworn Sugar to secrecy and Sugar honored that.

Her best friend's words bounced around in her brain as if spoken afresh. "I'll take it to my deathbed, Ida Mae. I won't say anything. There may come a day where you'll need to, though. Secrets grow stale and stagnate. They plant us in the past and prevent us from moving forward." Even in her youth, Sugar Perkins had it all together. How could she be so young and still so wise?

Ida Mae had been wise once. Certainly, smart enough to know right from wrong. Mom and Dad raised her that way. Why had she given herself to the smooth-talking charmer who said all the right things? Why had she believed the lines and lies he'd fed her?

The memory nearly paralyzed her. One careless night at Jaden Pond, unfortunately, taught her the hard way that anyone could *say* the right things. In truth, character defined saying and doing.

Greed robbed. It destroyed. *Character* cherished and respected.

If Ida Mae were to confide in Chuck now, she risked revisiting a place from which she might never return. It had taken years to insulate herself against the pain. To build a good life. To further establish herself in the community that had been home to the Hoscutt family for generations.

The Come and Get It thrived under her steady hand and watchful eye. Business grew. Having Chuck as her right-hand man had been a wise move too. She'd done Mom and Dad proud.

"Thanks for telling me that." Ida Mae gripped the pound cake container and forced a cheerfulness she didn't feel. She made a terrible actress.

"So, that's that? Not gonna say?"

"This isn't the time or place to get into anything deep." *Oops.* Why didn't she word it differently? "I mean, church is almost ready to start, and I need to run this downstairs to the fellowship hall."

"Understood." Hurt lingered in his voice and he exited the vehicle without further comment. He walked around to the passenger side and opened Ida Mae's door.

Their eyes met and her heart clenched. "Please know if I could talk about it, I would. It has nothing to do with you, okay?"

"Sure." He acknowledged her explanation with a nod. "Let me grab your things from the backseat and I'll set them in your regular pew."

He could feign nonchalance all he wanted. Because of their history, they realized when the other ached. She touched his arm. "Hey. It isn't you." Not a lie. Not exactly the complete truth either.

"You mentioned that."

"We each have our things, you know?"

"Yeah. But you know my stuff. There's about a four-month gap after high school that we've never talked about."

Dread squeezed her chest, making it difficult to breathe. She'd always kind of wondered if her absence mattered. For twenty-one years, she'd wondered. Now, she knew. The heartache mirrored in his eyes confirmed that he'd cared. Why hadn't he told her? Why had he tried to hide his feelings back then by pushing her away?

"I've seen what happens when marriage goes sour," Chuck had said. "Anyone who abandons their marriage, kids, or commitment is a poor excuse for a human being. Marriage is one thing. There are other terms for those who desert their kids and hang them out to dry." Words, laced with anger, shared in confidence so many years ago. How could she ever forget?

And then, their senior year in high school after Ida Mae tried for the dozenth time to tell him how she felt, this. "Save your breath, Ida Mae. You're a great friend—my *best* friend—but I'm not the marrying kind. Too much baggage. Stuff I'd never foist on a wife or kids. My old man may have packed his bags, but he sure left Mom, Voni, and me with the leftovers. Bitterness. Resentment. Distrust. All that and more. Generous, huh?"

"But you're not your dad. You have a big heart, Chuck. I know." At seventeen, she'd been so sure. "I'm not just your friend. You know that." She'd tried to put her arms around him.

"Stop. Don't do that and don't say it."

"I love you, Chuck. I have since we were kids and we

danced up a blue streak together. Since your daddy left and you cried in my arms. Since our first prom and I felt your heartbeat next to mine. Since—"

"Cut it out, Ida Mae. We're high school seniors now, but we're not ready for attachments."

"What is wrong with you? I'm trying to tell you I love you, baggage and all."

"You're naïve. Other than our junior prom, we've never even dated. You've *never* dated. Period."

"And you have?"

"Some. You know that."

"Sodas down at the diner don't count and neither do study sessions at the library."

"Gosh, girl. What's it take? Want me to rent a billboard? I don't love you. I'm not the marrying kind. I'm. Not. Interested. Got it?"

Oh, had she gotten it. And not long after, she began the disastrous, doomed-from-the-start relationship with bad boy, city kid-turned-Ruby-transplant, Tyler Fenston.

Tyler with his charming façade, and soon apparent, wild-child ways. Tyler with his fancy red Mustang and his penchant for driving too fast. Tyler and his promises in the dark...and contradictions in the light. Tyler, the boy her parents eventually forbade her to see, and regrettably, the one she continued to date behind their backs.

The hows and whys mattered less than the ramifications that followed. Breaking up with Tyler came easy. What followed did not. When she finally recognized him for the arrogant, self-absorbed egotist he was, she was several weeks pregnant, wracked with shame and remorse, and facing adult decisions on the verge of her eighteenth year.

An involuntary shudder ran through Ida Mae. The sound of Chuck clearing his throat jarred her from the past. He softened his voice as he spoke.

"I probably shouldn't say this, and I guess this isn't the time, but I know something big is bothering you. Every fall, you withdraw for a while. For a few days, it's like you become someone else. A person I don't recognize."

When she didn't respond, he continued. "I think you'd agree that last night's episode…er…reaction…was pretty extreme. It worried me. I didn't sleep much because of it."

Ida Mae's stomach churned. Why must he push this? Did he want an encore?

"Sorry."

"I'm not after apologies, and I don't mean to needle. Watching you get sick like that gutted me."

"Yeah, it wasn't a picnic for me either."

He kicked at the loose asphalt with the toe of his shoe. "What bothers me most is that it's different this year. I've been turning over what you said. The thing you blurted right before you jumped out of the car."

Ida Mae tried to remember. There'd been so much on her mind at that point. The radio DJ's call to action and the commercial that followed. Her birthday. The party. The significance of another milestone. What did she say?

"Twenty-one years ago. You added 'tomorrow.' Which is today, now." Chuck paused. "It's the anniversary of something. Something terrible enough to have you react this way. I've turned it over and over in my mind, and I'm drawing a blank. Approximately twenty-one years ago, we'd graduated high school and you'd returned from your sixteen-week hiatus. What happened while you were gone? When you were silent all those months?"

"I told you I don't want to discuss this now. We don't have time." Sadness coiled in her stomach and panic took root. "You'd never understand. Besides, what's past is past."

"Maybe. Maybe not. When the past affects the present, don't you think it makes sense to reassess?"

"That's odd coming from you." Her hands started to tremble, and the cake container jiggled in her palms.

Why was he goading her like this? Friends weren't privy to every jot and tittle of each other's lives, and he'd certainly made it clear all those years ago that's all they'd ever be. *Friends.* Still, over the years they'd regained some of the ground lost during that poignant period in high school. Working together for the last decade at the diner, they'd fallen into their easy camaraderie. Once or twice, it almost blossomed into something more. Or it could have if Chuck would have let it. Lately, Ida Mae shoved the hurt aside for the sake of companionship. Weighted against life as an old maid, settling for crumbs seemed more palatable than the other choice of a cake-less void.

"You're right." Chuck answered. "I'm not proud of the things I verbalized as a mixed-up kid. It breaks my heart when I remember our senior year in high school. I'm sorry, Ida Mae. Sorrier than you'll ever know. I wanted to be honest, not cruel. Heaven knows, I was—I *am*—such a mess."

"Why now? Why tell me this now, twenty-one years later?"

"Because I sense that I'm connected to whatever it is

that's troubling you. The time frame fits. I'm hoping we can get everything out in the open and talk about it."

"Hope's a powerful feeling. Sometimes, it's realistic, and sometimes, it isn't."

"Yet...you said it. There's always hope."

Chuck pointed toward the sky behind her. When Ida Mae turned around, the brightest, prettiest rainbow she'd ever seen stretched from one end of town to the other.

When he thought about those few, brief moments in the church parking lot, Chuck regretted his timing, but not the words. He'd known for a long while they needed to address that ill-fated conversation. The one where he'd let his big mouth overrun his teenage brain. The one where he'd intentionally pushed Ida Mae away because anything more than friendship was a risk. One he'd refused to take.

Had he been wrong all those years ago? Had he unwittingly labeled himself as unmarriageable when maybe it wasn't so? The hairs on his arms stood at attention. Had he treated Ida Mae terribly and abandoned her *before* she could abandon him? The twisted logic of his words and actions from twenty plus years ago sucker-punched him. If it hadn't been for seeing Ida Mae into the church with her things, he would have hightailed it out of there. He needed to think apart from the Sunday crowd, God love 'em.

The rainbow clung to the sky for the longest time. Now, as he remembered his poor excuse of a prayer, Chuck wondered if the Lord hadn't painted that rainbow as much for him as for Ida Mae. He hadn't hoped for anything in a very long while. Perhaps, he should start.

From across the aisle, Chuck noted Edwin Ramsey watching him. The old fellow tipped his head and Chuck did the same. Around town, Ramsey was known for his unshakeable faith. Sort of a powerhouse prayer warrior. A native Ozarkian and a lifelong Ruby resident, Edwin was known as the go-to guy for wisdom and insight.

Pastor Bill shepherded his flock with a loving hand and a straightforward approach, though physically, he couldn't be everywhere at once. He often said he appreciated when those within the church body, like Edwin and others, ministered to their fellow brothers and sisters if a need arose. Chuck had considered, more than once, going to Edwin to make sense of the past. Edwin knew everything about everyone in their small community, including the history of Sy Farrow, Chuck's dad, and the impact his sudden departure had on the Farrow family.

What good would it do to resurrect old ghosts? It had been nearly thirty years since Dad deserted Mom, Voni, and him and left for parts unknown. Where the drunk was now was anyone's guess. That is, if he were alive.

Chuck could not care less about the man he'd loved for the first ten years of his life. The man who once returned love so freely...then turned to the bottle because he loved it more. The man who kissed his family goodnight one cold, winter eve and left the next morning without so much as a whisper to anyone—including his sleeping family. The one-hundred-dollar bill he'd placed on the kitchen counter for Mom might have covered groceries for the month, but it provided for little else.

Utilities, a mortgage, car repairs, and Christmas. All

of it dumped on Chuck's mother, a homemaker, with no warning. If it hadn't been for friends and neighbors, Liza Farrow and her kids might have gone belly-up. As it happened, they never went hungry, bills got paid, the clunker got fixed, and Christmas, sparse as it was, came and went that year along with other Christmases after that.

Heartache, fresh and raw, dimmed after those initial seasons. Mom worked two jobs, Voni helped run the house, and Chuck mowed yards in the summers and shoveled driveways in the winters. In between, he delivered papers and worked as an errand-boy at Ernie's Automotive. He grieved the sudden exodus of his father the way any ten-year-old boy might. He shed a few tears, stuffed down the grief, and shielded his heart from further wounds. He grew to manhood raised in the church. He became everything his old man hadn't been. Educated, successful, and happy. Well, happy enough.

A movement caught his eye, and Chuck observed Ida Mae shift in the pew beside him. She pushed stray, blonde tendrils behind an ear and ever-so-deftly wiped away a tear that leaked from her eye.

The cadence of Pastor Bill's voice, heartening and familiar, mesmerized his parishioners. Today, he preached from the book of First Corinthians, Chapter Thirteen. The "love chapter." It had been a while since Chuck read it, but he knew many of the scriptures by heart. Verses four through eight, particularly, stood out. Regarding love…*"Charity suffereth long, and is kind; charity envieth not; charity vaunteth not itself, is not puffed up. Doth not behave itself unseemly, seekth not her own, is not easily provoked, thinketh no evil; Rejoiceth not in iniquity, but rejoiceth in the truth; Beareth all things, believeth all things, hopeth all things, endureth all things. Charity never faileth..."*

Charity—love—rejoiced in the truth. The truth. Was that the part that made Ida Mae cry? Or was it *charity never faileth?* Hmm...he wondered. If he ever married, he'd want the entire chapter included in the wedding vows. It characterized everything marriage should be.

Like a lightning bolt between the eyes, the thought slammed into him. *What are you thinking, man?* He fidgeted with his Bible, fingering the pages with his thumb. Marriage? That'd be the day.

"And now, let us ponder Apostle Paul's fine words. Always timely, forever true." Pastor Bill referenced additional scriptures, then closed his sermon with a prayer.

Tantalizing aromas of fried chicken, roast beef, and ham wafted upstairs from the fellowship hall, and fortunately, expedited the preacher's usual three-minute petition to the Almighty. Lots of love rebounded off these hallowed walls today. No one did dinner-on-the-grounds better than the church body of Grace Fellowship, and Chuck's stomach rumbled, traitor that it was.

As the crowd exited their pews and began moseying toward the basement, he fell in step with Ida Mae. It seemed only natural they'd walk together, as they did every Sunday.

The crimson-colored ruffles at the hemline of Ida Mae's blouse swished against her hips, accentuating the flattering cut of her blue jeans and completing the picture of a very attractive, full-figured woman.

Heart, brains, and beauty. She had it all. Why a fella

hadn't snapped her up and married her by now puzzled him…and relieved him too. It'd take a special someone to be worthy of Ida Mae. He squashed that thought before it took center stage. He knew very well where stupid fancies could lead. Dreams of the heart didn't build a lifetime. Reality put her stamp on that one.

"Great message today." Certainly true, but he said it hoping to spark conversation.

Ida Mae nodded without meeting his gaze. "Yes."

Okay. That didn't work. He tried once more. "Wonder how many messages Pastor Bill's preached in his thirty years here."

"A lot, I guess." She rolled her shoulders, not missing a step.

"I think today's sermon was one of my favorites. Can't go wrong in the pulpit with a healthy dose of love." When Ida Mae didn't reply, he continued. "I mean, it's basically the glue that holds everything together."

Now, what made him say that?

This time, Ida Mae stopped short of the basement stairs. "What are you trying to do?"

Chuck gulped. "Discuss the sermon?"

She waited while other church members filed past. Voices and laughter swirled around them.

"That's nice and all, but I don't think we should discuss the subject of the sermon right now. Obviously, it leads us into very touchy territory."

Yep. He deserved that. The last twenty-four hours confirmed it. He honestly didn't know where he'd hoped this went. He knew he wanted to clear the air between them and get their friendship back on track. Was that possible if Ida Mae wouldn't trust him with whatever it was that gnawed at her?

She turned and headed down the stairs. On the opposite end of the sanctuary, Edwin made his way along the descending ramp that accommodated the church's elderly population. Once again, Chuck locked gazes with the man. Had he seen their exchange? Why'd he get the feeling Ramsey could see right through him?

Chapter Six

Somehow, she'd survived church today and dinner on the grounds. When Chuck delivered her to her parked car at the diner, she'd thanked him without making small talk. Clearly, he wanted to chat, but to his credit, he didn't prod.

Now as she settled onto her sofa, she leaned back into the comfy throw pillows and pointed the remote control at her television. *Yours, Mine, and Ours*, the old movie classic with Lucille Ball and Henry Fonda, lit the TV screen. All those children. Ida Mae couldn't imagine having that many. She'd failed with one child. The Lord would never see fit to give her another. Besides, another child or even ten couldn't plug the hole in her heart left by the one she'd never held, but forever remembered. The one she'd carried below her heart for nine, long months. The one she loved and always would.

Whether the child was a boy or girl, she'd never known. She'd asked the doctor not to tell her. The strawberry birthmark on the baby's tiny hand was the only identifying feature she remembered with certainty these twenty-one years later. She'd glimpsed those precious hands right before the nurse swaddled the crying infant into a tight, blanketed bundle. The moment imprinted itself in Ida Mae's memory bank along with a few others.

As a tear slipped down her cheek, she flicked it away

with her fingers. She'd already decided there would be no more tears today.

She redirected her thoughts toward the other person who occupied them. What harm was there now? Part of the aging process was a new willingness to accept those things she couldn't change. They could talk the past to death. It did nothing to advance the future. Maybe it was time to reconcile this facet of singlehood with her sins of the past.

Unloved. Unmarried. No children of her own, that she could claim. Fitting punishment for the girl who'd compromised her future for a few false promises under a moonlit sky.

Chuck hadn't wanted to leave the diner parking lot today without answers, and she'd almost caved. They'd worked together in close proximity for the past decade, yet now, things seemed different. Something drummed at the man. Feelings she didn't dare examine. What good would it do? After all these years, if Chuck Farrow didn't know what he wanted, or worse, if he denied it, dredging up history at this point would only reopen a barely sealed wound.

Teenage squeals erupted from the television, and for a while, Ida Mae allowed herself to be drawn into Helen North's crazy, mixed-up world. It took her a moment to realize that the doorbell chime was actually her own and not Helen's.

Typically, visitors didn't call on Sunday evening. She checked off possibilities. Surely, it wouldn't be Chuck. She'd made it clear that she didn't want company. Not Mom and Dad. They'd fired up the RV this morning and left for their fall vacay. Not her neighbors. When Ruby rolled up the sidewalks at six, Nora and Ned Brewster helped. Other friends, maybe?

Dinnnng-donnng. There it went again. Well, she couldn't very well answer the door in pink-and-white polka dot lounge pants and matching tee-shirt. Where was her bathrobe?

Rising from the sofa, she tiptoed to the front door and stole a peek through the peephole. The familiar grin eased her self-consciousness and need for decorum. She swung open the door and grinned back.

"To what do I owe the pleasure?"

"Since when do best friends need appointments?" Sugar sashayed past, lobbing her jacket at one of the living room chairs. "So, how's the birthday girl?"

Ida Mae shut the door. "My birthday was yesterday."

"Yes—I—party-planner extraordinaire that I am, I helped Chuck arrange your surprise shindig, remember?"

"Yep, and so do my hips." They laughed and hugged, and Ida Mae grabbed her friend's hand and led her to the sofa. "I'll have to calorie-count for the rest of the week to make up for my moment of weakness."

"Oh. I thought you meant your hips ached from last night's dance-off."

"Not hardly." Ida Mae lowered the volume on the television and eased back against the throw pillows. "I may not be in tip-top form anymore, but being on my feet all day at the diner gives me quite a workout."

"Yeah, I know. I'm teasing you." Sugar leaned forward and patted her knee. "You're a regular powerhouse, which is why I'm here."

What was that supposed to mean? "I'm tired so pardon me if I'm not following."

"I'll cut right to the chase. I'm worried about you."

"You've spoken to Chuck?"

"Of course not," Sugar returned quickly. "I'm your best friend, remember? I'd never discuss personal stuff with him."

"You two planned my surprise party without my knowledge."

"That's different. Thus, the word *surprise*. We weren't talking private matters." Sugar snagged a throw pillow and clasped it to her midsection. "This season is always difficult for you. Why don't you close the diner and take off a few days?"

"Wow. You do cut right to the chase."

"Uh-huh. Told you I would."

"I'm fine. Besides, I can't close the diner. There's my personal income and additional staff to consider. Chuck, the other waitress, dishwasher, busboys, and janitorial. It's not a big crew, but other than Chuck and me, the rest can't afford those missing hours."

"Then you take off. The Come and Get It won't fall apart. Chuck'll make sure of that." Sugar narrowed her gaze. "I know the significance of this birthday. Yesterday, your thirty-ninth...and today, someone else's twenty-first. It's a big milestone. I realize that opens old wounds. It's understandable."

Sugar spoke with compassion, the expression on her face, tender and thoughtful. A constant in her life since childhood, Sugar Perkins was the one person who she could always count on, hands-down. Even though she'd been married for eighteen years to Lowell, most everyone referred to her as "Miss Sugar." The "miss" a term of respect for many women, married or not, down South, and in the Ozarks too.

No one ever called Sugar by her given name. Word had it that the birth certificate designation "Beatrice" died an instant death one Christmas Eve when the toddler's mama and daddy discovered she'd sampled all the candy canes on the lower branches of the Christmas tree and then strategically rearranged them. After that, Beatrice was forever known as "Sugar."

"Too sweet for her own good!" her parents proclaimed to anyone who listened, which in fact, was everyone in Ruby and at least three counties over.

"Thank you for understanding." Ida Mae squeezed Sugar's hand. "The diner's closed on Mondays so tomorrow's a day off too. By Tuesday, I'll be as good as gold."

"You need a vacation."

"More time on my hands won't fix this. You know that. I know that. I've reconciled it. Staying busy is my balm. The diner's my jam. My heart and soul."

"Who are you trying to convince? Me? Or you? I know you love the diner and your customers love you right back, but work doesn't put a ring on your finger. It doesn't hold you in its arms or warm your bed at night."

"*Whoa.* How'd we go from time off to marriage and its perks?"

"*Tsk. Tsk.*" Sugar clucked. "A vacation would provide clarity. Help you reevaluate life and brainstorm new goals. No, time off can't fix the past, but it can help you refocus. Ever consider getting out more? Maybe join a book club, take up dance, explore a new hobby? Have you researched any area singles groups?"

Had her BFF gone nuts?

"Singles groups?" Ida Mae snorted. "Don't make me

laugh. Since when does our fair town have one of those? This *is* Ruby, Missouri we're talking about. We're not exactly bursting at the seams with any of those things."

"Well, my dear. We have single men in church. How about Jake and Billie Gail Brewer's three boys—Gabe, Garrett, and Mike? Respectable stock, have their heads on straight, pretty handsome fellas."

"Melinda Brewer's older brothers? Why, they're all at least ten years younger than me."

"Aww, age is relative, but okay. How about that new social worker at Sunset Meadows? Nice grin, rugged-looking, and cute. Word has it, a real innovator too."

"Matt Enders? The Social Service Director? Same. Late twenties. Too young for me. And in case you didn't notice, he's set his sights on Miss Melinda."

"Wow. Guess I didn't realize that. Doesn't seem like the feeling's mutual."

"I don't think she wants to admit it yet."

"Ahh. A fire-and-ice kind of thing, huh?" Sugar tapped her fingers against the sofa cushions, thinking. She ticked off additional names, single men in town who were either too young, too old, or spoken for. Then, she snapped her fingers. "Of course! The very man you're pining for!"

Ida Mae shook her head, blonde waves bouncing. "Ohh, no. That ship has sailed. I'm done yearning for Chuck Farrow."

While she couldn't blame her past indiscretion on him, because after all, she'd ultimately made the choice to date Tyler, there was the little matter of the past twenty-one years since then. During that period, despite mixed signals, it had been difficult to discern what the man wanted. If he wanted something beyond friendship, then Romeo he wasn't.

Hadn't those mixed signals landed her in her current state? An old maid. While thirty-nine wasn't ancient, years that she might have married and borne children had all but withered away.

Yes, God had doled out fitting punishment for her teenage rebellion, but if it hadn't been for Chuck's subtle on-again-off-again cues, especially over the past ten years, maybe life would have taken a different direction.

Today, she questioned whether she'd loved the man at all. Friendships, intense friendships, could skew how things actually were. Ida Mae hardly knew fact from fiction anymore. In her exhausted haze, maybe she didn't know Chuck as well as she thought she did.

Sugar studied her, as if weighing her next words. When she spoke, her voice was soft and empathetic. "I think Chuck cares for you more than you know. Probably more than *he* knows."

"Big difference between that and love. Caring rescues a drowning man. Love sustains him."

"Point made."

Ida Mae wondered if Chuck thought about that. Not that it mattered.

Across the room, Helen North, played by Lucille Ball, and Frank Beardsley, portrayed by Henry Fonda, recounted all the reasons why their crazy, mixed-up relationship would not work. But Ida Mae knew this movie by memory. Helen and Frank would decide to take a chance anyway.

Old movies, like this one, almost made her believe anything was possible. Though Ida Mae's story differed, taking chances, a similar theme, resonated.

Risks—healthy ones—sometimes recrafted a future.

The notion appealed. Nevertheless, short of lighting a stick of dynamite under Chuck's behind, she highly doubted he'd trade comfort zones for chaos. Wasn't that what happened when one risked one's heart?

Chuck didn't sleep well. He rose that Monday morning, his day off, jogged his usual distance of a couple miles, and lumbered back inside with no more clarity than he'd had last night.

There'd been no answers from Ida Mae. Nothing forthcoming to help him understand where that woman's head was. The few clues she'd dropped yesterday and the day before further muddied the waters. How was a guy supposed to make sense of a milestone if he didn't have the faintest idea what all the veiled references meant? They weren't kids anymore. Why couldn't they talk about this?

You know why. You wounded that girl, big time. Chuck opened a sports drink and took a swig. Back then, he may have been a kid himself, but his mama raised him with manners. He knew better.

Yeah, they'd moved past it, but only because they never spoke of it. Other than yesterday, he'd never apologized about what he'd said when she'd professed her love. Essentially, that apology stunk. If he'd had a chance to practice, get his words right, maybe he would have done a better job.

Twenty-one years. The words, the day, tumbled around in Chuck's mind. Most of the time on his day off, he'd tinker with tomorrow's menu, line up the Pink Pig Special in his mind, and go over the dessert selections.

He'd putter around in his yard, maybe catch a movie on TV, visit his mother, and Voni, and her crew too. Occasionally, he'd do volunteer work at Sunset Meadows, the retirement living complex on the other end of town. Sometimes, he'd work on his secret project. Not today.

He plopped down at the tiny kitchen table, sports drink in hand, and ruminated. He resisted the urge to grab his cell phone and tap the familiar number. Nope. Why do that when he could go see her?

He showered and changed, and he considered what he might say. He ran it forward and backward in his mind. Fifteen minutes later, he stood on Ida Mae's front porch and rang the bell.

Sunlight filtered through the crimson-colored leaves overhead, and Chuck checked the time. Seven-fifty. Was he that early? He didn't think Ida Mae slept in on her day off, but then again, he rarely paid her a visit at this hour. His third visit here since Saturday night—it must be a record. Though they saw each other daily at the Come and Get It, they didn't often visit the other's home. They'd stopped the practice a few years back. Why, Chuck couldn't recall. Once tight friends, in recent years, their friendship shifted. Something seemed off. Had he grown too comfortable? Taken their bond for granted?

A minute passed. Maybe she hadn't heard the chime. He rang it once more.

This time, Ida Mae's voice echoed from within. "Hold your horses! Give a girl a chance to zip up her bathrobe!"

Uh-oh. Poor timing.

Chuck tried to erase the pictures that drifted through his mind. Should he stay...or should he go? As he stood on the porch debating the pros and cons, the front door swung open. There she stood in her pink chenille bathrobe, blonde mane tousled and unbrushed, eyes caked with sleep, and the telltale mark of a pillowcase crease on her rosy pink cheek. She stifled a yawn and he refrained from gawking. Or attempted to.

He'd never seen anyone so beautiful. The picture almost knocked him senseless. "I—I'm sorry. I didn't know you…slept in. I should go."

"Why wouldn't I sleep in? It's our day off, silly." She motioned him inside. "It's a rather brisk morning to stand here in my PJs, if you don't mind."

"Oh. Gosh. Sorry about that." He stepped inside and closed the door. Fresh-brewed coffee scented the home, teasing his nostrils and taste buds. He sniffed the air and sighed. "Ahh."

"I flipped on the coffeemaker as I made a beeline for the front door."

"Quick thinking."

"Yeah, well, I had it set for eight, hoping I might catch a few extra winks this morning."

"Wow. I'm an idiot. I should have called first." He stuffed his hands in his blue jeans pockets but didn't quite know what to do with his eyes. Where to look? Obviously, nowhere below the shoulders. Her face. Her face was good. Safe. Gorgeous.

Ida Mae's early morning state upended him. Normally, when they arrived at the diner pre-dawn, she usually wore make-up and one of those frilly pink and white waitress dresses. Sometimes, after closing, she unpinned her hair. When she did, the gesture gave his heart a curious squeeze. He wished she'd wear it down more.

"Yes. Well, since you're here, why are you? Here, I mean."

Her question roused him from his trance-like state. Every sentence he'd practiced, every word he'd rehearsed, embarked on its own journey. He couldn't remember any of it.

"The Pink Pig Special."

"What?" Ida Mae stared at him like he'd lost his mind. "You came all the way over here for that?"

"I'm thinking about changing it tomorrow. Trying something different. Maybe chicken tetrazzini instead of pork chops and apple sauce."

"Fabulous. You don't need my permission. You're our chef now. Our kitchen manger. Second in command. Do it." She padded toward the kitchen and left him standing near the door.

An awkward pause ensued. He didn't know if he should leave or follow.

"Do you want coffee or not?" She raised her voice a notch over the sound of clinking coffee mugs.

Chuck assumed that was her way of inviting him to stay so he strode after her. "Please, if you have enough."

She'd already poured two cups when he entered the kitchen. She held one and set down the other. Should he sit? Stand? Make small talk?

He took his cue from Ida Mae. When she sat, so did he. Steam rose from the coffee mug before him and he waved a hand over the steaming brew, as if the action would cool it any faster. He liked his joe strong and black with no sweetener. She did too.

They sat in companionable silence for a moment as Chuck worked up his nerve. Why had he come? What did he hope his visit would accomplish? They'd been friends all their lives. This shouldn't be so hard.

He sipped at the coffee, trying to remember the things he'd intended to say, but a new awareness brought him up short. If he resurrected the past, what then? He couldn't stroll down Memory Lane without addressing the weeds that needed whacked. But wasn't that why he'd beat a path over here? To mow down a few of those weeds and attempt to make things right? Bright guy that he was, he'd certainly waited long enough. Twenty-one years, to be exact.

"Look, I don't make a habit of having coffee with men while in my bathrobe." Her not-so-subtle way of saying, "Hurry up."

He smiled, lacing his fingers around the coffee mug handle. "A good thing."

"What's on your mind, Chuck? I know it's not the Pink Pig Special. It's not the menu re-do or the diner updates. The reason you're here has nothing to do with the diner at all, does it?"

What could he say? "You're right."

Sunshine trickled through the window and fell across the table, warming them. He noticed Ida Mae's hands. Fair-skinned, and youthful-looking, in spite of hard work. Nails recently polished. Fingers, bare, and no wedding band in sight.

His heart twisted. She'd waited for him. Waited to the point of no other prospects, and indeed, no babies. Sure, there'd been that teenage preoccupation with Fenston for a while, but that didn't last long, as he knew it wouldn't. Tyler was her rebound guy. The wild and rowdy rebel who could turn a clever phrase and spin a lie into truth.

A smooth-talking charmer who loved girls and fast cars almost as much as he loved himself.

Wow. Did I ever mess up. Chuck reeled with the truth. When he spurned Ida Mae and inadvertently propelled her toward Fenston's all-too-ready arms, a landslide began. It rocked the foundation of their friendship. It cracked the façade of what he imagined they'd always have. It robbed them of time and possibilities.

His actions—words so carelessly tossed about—influenced where they'd arrived today. *But I was eighteen. I was a kid myself.*

True. But old enough to know better.

Chapter Seven

Were they going to sit here until their coffee grew cold or was he going to elaborate? Why had Chuck come?

Ida Mae glanced outside. Must be a breeze. Treetops, thick with color, swayed in the wind and bowed to their Maker. Last week, fall's official kick-off. This week, a new season.

She watched as sweet Nora and Ned Brewster tootled out of their drive in their old model station wagon. Before Ned guided the vehicle onto the street, he leaned over and kissed his wife flush on the cheek. Then, for good measure, he gave her another. *Oh, to be loved like that.*

They'd owned Nora and Ned's General Market here in Ruby for fifty-three years and they'd been married at least a year longer. In their mid-seventies now, the couple was inseparable.

"Good-natured pair, aren't they?"

So, Chuck had observed them too. "Yes. They never seem to have an off day. I'm usually at the diner when they leave to open the market. Except on Mondays, when we're closed. And it's always the same between them. Ned sneaks a kiss or two on their way out and Miss Nora breaks out in a massive grin. It's the most precious thing. They work together, see each other twenty-four-seven, and they are so in love."

"Ahh, I wonder if they know you spy."

"Something tells me they wouldn't care." Ida Mae

brought the coffee mug to her lips and sipped. Chuck fiddled with his mug but didn't drink.

"That's how it is when people are in love, I suppose. When a couple's in sync, what the rest of the world's doing or thinking doesn't matter."

He gazed at her long and hard, his words unearthing various emotions. What was he trying to say? This being in sync business confused her. Was he admitting to loving her? Doubtful. Maybe he wanted to beat around the bush today, but she did not. Every minute that passed nudged her closer to the age forty mark.

"Why are you here?" She put it plain and simple. There was no need for preamble.

He nodded and leaned forward. "We need to clear the air. This past weekend seemed to be a turning point of sorts. I hoped a birthday party might be fun, but I'm afraid I misjudged. It only served to remind you of something from the past. Something painful, right?"

"The party was fine. It *was* fun. I appreciate all the planning and effort that went into it."

"Saturday night when we tried to talk, it made you ill. Yesterday, before church, you indicated there wasn't enough time. In the past twenty-four hours, I've rolled this around in my mind, and I've come to realize that I'm connected to whatever is troubling you. This might be a hard conversation to have, but I don't know that there will be a better time than now."

Ida Mae's stomach lurched. Why had she thought they'd never have to talk about her pregnancy? Maybe because, with each passing year, they'd drawn closer. They'd moved forward in many ways. They'd set old hurts on a shelf and put a lid on that box. And yet, old memories remained. Memories that sprang to the forefront because of the milestone that was her child's twenty-first birthday.

When she didn't speak, Chuck continued. "When my dad deserted our family, it played havoc with my head. It's tough on any kid when the person who should love you abandons you, but for a ten-year-old boy, when his dad leaves, it messes you up in ways you can't imagine. It devalues you. It affects your self-esteem, your ability to bond, and how you see the world. It affects other things too, like one's view of marriage. It makes you think it might not be such a wise thing for you either.

"To make matters worse, we never saw it coming. Voni was too young to grasp everything, but Mom and I knew Dad's drinking had increased. He wasn't one of those fall-down-drunk types, but his breath always reeked of alcohol. It permeated his pores. Occasionally, behind closed doors, he and Mom argued about his drinking, but it never seemed to get better. Still, we got the idea Dad loved us. The night before he left—when we last saw him—he kissed us goodnight and said he'd see us in the morning. That was thirty years ago."

Ida Mae remembered. They'd been in the same grade at school. When he confided to her that his father left, it was as if all the air whooshed from his lungs and emptied him of oxygen. She'd found him crouched behind the bus barn at school that day, his face a mask of sorrow, his entire body trembling.

"Go ahead and cry. It's okay. It's only you and me, and I'm not gonna tell anybody." She wrapped him in a hug as deep, gut-wrenching sobs shook his ten-year-old frame, and she immediately hated Sy Farrow for hurting her best friend.

Chuck returned her hug, and she handed him a wad of tissues. As he blew his nose and collected himself, he said in a low voice, "Thanks. Maybe he'll come back."

But Sy never did.

The snippet of that childhood memory forever embedded itself in her brain. Decades had passed, but that recollection was as fresh today as if the incident had just happened. Life meandered on, but the scars lingered.

"I'm sorry. No parent should do what your father did. I know your dad leaving shaded your views about a lot of things."

"Yeah. It was the way he did it too. He and Mom tucked Voni and me in bed, as usual. Said our prayers, kissed us, and *bam*. Next morning, he was gone. No note. No word. No reason. What kind of man does that to his kids? His *wife*?"

"I honestly don't know." Ida Mae rose and topped off their coffee. She took her seat again and positioned herself closer to the table. They hadn't talked of these things in a long, long while. "I've never been through anything like that, so I can't possibly know how that would feel. I do know what I felt when it happened to you. I despised your father for wounding my best friend. As terrible as it sounds, I prayed something bad would happen to him. Since then, I've had a chance to…reflect. We don't know why people do the things they do. Maybe they feel boxed into a corner. Maybe your dad left to get help and was afraid to return. Maybe it was a choice he later regretted. We all choose differently. Occasionally, we make bad choices."

"That's way more grace than I'd ever extend the guy."

Chuck gave a wry laugh. "The thing is I could've understood more if he'd at least tried to contact us. Kept the line of communication open. But he didn't. We never knew where he went or why he went. To this day we don't even know if Sy Farrow is dead or alive, not that I really care."

Did he really believe that? Wounds colored perspective and skewed objectivity. That was a cold, hard reality.

"I think you do care. I think you care very much." Ida Mae rested her arms on the table and gauged his reaction. "When those we love hurt us, it's easier to insulate ourselves than take a chance on loving that deeply again. We draw a line in the sand of non-negotiable matters we won't risk, and we develop an aversion to all sorts of things."

"Like matters of the heart, huh?"

"Yes, especially those."

Chuck reached out, resting his fingertips on hers. The action surprised Ida Mae. Pleasantly so.

"Like I tried to say yesterday, poor timing though it was, I didn't mean to hurt you all those years ago. I was a stupid, messed-up kid. By the time I was a teenager, I'd promised myself that I'd never gamble my heart the way Mom had hers. The way she cried after Dad left broke me. Every tear she shed, all the sadness she bore, let me tell you—I noted that." He swallowed and composed himself. "I always thought I'd make a lousy husband. Like father, like son, you know? Like maybe it's imprinted in my genes."

"You're not him. You could never be that kind of man. You're kind and gentle and thoughtful. There isn't an irresponsible bone in your body, Chuck Farrow."

"I wasn't kind or gentle or anything else when I blew you off all those years ago. I crushed my best friend and sent her straight to an egomaniac's arms. A responsible person, a mature person, wouldn't have said that stuff or acted that way."

"I can't lie. Yes, what you said then about not loving me back, and the way you said it, stung." *Stung?* It shattered her. "But no one forced me to date Tyler Fenston. I made that decision, as poor as it was."

"I'm glad you came to your senses and ditched the guy. Otherwise, you might have been in that car accident too. And I couldn't have handled that."

Ida Mae gulped. Her knees quaked and her heart raced. Why had he never told her this? Nevertheless, she lived with one, huge life-changing choice and always would.

Their fingertips still touched. Flesh meeting flesh. The barest of touches, yet symbolic all the same, and a hair's breadth away from holding hands. Did Chuck realize it too?

"Me pushing you away...It wasn't you. Not then. Not ever. A relationship was the problem." He rustled his fingers against hers. "At eighteen, I couldn't commit. Few kids that age can, but my reasons were twofold and ones I could barely understand, much less tactfully convey. At that point, I was angry and bitter. Afraid too, I suppose. Even though it'd been eight years, I spent those years allowing all that emotion to fester."

"I understand that better now."

"You know, wounds are curious things," Chuck mused. "Some folks heal quicker. Others never do."

I know. Oh, how I know. So much for telling Sugar she was done yearning for the man. Something soft and warm fluttered in her soul. Words unspoken hung suspended between them.

"Ten years ago, when you agreed to work for me, why did you?" An answer to prayer, but she'd always wondered. "Why did someone with your professional background agree to shift gears and work for a lot less pay and a lot less acclaim?"

Effortlessly, and seemingly without thought, he laced his fingers through hers. At last. Hands entwined. Hearts, fragile, yet fused.

"Because you asked me to."

There. He gave her the reason. Another point—he was thirty then. He'd had ten years to contemplate their teenage exchange. The one that altered their friendship and shaped its trajectory. At that point, he would have walked through fire to right the wrongs between them. Going to work for Ida Mae at the Come and Get It seemed like a real pleasant alternative.

Though they talked a bit about the past, until today, they'd never fully discussed it. Being in close proximity all day, every day, he'd hoped to prove how very sorry he was and show her how much he cared. But he'd failed miserably.

In trying to navigate the employer/employee slippery slope, as well as identify his personal feelings, years scuttled by and complacency took hold. Their relationship grew comfortable. Easy. *Predictable.*

Ida Mae's coffee cup remained almost full. She pierced him with her gaze. The one that seemed to look right through him and know exactly what he was thinking.

"If I'd asked you to swim through hot lava, would you have?"

"Yes'm. Pretty much."

"Wow. Great to know." She glanced at their hands, still linked. "What does this mean?"

"Honestly? I don't know. I wanted to clear the air. I wanted...you to understand how important you are to me."

"Ahh. I see. Best friends and all that, huh?"

"Well, I know you and Sugar are tight, but I always thought of you as my best friend, yes."

Ida Mae was a smart woman. Didn't she appreciate his candor? Now, Chuck wanted to ask a few questions. They'd danced around that time long enough.

As if guessing his thoughts, Ida Mae sighed. She relaxed her hand but didn't pull away. "You crushed my spirit. Maybe if we hadn't shared so much history then, maybe if we'd been older and more mature, we'd have responded differently. I would have exercised more caution in telling you how I felt, and you wouldn't have lashed out."

"We were high school seniors. A pair of small-town kids and inexperienced in adult matters."

"Yeah, but inexperienced or not, we shared a special bond. I guess I kind of thought you felt the same way about me that I felt about you. I lost sleep pondering why you reacted the way you did. I couldn't concentrate on simple tasks and my mind started to wander. For a while, my grades even plummeted."

The depth of how much he'd hurt her rocked him to

the core. "I'm so sorry. I've wished a thousand times I could take back those words. It wasn't until you left after graduation that I understood everything."

Ida Mae frowned. "Understood everything?"

"I understood the reason you left wasn't because of Fenston, and it wasn't because you wanted to travel before you settled down in Ruby. You left because of me, right? Because I messed up. When you came home, you weren't the same. You hid it well or tried to anyway. You were different, though."

"Different?"

Was she really going to deny it? Intuition told him he needed to tread easy. He bobbed his head. "Yes. Almost like you'd lost a piece of yourself. I'm not sure how to explain it."

She swallowed hard, and with her other hand, reached out to clasp the coffee mug handle, as if to take a drink. But she didn't. Instead, she let her hand rest there and trained her eyes downward, making it impossible for Chuck to guess what mysteries they held. "I know I drove you away, but where did you go? What happened while you were gone?" The hand that remained in his, trembled.

"It doesn't matter where I went, but you're right. You were part of the reason I left. And to answer your other question..." She raised her chin. "I grew up. In four months, there are bound to be changes. People change."

"Yes, but the changes I'm talking about have less to do with time that elapsed and more to do with your countenance. How you saw the world and how you carried yourself. You seemed...older. Way older than the seventeen-year-old girl that left."

"I *was* older. I turned eighteen while I was gone."

"No, you know what I mean, Ida Mae. It was like you'd climbed Mount Everest and suffered altitude sickness. For weeks, you weren't yourself. You kind of walked around in a fog."

"You'd started college and were awfully busy. How do you even remember that?"

"When my best friend, once a social butterfly, retreats to a cocoonlike state, it's pretty memorable. You may have fooled others by slapping on a smile and acting like business as usual, but I saw something deeper beneath the happy-go-lucky mask." He carefully weighed his next words and plunged ahead. "That bit you told your parents about traveling over the summer... Where'd you go? How'd you even afford to be gone that long? Don't those extended stay places get expensive?"

Ida Mae ignored his first question. "I worked for Mom and Dad at the Come and Get It all through high school. I saved every penny."

"Yes, I remember. But I also remember you'd planned to attend community college in the fall after graduation, like me. What happened to that plan?"

"I realized I didn't need a college degree to eventually own and run the diner. Most of what I needed, I learned from my parents." Ida Mae paused, her expression pensive. "I always wanted to travel a bit before settling down here. Ruby's my home and I wouldn't live anywhere else. I love it here. But there were places...I wanted to go first. Things I needed to do."

Why did he get the feeling she was stalling? Maybe because this was the third time since Saturday night that he'd tried to pin down what happened. He reminded himself everyone had a right to their privacy. He should let this rest. Obviously, Ida Mae didn't want to talk about those mysterious four months. Still, it baffled him. Her secrecy seemed so out of character. Why would she not tell him?

"Okay. Don't keep me in suspense. Where did you go? What did you do?"

"It's been twenty-one years. Why does that matter now?"

Was she serious? *Because every year at this time, you withdraw. You have since your whirlwind trek, Lord knows where, after high school.* If Chuck had any doubts about her trip's significance and the role it played in her current mindset, her reluctance to address the issue further cemented additional questions. Yeah, a lot of years and water under the bridge, but in a lot of ways, the emotional bog called "the past" hindered her.

"It matters because the toll this thing's taking on you is getting worse. It's like whatever it is still hounds you. Am I wrong?"

Ida Mae unlaced her fingers from his. Uh-oh. He shouldn't be surprised. He'd nudged and she'd withdrawn. Slowly, she backed her chair away and stood, indicating their conversation was finished.

Chuck didn't want to leave it like this. He came over to talk, not to irritate her. He stood too and touched her arm.

"Hey, please don't get mad. I'm not trying to pry or delve into your personal business."

"Really? Sure seems that way."

"I care, girl. I always have."

She considered his statement, then Ida Mae gathered

their cups and padded over to the sink counter. With her back turned, she spoke in a hushed tone. "For years, folks around town pegged you and me as an item. I almost let myself believe it. During our school years...before Tyler...and then, as we grew into adulthood. Does the town chatter ever bother you?"

"Nah, I know people talk. It's not malicious or anything. Why? Does it bother you?"

Dumb question. He knew they weren't getting any younger. She'd bared her soul more than once without much encouragement from him. However, until recently, he hadn't had the nerve to explore possibilities. His feelings, and hers, were a mixed bag of contradictions. Of course, all the nuances must bother her. Even he'd started to sense the hitch in her spirit. If he were honest, that part troubled him too. Her unease over the future, their disconnect over the past, and the fact he couldn't seem to move forward without the two merging stirred his emotions in a gut-wrenching way.

How had they gone for years on a fairly even keel, and now it seemed they'd reached a turning point? It confused him.

Portions of Pastor Bill's Sunday sermon flitted through Chuck's mind. The pastor's words, so poignant and thought-provoking, danced around the outer edges of his subconscious and lingered there. *Love* and the scriptures and analogies Pastor Bill used to reference it begged him to revisit long-held convictions. Specifically, the part about love persevering. That passage in the thirteenth chapter of First Corinthians really gripped him.

There were other verses that compelled him.

Specifically, verse eleven. *"When I was a child, I spake as a child, I understood as a child, I thought as a child: but when I became a man, I put away childish things."* That was a tough one. Mired deep in the trenches of resentment and sorrow, he doubted that he could ever understand his father's abandonment, much less dispense with the memories and emotion associated with the guy. One day, maybe, as Scripture promised. But not today. Not in this lifetime. A pillar of righteousness, he wasn't.

But, man. For Ida Mae's sake, he wished he were. Face to face with this woman, the epitome of virtue and goodness, he hated his dad all the more for tainting his ability to commit to her.

She pivoted around and stared. "Folks' talk doesn't bother me as much as what's at the center of it. You. Me. The *us* I hoped we'd eventually be."

The words stabbed his heart and he flinched. Her answer yanked him back to the here and now. Ida Mae's face bore a thousand regrets and wishes too. If only he could tell her what she wanted to hear. That he loved her. Intentions weren't cutting it. He needed to put gas in the engine if he expected them to go anywhere.

Chuck stood there, silent, ramrod straight. Blast it! What he wouldn't give to take her in his arms and hold her again...like he had at their school dances so long ago. The memory, especially, of their junior prom—when they'd slow-danced to the Righteous Brothers' oldie, "Unchained Melody"—brought goosebumps. Thankfully, he wore long sleeves, which hid his reaction. "Knowing what I've shared and the baggage I come with, you have to admit a relationship would be a mighty big risk."

"Slipping in the shower is a risk. Manning a hot grill down at the Come and Get It is a risk. Life, in general, is one big risk." Ida Mae twisted a dishtowel in her hands. "Sometimes, we get burned and we give it another go."

"My head says you're right. My heart isn't quite there." He stepped forward and encircled her palms with his. The intimate gesture underscored the obvious. He hoped his heart would be ready soon. He refrained from overanalyzing it, but the word *commitment* teeter-tottered in his brain and made him dizzy He wanted to plan a future together, yet his head remained a jumbled mess. Would Ida Mae marry him if he asked? Did she even still love him? He'd like to believe he knew the answer to those questions, but the truth eluded him.

That is, until she stood on her tiptoes and quickly kissed his lips.

Chapter Eight

Yes, she'd taken a risk. She hadn't planned to kiss him, but she wasn't sorry either.

Thinking of that encounter made her smile. It had been three days ago, yet when her and Chuck's paths crossed at the diner—which happened often since they worked together—one of them sent the other a knowing glance. The glance that insinuated "maybe." "Maybe" was a hopeful and motivating word. It awakened possibility.

When Mom and Dad phoned her Thursday afternoon, Ida Mae took the call in her tiny office at the Come and Get It. She tapped her cell's speaker function and sank into the chair overlooking the hills and hollows she'd loved since childhood. Sunlight bathed the changing trees in golden hues, and like always, the land's sheer beauty caused her breath to catch.

"We thought we'd call and check on you, sweetheart. How's our favorite daughter?" Her father's voice washed over her.

She pictured Dad on the other end of the line, grinning. Most likely, he wore blue jeans and a comfy sweat shirt and one of the fourteen caps he owned. The cap he liked best was one Mom had purchased for him. The words "Ozarks born and bred. Not a tourist." were emblazoned above the bill.

"Your only daughter's great. How's Branson treating you and Mom?"

"Wonderful, dear. As usual, we're eating way too much," her mother chimed. Obviously, her parents had her on speaker. "We know you like texting, but our fingers don't move like they used to, and besides, we wanted to hear your voice."

"I'm glad you and Dad called, Mom. Now's a perfect time." The diner's second rush of customers would swarm the place in about thirty minutes. Ida Mae needed a breather before the next wave hit. "Are you guys enjoying the cabin?"

The cabin, a one-thousand square foot, hand hewn gem overlooked Table Rock Lake. Her mother and father purchased it when they'd retired ten years ago. Only an hour's drive from home, it offered the perfect vacation haven or weekend getaway. With the exception of Ruby, their lake retreat served them their very own slice of Ozarks' heaven.

"The only thing that would make it better would be if you were here to enjoy it with us."

"I'd love that, Dad. You know I would." Ida Mae patted a few loose curls back into place as she spoke. She'd seldom been to the cabin over the years because she rarely stepped away from the diner, but lately, the idea of a week's respite sounded heavenly. Maybe Sugar had pegged it right. She toyed with the idea of a vacation and filed it away for future reference.

"Well, you come on down whenever you want, sweetheart," Dad said. "If you'd like to spend some time with us oldsters or even if you want R and R to yourself, the cabin's all yours. You have your key, right?"

"Sixty-five isn't old, but yes, I have my key, and I may take you and Mom up on that one day."

"Wonderful. Now, how are things there?"

She told them about the new menu selections and additional ideas she had regarding diner updates. She enlightened them on the latest goings-on in town, noting the tension between Melinda Brewer and one Matthew Enders. Word had it that Sunset Meadows' new social services director was about to butt heads with Melinda. Enders' get 'er done attitude and high-amp energy seemed to jerk Miss Melinda's chain, and in a most exasperating way.

Zeke Ledbetter recently brought Delia Scroggins into the diner. They ordered the Pink Pig Special and chatted away until close. And let's see—the county finally issued Horace Sapp a brand, spanking new patrol car, complete with all the bells and whistles necessary for maintaining law and order in Ruby and the surrounding community.

Rumor had it that Buster Boy, Jerry and Ann Marshall's black Lab, rode as the first passenger. Buster Boy dug under Jerry and Ann's fence, as he liked to do, and the good deputy hauled his furry behind back home. If only that skunk hadn't sprayed Buster first. And no, Jerry didn't have the faintest idea how to fumigate vehicle upholstery, though, he most certainly appreciated Horace's help in delivering their fur baby back home.

Blessedly, old Ernie knew what to do down at the auto shop and promptly went to work on the...er...situation.

"Skunk, huh?" Dad howled. "How's Buster Boy?"

"Ann says a few baths in tomato juice neutralized the odor. The patrol car's going to stink a while, but Ernie used a special cleaning solvent on it and the odor should eventually dissipate."

Her parents laughed so long that Ida Mae wondered if they'd forgotten she was on the line.

"In the meantime," she interjected, "Horace wears a mask as he patrols. The county health department offered him a box of those disposable paper thingies. No charge, of course."

"You mean that's allowed? For our local crime fighter to wear a mask?"

"Well, what's his boss—the high sheriff—gonna say, Selma?" Her father blew his nose as he continued to laugh. "No masks allowed unless you're the criminal?"

That did it. The three of them started hooting and Ida Mae had to reach for a tissue.

"I'm trying to picture it." Her mother made a valiant effort in gaining control. "Our Horace tootling around town, tipping his hat to passersby, kind of like the Lone Ranger. But his mask was black, wasn't it, Emory?"

"Yes, if memory serves. The health department's masks are mint green aren't they, Ida Mae?"

"No, sir. I think the shade is Poppy Pink. The county nurse switched them up last year."

"Ohh. This is rich!"

Eventually, the laughter worked its way out of their systems. Before their conversation wound down, her mother cleared her throat. "Well, we've heard about everyone else. Anything new with you, dear? With Chuck?"

Was there ever? But after Monday, hope lit on Ida Mae's shoulders, expanding her odds. "I spoke with him."

"Chuck's a worthy man to have in your corner, daughter. With him by your side, we never worry about the diner." Dad raised his voice a notch over the sound of running water. She heard him gulp and smack his lips, as if taking a long, satisfying drink. "Not that your mother and I have any qualms about you running the place on your own. You've done us right proud in the years since we transferred ownership."

"What your father's trying to say," Mom offered, "is that we know you're a tip-top businesswoman. We're glad too, that you have a dependable right-hand man you can delegate some responsibility to."

"Yes. I like the way you put that, Mom." Ida Mae grinned and stretched. "To clarify, however, I meant that Chuck and I...we...spoke about things other than the Come and Get It."

"Oh?"

She envisioned her parents pausing, mid-motion, in their tracks, training their eyes on Dad's cell. They'd known Chuck and his family forever, and it was no secret Mom and Dad wondered why romance between their daughter and her childhood friend never blossomed.

From the time Ida Mae and Chuck were kids until their teenage years, her parents, like everyone else, assumed something more than friendship would happen.

As life marched by, it was only natural her parents would assume love eventually found her and Chuck. Except it hadn't. Love couldn't find its way when there was only one willing party.

Ida Mae stood, noting the hour. "Mom, Dad, I love you and I really hate to go, but I have to get back out there. We're about to get our second wave of hungry customers."

"Wait, dear!" Mom sounded flustered. "Can't you

further explain that comment? You and Chuck spoke about what?"

"The best medicine for burns, Mom. But joking aside," Ida Mae added, "about the future."

Chuck watched as Ida Mae glided onto the floor, straightening her frilly, white apron as she went. She moved effortlessly as if the world were her oyster, and from her countenance, one might readily agree.

Chuck had unearthed no mysteries, but for now, they'd tabled the past. The little matter of that kiss on the lips caused his heart to thaw. He wouldn't put a name to it, yet.

"Your folks doing okay?" He continued kneading the dinner roll dough but caught her as she waltzed out of her office into the kitchen. She was about to enter the dining area, and she turned around, humming.

"Yes. Their lake cabin is their home away from home."

"I remember when Emory and Selma bought the place. Your dad wanted to fish, and your mom wanted to take up photography. How'd that work out?"

Ida Mae smiled. "Dad got his fishing boat. Mom took photography classes and got a fancy Nikon. She's actually pretty decent. They also frequent the country music shows and other Branson venues, and they spend a lot of time together having fun. They worked hard all their lives, so after they retired ten years ago, they're living their dream."

"Well deserved, I'd say." He finished kneading the dough and set it aside. "They ever miss it here?"

"Occasionally, I think. They built the diner from the

ground up, so it's in their blood, you know, but they reached a point where they welcomed retirement. They're able to enjoy their hobbies and each other."

Obviously, Emory and Selma's happiness mattered to their daughter. There was a measure of wistfulness in her voice too, and Chuck knew why. Most likely, she'd envisioned her life differently than how it had turned out so far. Frankly, he knew that feeling.

While he'd never fully allowed his mind to consider marriage and a family, he had to admit, life could be lonesome. Yeah, food and cooking inspired him, but did they fulfill him? What would his days be like in twenty years? When he stared retirement in the face—with no one by his side. Sure, he had his secret goal, but without someone to share it with, it wouldn't be nearly as fun.

The Ozarks and Ruby, Missouri were home. They were his heritage. He couldn't imagine ever leaving. He also couldn't imagine the rest of his days here alone. He had his mother and Voni, but his family couldn't fill the void of a helpmate.

At forty, he more than recognized a person either reached for the stars or watched others lasso theirs. The thought deflated him. How long had he convinced himself that life spent alone was better than a future filled with risks? The answer, if he were honest? Since that loser father of his walked away without so much as a backward glance.

Maybe he should ponder another alternative that risk-taking offered. His life might be weighed down with memories and heartbreak, but perhaps, new interests and celebrations could tip the scale.

"...I love it here too. Wouldn't trade our regulars—our

friends and neighbors—for anything, but I've been thinking. There might come a day where I do something different. Don't know what yet, but now that I'm thirty-nine, I want to keep my options open."

Huh? What had he missed?

"Like?"

"Well, for starters, maybe reduce the hours we're open." Her eyes scanned the kitchen and landed on the serving window. She stepped over and peered out, then turned to face him again. "Golly, I've worked here since high school. I transitioned back into my hostess and waitress role except added to that all the responsibility that comes with owning and managing a business. Without you as my right-hand-man, I might go nuts."

The diner definitely didn't lack fans. Business boomed. Besides their regular customers, visitors and tourists now frequented the place despite the fact that they rarely advertised. As a long-established diner, the Come and Get It had a solid reputation in the Ozarks and beyond. Word of mouth proved their best friend.

"I know we put in awfully long days here. I also know work can be a fickle mistress. We love our professions, but too much of a good thing isn't necessarily the *best* thing."

"That's it exactly." Ida Mae tipped her head from side to side and ran a hand over the back of her neck. "I've run the numbers. Decreasing our hours won't impact our bottom line a whole lot. In fact, with the slight increase in menu prices and the business we continue to generate, we'll still make a dandy profit, and we can offer our limited staff an increase in wages to balance the decrease in workload. I'm toying with what might work better, but I'd like to hear your thoughts."

It pleased Chuck that his opinion mattered. In all the years he'd worked here, never once had Ida Mae treated him as "hired help." He might not be listed as co-owner, but for all intents and purposes, they worked as a team and that had served the Come and Get It well.

"I think this makes sense. Let me chew on it for a while, okay?"

She waggled her head and continued rubbing the back of her neck. "Sounds good."

"Here." He washed his hands and dried them. "Let me help."

He walked behind her and placed his palms on her shoulders and began massaging, working his way around to the middle of her shoulder blades and up toward the base of her neck. Gently, he manipulated the knots of tension until they softened beneath his fingertips.

"Oh, my! Where'd you learn to do this?"

"When I was a kid and Mom worked two jobs, I used to massage her neck at the end of a long day. We couldn't afford doctor visits, so I got pretty good at this sort of thing."

Ida Mae melted into his hands. "Mmm...You could spoil a girl."

Her innocent words gave him pause. He knew she hadn't meant to infer anything romantic, yet his heart tripped against his chest as if he'd touched a live outlet.

Certainly, rubbing a woman's neck while on the clock, much less in a work environment, would normally be taboo. But he and Ida Mae shared a unique history. There was nothing dishonorable in easing his friend's discomfort. Was there?

She turned around, her beautiful face mere inches from his. "What's the matter? Why did you stop?"

"I...uh..."

Her smile faltered. Lips, full and pink, curved downward. The air arced between them and his thoughts scattered. He'd known this woman since she was a girl and had seen her face thousands of times. Why had he never noticed that tiny black mole to the left of her mouth? And could her skin be any fairer? Her eyes, any bluer?

The revelation kicked Chuck in the gut. After all this while. What he'd tamped down and denied bulldozed its way to the forefront. Camaraderie was one thing. Chemistry, quite another. Toss in a fair bit of emotion and one might even use another word to describe this thing. *Oh, Lord. You can't be serious. I'm not ready.*

"Your face is red. You all right?"

"Sure." He backed up and pointed to his Fitbit. "The next rush is about to hit. We best get shaking and baking around here."

As if by divine appointment, dishwasher Salty Hobbs ambled out of the break room and went back to work as both busboys delivered tubs of dirty dishes to the rinse counter. Ava Kruse, the temp they'd hired to help waitress, clipped a batch of fresh white tickets to the order wheel at the serving window.

"Orders in!" she hollered before bouncing away to freshen customers' drinks.

Whew. The diversions couldn't have happened at a more opportune time. The shade of his face seeming to be a non-issue now, Ida Mae nodded and scooted through the swinging door.

He snatched the tickets from the order wheel and stole a quick peek through the window. Full house, lively chatter. The way he liked it. If he didn't know better, he'd say Ida Mae had a new spring to her step and that caused his mind to wander.

Before he drew his attention to the task at hand, he watched the woman zip around the room, greeting and charming the customers in her usual, carefree, Ida Mae way. That Chuck met Edwin Ramsey's gaze in the process shouldn't embarrass him. It was only natural he observed the head count so he could whip up more of the menu favorites, as needed. What wasn't natural, maybe, was the way his face warmed as he studied Ida Mae and then realized Edwin studied him.

Chapter Nine

The remainder of the week dashed past, and by closing time Saturday, Ida Mae dragged, exhausted.

Thirty-nine, now, a whole seven days. How would forty feel next year? She didn't want to think about that. Instead, she sank into a booth as her staff clocked out. Other than Chuck, Ava Kruse, the new kid on the diner block, was the last to leave.

"Silverware is wrapped and napkins restocked. Oh, and I gave the wall art a light dusting. Looked like those dust bunnies had bedded down for a couple of years." The girl giggled and poked her arms into a rhinestone studded jean jacket. "Are you sure you don't need me to do anything else? Maybe take spray cleaner to the windows or door?"

"No thanks, honey. You've done plenty for today, and I sure do appreciate your effort. You're one of our best workers, in fact."

Ava's pretty features lit up like a Christmas tree. "I'm really glad you think so. Nothing like hard work to expand our mindset."

Ida Mae tipped her head to the side and squinted. Was she teasing?

"It's also good for our constitution." Ava's giggles rose from her chest and danced past her lips. "That's a Mom-ism."

"Ahh. I see. Funny, my mama used to say that too. I've probably even repeated it."

"Guess I'm an old soul then." Ava's hand flew to her mouth. "Wait! I didn't mean that like it sounded."

Ida Mae laughed too. "No offense taken. I know what you mean."

"Guess I'll run along now. I've done all the damage I can do for one day." She waggled her fingers at Ida Mae. "Good night." Ava bounded toward the door, still in stitches.

Hard worker, indeed, that one. Even though Ida Mae had given Ava permission to take off at noon to accompany her parents on a camping trip, she'd stayed until close. Her work ethic would carry her far when she graduated college next spring, and her sense of humor would ease any challenges.

As was the norm, Chuck flipped the sign on the door to Closed and drew all the window blinds. Bud, their janitor, had already swept, mopped, emptied trash, and cleaned restrooms. Plates, silverware, and pots and pans gleamed spotless, thanks to Salty. The high school kids that served as the Come and Get It's busboys, as well as assisting where needed, had refilled salt and pepper shakers and napkin dispensers. Everything done, she and Chuck only needed to skedaddle. If she could drag herself back up, that was.

Before she moved, Chuck eased himself onto the vinyl seat across from hers. What did he want to say? No doubt he too, remembered last week's birthday party and how it all ended.

"Don't look so skeptical." A grin formed on his tired, but handsome face. "We spoke about revamping the diner's hours, thereby decreasing our work load and giving ourselves more downtime. I think, after today, you'd agree these fourteen-hour days are getting old. I realize you and I spend the most time here, but even so, the rest of our crew puts forth a lot of effort, as well."

"Yes. I couldn't ask for a better bunch. We're blessed. I know what you mean though. Something's gotta give. Working 'round the clock doesn't leave much time for R and R."

"Right." He plucked a sheet of paper from his pocket and handed it to her. "This is what I'm proposing. See what you think."

She perused the figures. Instead of their usual work hours, he suggested significantly decreasing their long days, with Sunday and Monday remaining closed and unchanged.

"It might take locals a while to adjust, but I don't believe we'll lose business over it. The cafe is a mainstay here. Folks will still come in by the droves." Chuck paused. "This is long overdue."

"Yes. I know."

"That's not all. I think we should hire an additional waitress. Even with raising current employees' wages a tad, it'll work. We can ease our workload while the Come and Get It turns a significant profit. Trust me, you can afford to do this. You *need* to do this. We should get lives, you and me."

He didn't say "get a life together." Was that the inference?

What he proposed made sense. Significantly shorter days versus the fourteen-hour days she and Chuck had grown used to? Revamped hours, overhauled shifts, and closing earlier, mid-week, with Sundays and Mondays off as usual? It sounded heavenly.

Trying something new excited Ida Mae. How they'd maintained their rigorous work schedules this long bordered on miraculous. She had a feeling Mom and Dad would approve of the changes. Maybe taking a vacation in the future would happen sooner than she thought.

"So, what do you think?"

"I think the quicker we implement this, the better. Any ideas on that end?"

"We'll need new signage. Nothing fancy. We'll also need a chance to spread the word, which shouldn't take long. Tell a few of our regulars, and it's off to the races. How about two weeks? Does that sound good?"

"A little scary, but good."

"Change always generates mixed feelings. Especially when life has remained stationary for so long. Once we negotiate it, we often find it's not so scary after all."

She sensed he said that as much for his sake, as hers.

The regulars welcomed most of the changes as Chuck expected. New menu options, along with beloved preferences, despite a slight price increase, appeased patrons. Hour cutbacks surprised people, yet they handled it with diplomacy rather than complaints. As anticipated, business increased because customers knew there were only so many hours they could catch up with friends and neighbors, as well as satisfy their hungry appetites.

Not long after the transformation, Edwin Ramsey wandered into the diner one day and sat down at his preferred table. Chuck made a point to visit him.

"Great to see you, Edwin." He extended a hand and

the old fellow readily grasped it. "Are you keeping 'em in line over at The Meadows?" The actual name of Ruby's retirement home was "Sunset Meadows," but people often interchanged it. That version stuck, as opposed to the one that implied dusk or end-of-the-day scenarios. As fetching as a sunset was, the older population there preferred a different connotation. An innovative community, The Meadows offered a unique approach to the golden years.

"I reckon I'm tryin'." Edwin laughed. "And how about you? Are you and Ida Mae holding down the fort here?"

"Yes, sir. As always." Mentioning them together didn't bother him in the least. Why wouldn't their friends think of them as a team? Many thought their relationship was more on the romantic side, though Chuck hadn't overtly fostered the notion. Admittedly, the romantic link didn't bother him either. Especially, lately.

"Looks like you've modified the place. New signs, new hours, new menu. Fresh paint and some swell upgrades. I like it." Edwin bobbed his head. "Good for you!"

"Glad you feel that way. Makeovers aren't always met with open arms, but so far, the Come and Get It's batting a thousand. We're busier than ever because no one wants to miss their favorite meal. They either come in a little earlier or order ahead to take it home."

"You haven't missed the long hours and heavier workload?"

"Well, we're still in an adjustment phase around here, but so far, I can't say that I have. As much as I love the diner, there's more to life than work." He believed it now more than ever.

"That's a fine sentiment and one I thoroughly

endorse. Life's too precious to allow work to become your life." Edwin admired the new menu and opened it. He examined the selections, then shifted his gaze back to Chuck. "Now that you have a few more minutes in your schedule, stop by The Meadows soon. We'll chat and have coffee."

"I'll do 'er."

The Come and Get It grew packed, and Chuck bid Edwin a good afternoon and retreated to the kitchen. Why did he have the feeling that Edwin wanted to say more? He'd had that inkling for weeks.

As late October settled over the Ozarks and the community, restlessness stirred in Ida Mae's soul. She enjoyed the downtime the extra hours off afforded her, however now she admitted the inevitable. More time on her hands meant more time to think.

She'd hoped after their impromptu coffee chat several weeks ago, the climate between her and Chuck would improve. Improve, as in they'd transition from friends to more. Beyond that, she'd hoped for clear-cut answers regarding their future. A future together. Instead, they'd treaded new water with only a few noteworthy differences.

Chuck called her cell more often. He dropped by her home on occasion. Frequently, he slipped into her office to chat about the menu, supplies, or even the weather. All fine gestures, as gestures go, but Ida Mae had no idea what they meant. His intentions were difficult to discern. Since that day in the diner kitchen when Chuck massaged the kink in her neck, any physical contact between them had been nil. Oddly enough, the emotional undercurrents intensified. It was enough to drive a girl crazy. They weren't children. He either wanted to pursue a relationship with her or he didn't, and that placed them exactly where they'd been as long as she could remember. *Nowhere.*

Well, one could only take so much. If this was the extent of his pursuit, or lack thereof, then maybe what Chuck Farrow needed was a puppy. Not a girlfriend, and certainly not a wife. Puppies were cute, cuddly, and made great companions. Ida Mae often thought about getting one. This guessing game exhausted her.

One Sunday, when the sky overhead was a robin's egg blue and the treetops were doused in lemon and scarlet, she decided to skip church and indulge in a spur-of-the-moment road trip. Surely, God would understand. She rarely missed Sunday services, but today, another place drew her. She could rest and recharge and worship in her own way there.

Quickly, before she talked herself out of her spontaneous venture, Ida Mae grabbed her cell phone and tapped the familiar number. Her mother answered by the third ring. "Your father and I are almost ready to leave for church. Everything okay, dear?"

"Sure, everything's fine, Mom." She slipped on a sweater as they spoke. "I was wondering... Remember a few weeks ago when you and Dad offered the cabin to me if I ever wanted to get away?"

"Of course. Are you considering it?"

"Yes, I am. I'd like to drive down there today and stay overnight, if that's all right."

"Dear, that's more than all right. You know that." The distant sound of a passing vehicle registered. Mom and Dad must be heading out the door. "Any reason for this sudden getaway? It isn't like you."

"No. No reason. Now that I'm not spending every waking moment at the diner, I've decided to make up for lost time. I need a breather. I think today's the day."

"That's wonderful! Why not stay longer than overnight?"

"Maybe later when I've had a chance to better juggle my schedule, but overnight is good for now. I plan on leaving soon and making the most of my trip there. I'll head back home tomorrow afternoon."

Her mother pressed the speaker function and Dad told her he loved her and to drive safely. "Oh, and the cabinets and freezer are well-stocked," Mom added. "Don't forget to reset the heat if you need to. Nights at the lake can get chilly during fall."

Instead of referencing her age and grown woman status, Ida Mae simply reassured them. "Gotcha, Mom. Thanks. Love you both."

She stuffed a change of clothes and toiletries into an overnight bag, double-checked the house, locked her doors, and headed to the car. The sun overhead shone bright and a light breeze ruffled her hair. The morning chill nipped at her nose, but the forecast projected a high of seventy degrees today. Perfect.

As she drove away, she passed Chuck, paused in his vehicle, at a stop sign. He raised his hand and waved. On his way to Sunday services, he probably assumed she was too. She wondered if he'd miss her. Should she text him? Normally, she would, but today, she fought the urge. He needed to realize, that without a commitment, she owed him no explanation.

Trying to get into Chuck's head and figure out what he wanted exhausted her. Still, a twinge of guilt tugged at Ida Mae's conscience. Maybe later she'd send him a quick text. Nothing too mushy. Just something about needing to get away overnight and where she was. After all, she didn't want him to worry. She only hoped her departure made him think.

Ida Mae increased her speed on the way out of town and noted the chimney smoke rings that curled above the hilltops. It was that time of year when folks used their fireplaces overnight and early morning to warm their bones, but by mid-afternoon, they opened windows for a dose of fresh air.

During her hour drive, she marveled at the Ozarks' landscape—endless hills, tinged in russet and gold—framed against a flawless, unfettered sky. True to season, not a tree nor a leaf remained untouched by the Creator's supernatural paintbrush.

Every curve, every peak and slope, beckoned her onward toward the burgeoning panorama that was Branson, Missouri. Mom and Dad's cabin, fifteen minutes from downtown, overlooked Table Rock Lake and afforded privacy, stunning views, and a marina within walking distance. Though Ruby had a similar, laid-back vibe, tourism hadn't yet affected her hometown. Her home remained on the fringe of a time warp, while Branson moseyed forward with the future in mind. Ida Mae liked aspects of each. Ruby was the entrée. Branson, dessert. Ozarkian roots ran deep through both.

She pulled into the graveled drive adjacent to her parent's cabin and inhaled clean, pine-scented air. She hadn't been here in over a year, and she chided herself for not making downtime a priority until now.

In the mid-morning light, hand hewn logs gleamed. The red metal roof sparkled. Rays of golden sunshine bounced off the native stone fireplace exterior, creating playful shadows across a dormant lawn. A nineteen-forties treasure, her parents had renovated the cabin while preserving its historic charm.

Inside, the dwelling utilized space well. Downstairs included a living room, kitchen, and half bath. Upstairs housed the master suite with full bath and enough room for a washer and dryer. The cabin was small but boasted all the comforts of home. In addition, each room featured spectacular lake views. No wonder Mom and Dad loved it here. She'd barely set foot in the place, and already a sense of tranquility enveloped her. She wouldn't lay a fire tonight since she wouldn't be here that long, but she looked forward to her next visit.

Glancing around the compact living room, Ida Mae surveyed her mother's handiwork. Mom's touch resonated in the cozy, comfy furnishings and the cabin's country flair. Not to be upstaged, her father had added his own stamp on the cabin, as evidenced by the smattering of paintings highlighting fishermen, boats, and the great outdoors. In the ten years her parents had owned the cabin, it shamed her that she'd never really noticed, until today, all the TLC they'd invested here. Her four or five trips to the cabin weren't conducive to long-lasting memories. Her visits were too few and far between.

How had she allowed the Come and Get It to become her life? *When work is all you have, there's no room for anything or anyone else.* The thought poked her subconscious. Like someone else she knew, work had become her safety net.

Well, no more. She loved the diner. She loved the customers—her friends. She loved...a man who couldn't commit. That was just it. Having downgraded her workload these last several weeks, finally, she'd removed her rose-colored glasses. If he didn't love her by now, or at least get real about it, chances were Chuck wasn't going to. Mixed signals might work for politicians, but they sure put a damper on romance.

Ida Mae shook off disappointment. She traipsed to the kitchen pantry and found a box of hot chocolate. Not as tasty as the real thing, but instant would do in a pinch. She warmed a mug of water in the microwave, stirred in the contents of one of the packets, and carried the hot drink outside to an adjoining deck overlooking the lake. Beneath a full sun, Table Rock shimmered.

She envisioned Mom and Dad sitting in the same spot, probably holding hands as they often did, chatting about life and all they held dear. There'd be no need for vague pleasantries or meanderings about the weather. Idle conversation and empty words weren't necessary between soul mates. Married forty-three years, her parents bypassed the verbal veneer and appreciated the art of intimacy. The kind that comes from knowing one's partner as well as one knows oneself.

Most likely, they speculated why their only daughter remained alone and unmarried. Maybe Chuck's name came up. Certainly, Tyler Fenston's didn't. Perhaps, grandbabies worked their way into the conversation along with the assertion, "There is still time..."

Ida Mae exhaled a wobbly breath. *Time.* In some respects, something she had a little more of now, if only the wind blew her way...or if God crafted a miracle. She wasn't aware of many modern-day miracles, but anything was possible, wasn't it?

When her cell phone buzzed in her pocket, Ida Mae almost jumped.

"Hi. It's me. Are you okay?" Might as well get right to the point.

"Sure. Why wouldn't I be?"

Given the fact he'd seen her this morning at the stop sign, Chuck wouldn't have guessed Ida Mae was on her way anywhere but church. Where else would she go at that hour?

He got the story from Emory and Selma. Though they didn't seem concerned that their daughter's overnight jaunt to the lake was out of character, Chuck wondered. He needed to hear her voice.

"You never said anything about your trip. I guess it surprised me." He tried to keep it light and upbeat, but her sudden departure gnawed at him.

"Oh. I'm not sure why it would surprise you. Remember, we agreed that we needed to reorder our lives."

"Yes, but you rarely miss church or break from routine." He searched for the words. "It...concerned me."

The pause gathered steam and seemed to last an eternity before she replied. "I needed to get away."

Okay. This wasn't going well. What did he expect? Chuck paced the floor of his tiny living room and finally plopped down in his rarely used recliner. *I needed to get away*. Code for *I wanted to be alone*. Without him?

"I see." The realization of what she meant jabbed him in the gut. Still, he couldn't help himself. "Would you like some company?"

Another pause. This one not as lengthy, but noticeable. "I'll be back tomorrow afternoon. Then, the next day, work. See you Tuesday?"

Her implication couldn't be plainer than if she'd whopped him upside the head with a two-by-four. He should thank her. At least her rejection was the less painful option. "You bet. Be safe."

"I will. Have a restful Sunday, Chuck."

Ida Mae ended their chat and left him staring at his phone. What made him think he could simply call her and act as though nothing had changed when they both knew it had? She wasn't playing hard to get. That wasn't Ida Mae's way. She stated her feelings up front, like when they were kids and he'd soundly rebuffed her.

When she returned to Ruby the fall after graduation, her attitude had shifted, but her feelings for him hadn't. Her eyes gave her away. So did the color that sprang to her cheeks whenever their paths had crossed. Now, the pendulum swung back again. They'd entered a new phase in their relationship. That he thought of their friendship in terms of a relationship was progress. Comfortably stagnant advanced to awkwardly evolving. Decades past due, he'd better jump in the saddle and prepare for the ride.

But first, he needed to talk to someone.

Chapter Ten

He'd been hurt and she was sorry about that. Nothing in her derived pleasure from his turmoil. Chuck needed to understand that roller coasters were best left to theme parks and county fairs. While she couldn't quell her feelings for the man, boundaries at this point, were necessary. She cared for him and they'd always be friends, but self-care was important. They could continue like this indefinitely, or they could explore new horizons. The latter held appeal the more she considered it.

She should focus on moving forward. For too long, she'd remained entrenched in the past, chained to guilt over poor choices and bad decisions. She'd allowed her feelings for Chuck to derail new possibilities.

Well, she couldn't undo her pregnancy or get her baby back, and she couldn't make Chuck love her. Circumstances were what they were. For twenty-one years, she'd wallowed in guilt and shame. She'd dined on one-way pursuits and settled for crumbs. That was no way to live life.

According to Pastor Bill, and more importantly—Scripture, God wanted the absolute best for His children. God wanted to free her from anything that would hinder a relationship with His son. He wanted her to know that her completeness didn't hinge on another person's rejection or acceptance. She was made whole through Him.

Ida Mae sucked in her breath. She clung to this, though she didn't fully grasp it.

Help me believe. Such a childish prayer. It probably didn't even count. She drained the hot chocolate from her mug and went back inside to make lunch. At the very least, something sprouted deep within her. She didn't know what, but whatever it was brought a sense of peace. With or without Chuck, she'd be okay.

Chuck noticed him at the far table by the windows. Sunshine streamed across the industrial-tiled floor and gleamed through meticulously cleaned windowpanes, illuminating the dining room in gold, bright light. Hardly the stuff of an "old folks' home," Sunset Meadows embodied a cottage-like appeal. Even the men and women who lived here functioned more like family than mere "residents."

Edwin grinned when he approached, and they exchanged handshakes. "Well, well. To what do I owe the pleasure?"

"I thought this afternoon might be a perfect day to join you for that cup of coffee. I hope I'm not interrupting anything." Chuck probably should have called first. Maybe Edwin had planned to take a Sunday nap.

"Don't be silly, my boy. We don't stand on ceremony here. 'Sides, this is perfect timing." Edwin motioned for him to have a seat at the table. "Sam and Charla and the girls joined me earlier for a mighty fine roast beef dinner. They left about five minutes ago, and coffee is the very next thing on my agenda."

Yeah, he bet. But it was nice of Edwin to say so. "Great. Allow me, sir."

Chuck strode over to the coffee bar and poured two steaming hot cups of coffee. From Edwin's habits at the diner, he knew he preferred his brew strong and black. No sweetener. The Meadows also made dynamite chocolate chip cookies, reminiscent of the ones Edwin's wife, Letta, used to make. When she passed away, everyone attempted to reproduce them, but so far, these ranked the best. Chuck gathered napkins and a few of the cookies and set them on a dining room tray with the coffee cups.

"About that 'sir' business..." Edwin waved a hand. "No need for that. I've known you all your life. That's long enough to forgo formalities. It's Edwin."

"Certainly." Chuck arranged the coffee and cookies on the table and took a seat. The Meadows' dining room had cleared out except for a couple women residents in the far back corner. Judging by their crochet baskets, he bet after they finished their pie, the recreation room was their next stop.

"Thank you, very kindly." Edwin curled his weathered fingers around the coffee cup handle and raised the cup to his lips. He sipped and smiled. "Mmm. Heaven's nectar."

Chuck agreed. He hoped heaven had a coffee bar. As they sipped coffee and dunked cookies, they chatted about a variety of subjects. Edwin's granddaughters. Gas prices. Politics. The Ozarks. When they'd exhausted those, Edwin leaned forward and tapped him on the arm. "How's Ida Mae these days?"

"Good." Oh, man. The old fellow was on to him. Wasn't that why he was here? To glean wisdom from one of the wisest men he knew? Chuck fiddled with a paper napkin, folding and unfolding the corners. "She drove down to her parents' lake cabin. She'll be back tomorrow."

"Ahh. I remember when Emory and Selma bought that place. Emory couldn't wait to catch bass and Selma wanted to shoot pictures. Great thing to see hardworking folks enjoying retirement and each other. Glad to hear Ida Mae's spending a weekend with her mama and daddy."

"Actually, Emory and Selma aren't there this weekend. Ida Mae's alone." Chuck's hands stilled over the napkin.

"Oh, yes. I remember seeing the Hoscutts in church this morning, come to think of it. A little unusual for Ida Mae to take an out-of-town trip, but the way that girl has worked all these years, I'd say it's way overdue."

"You're right. I only wish…"

"Only wish what?" Edwin's gray eyes held kindness. "I'm listening."

"I wish I were there with her." There. He'd said it. What would Edwin think? "She…made it clear she needed to get away. Alone."

"Did you two have a falling out?"

"No, sir. That is, Edwin."

Edwin raised an eyebrow.

"What I mean is I wouldn't really call it that. I know a lot of people think of Ida Mae and me as a couple, but the truth is…we're not. We're friends—real fine ones—and I know Ida Mae hoped for more, but we never managed to…get off the ground, so to speak." Chuck flattened his palms on the table and shook his head. "I've been stupid. Because of what Sy Farrow pulled when I was ten, I let that experience define what I became."

"Which is?"

"Bitter. Distrustful. Gun-shy. Of relationships and attachments. I hate it, but it's the truth." What prompted him to tell Edwin this? The old guy seemed to draw it out of him. Besides, from years of knowing Edwin, he knew the depth of wisdom and kindness the man possessed. Folks in the community trusted his insight and his ability to home in on the slightest detail others might overlook.

"I know when your father left, it deeply affected your family and you. Understandable, but I sense something's changed. That maybe you're ready to open your heart?"

"Yes. I want to, but I hope it's not too late."

"It's never too late for transformation. The Author of grace teaches us that." Edwin met his gaze and craned forward. "Let me ask you this. What are your expectations? What is it you want to happen?"

"Between Ida Mae and me?"

"No. Between you and that coffee cup there." The elder man snickered. "Of course, I mean between Ida Mae and you."

"I don't know. I'm not sure. We're not kids anymore. So much water has flowed under the bridge that part of me says leave it alone. We can't recoup lost years." Sorrow gripped Chuck's heart. He allowed another thought. "The other part of me says 'grab this woman if she'll have you.' We're not too old to make new memories together."

Edwin nodded. "That's the part you should listen to. Don't waste another minute wallowing in the past. It'll play tricks on you."

"Yeah, but what if stuff in the past keeps rearing its

ugly head—for both Ida Mae *and* me? Is it wise to pursue a relationship when we're still dealing with some issues?"

"You raise a valid point. I think it would depend on what those issues were. If they affect your current relationship, then you gotta deal with 'em before exploring other options. Keep in mind, however, relationships and marriage don't come with guarantees. What makes 'em stick is the commitment to press on, despite blemishes. That's the hallmark of faith, my friend."

"Meaning, we address and deal with the crud. I get that. It's the other stuff you mentioned that trips me up. I don't know if I can risk it." After dragging his family through the coals without ever looking back, Sy upended three lives and discarded them among the ashes. How could Chuck be sure he wouldn't foul up like his old man had? Or, as much as he hated to think about it, that Ida Mae wouldn't? The thoughts swirled in his head, dredging up more questions than answers.

"When we truly care about others, we're willing to accept them, faults and all." Edwin placed a wrinkled palm on Chuck's arm. Understanding sparked in his eyes. "Because life isn't perfect, we place our fears and quandaries in the One who's flawless. He takes the old and makes it new. Our confidence isn't found in people, things, or circumstances, but in Christ who shapes outcomes according to His will, plan, and purpose."

"Thanks, Edwin. I needed to hear this." He'd been more of a father figure to Chuck in one hour than his biological dad had been in the first ten years of his life. "I wish I'd had a father like you."

"That's quite a compliment." A slight catch

punctuated Edwin's reply. He spoke softly. "Never think for a moment that your father didn't love you."

Chuck swallowed. His heart hammered against his chest. "Pardon?"

"Sy. He didn't leave because he didn't love you. He left because he did."

The asinine logic of that almost made him laugh. Edwin was a wise man, and someone he respected, but maybe his seventy-odd years had finally caught up with him. Loving parents didn't desert their kids. They didn't leave with nary a word for thirty years. They sure didn't forget what they'd done. They simply didn't care.

"Edwin, I admire you. I always have. But you're way off base. If my dad..." He hated to even use the word referencing his biological father. "If Dad had loved us, he wouldn't have abandoned his family when we needed him most. He wouldn't have chosen the bottle and easy livin' over his wife and children. That's the problem with society today. We're too willing to make excuses for bad choices."

Edwin pursed his lips. Was that irritation or empathy Chuck read on his face?

"Not excuses, young man. The word is *grace.* Sometimes, we must look beyond the surface and see the deeper layers as Christ does. Untended wasteland is ugly and fraught with weeds, but with a little TLC, it's those deeper layers that produce keeper crops."

It's what Pastor Bill, and others, espoused from the pulpit. We accepted that people were works in progress. It didn't mean we had to like the process. "Yes, I remember. But earlier when we were speaking of that, it was in a different context. Guess it's a moot point though. The likelihood of low-life Sy Farrow ever transforming is about as likely as a snowball's chance in h—"

"Do me a favor." Edwin squeezed his arm. "Reserve judgment. As you know, there are reasons people do what they do. They may not make sense to us. They may be self-serving and sinful. Or they may reveal additional truths and transparencies. Some bad. Some good. God's hand is always at work."

Yeah. He didn't doubt God's methodology. He had a problem with people's tendency to rationalize.

Chuck's gut dropped to his knees. Thoughts of his father fled. Was that what he'd been doing with Ida Mae? Had he wasted all these years because he'd overthought the process? Because a relationship—any relationship— might not succeed?

He hadn't consciously pushed Ida Mae away, but then again...maybe because of Dad, he had. In a way, Chuck had made her pay for something that really had more to do with his own insecurities and abandonment than it had to do with her desire for a lifelong commitment. As long as he kept her at arm's length, he'd played it safe. Never mind the fallout—the fact that safe didn't always equate to living a full and happy life.

She lay in the moonlit room, comforted by her parents' presence although they weren't there. Wrapped in her mama's handmade quilt and surrounded by treasured family heirlooms, sleep should come easily, but it eluded her.

What would Mom and Dad say if they knew her secret? If they knew the real reason she'd left Ruby after high school? That somewhere, the grandchild they dreamed of having one day actually existed? Her deceit would break their hearts. Would they ever be able to forgive her?

Guilt positioned itself like a battering ram ready to strike. She'd all but reconciled that she and Chuck might never go anywhere, much less marry. But her parents? How would she bear it if they viewed her differently? Or even distanced themselves from her? Granted, bitterness and resentment weren't part of her family's gene pool, but then again, they'd never faced a situation like this.

Ida Mae rolled over and plumped up her pillow. She repeated the words. *Help me believe.* A prayer? This time she wasn't sure. She simply knew the words brought peace. They calmed her spirit. Like before, the plea breathed life into her heart's desire. She had to believe that God loved her and wanted the best for her. Whatever God had in store for her, He certainly understood her insecurities and longings.

Her eyelids grew heavy. Thoughts of Mom and Dad and Chuck hovered along the perimeters of her subconscious. The three people she loved most...How would God use her past for good? As she drifted off to sleep, her cell phone vibrated on the nightstand. Or...was she dreaming?

Her phone buzzed a fourth time. At last, the noise ceased, and a familiar ding sounded. A text too? Who would contact her at eleven p.m.? Unless it was an emergency. She scooted into an upright position and shook off vestiges of grogginess. She almost knocked the phone to the floor in her sleep-addled state but caught it before it dropped.

Hi. I know it's late. Sorry about that. I wanted to say you're on my mind.

That was it? Where was Chuck's head? Ida Mae returned her cell phone to the nightstand and flopped back against the pillow. The master of mixed signals, he sure knew how to unhinge a girl. Why had he called her? And why the odd text? When sleep finally found her, she'd exhausted all the reasons but one.

His morning jog complete, Chuck bounded up the back-porch steps and into his house. At forty, he creaked a tad more now, but not as much as the screen door that slammed behind him.

He swigged the sports drink he'd opened earlier and checked his phone for missed calls or texts. Nothing. Why hadn't Ida Mae at least texted back? He guessed she could be sleeping in on their day off. He remembered several weeks ago when he'd arrived on her doorstep and caught her in her bathrobe. Boy, he sure couldn't forget that. Heat stole up his neck as he recalled those blonde curls, pink cheeks, and sleepy eyes that turned his insides to mush. The fact the woman had curves in all the right places hadn't gone unnoticed either. He'd had to tighten the rein on his emotions after that or a guy's mind could wander.

Okay. So much for that. He chugged down the rest of his drink and headed for the shower. If he'd been thinking, he wouldn't have called or texted her so late last night. He would have waited and called this morning or held off until later today when maybe she'd returned home.

Doggone it. Since when did he call anyone at that late

hour? Except for Ruby's teen population, almost everyone he knew sawed logs at that time. What if he'd awakened her? She might be ticked.

Chuck worked the soap into a lather, bathing quickly. He attempted to shove the negative vibes from his brain in an effort to refocus. What he needed was a diversion. Normally, he enjoyed his days off. Though, recently, his thoughts centered around a blonde-maned gal and how she occupied her spare moments. Did she think of him too?

Lately, he'd begun to see Ida Mae in a new light. Secrets or not, the woman captivated him. How could he know someone for thirty years, see her almost every day of his life and then... *bam.* The warmth that spread in his belly smacked of last night's dessert. Homemade apple pie—sweet with a hint of tartness, piping hot, and off-the-chart delicious—was there anything better?

Oh, Lord. I'm a goner, aren't I? It hit him between the eyes. Then another thought blindsided him. Had it always been so? Had he always loved her? *Aww, man. There I go using the L-word.* But he was probably right on both counts, if he were honest. Why it took so long to settle this in his mind he didn't know. Scratch that. He knew. All the stuff about his old man rubbing off on him and his fear of not being husband material had shaped his identity and self-worth. Toss in a good measure of bullheadedness. Probably thanks to dear old Dad too.

Soap bubbles swirled beneath his feet as he rinsed and collected himself. How to tell her he loved her? He couldn't very well shout it out during the diner's supper rush hour, nor did the diner's atmosphere exactly lend itself to the intimacy of the moment. The possibility of

Deputy Sapp's foghorn belches somewhat downplayed the seriousness of his proclamation. He'd have to revisit this. Tabling the subject for now, other things called his name.

He finished showering and changed clothes and went to work on the surprise. Ida Mae said she'd be back this afternoon. If he delivered it later today, that would give her plenty of time to unwind before he arrived with the goods. Recalling her words "see you Tuesday," he wouldn't foist himself on her. He'd drop everything off and honor her wish for privacy.

He worked the rest of the morning preparing a scaled back version of Beef Bourguignon, often referred to at the Come and Get It as "Billie Gail's Bust-My-Buttons Beef Stew." Another diner favorite, most folks didn't ask about the secret ingredient that gave the stew its flavor, but judging by customers' died-and-gone-to-heaven smiles, everyone agreed. This recipe could drop you at the pearly gates. If Pastor Bill and Sister Sharon endorsed it, then certainly, it earned its stars.

Once transferred to the slow cooker, Chuck went about other tasks. He peeled and cubed a few red-skinned potatoes and set those aside in a pot of cool water to boil later. Most of the locals concurred that the bourguignon paired best with mashed potatoes rather than rice or noodles. Later, he'd make a pan of garlic-cheddar drop biscuits.

Dessert called for something fall-themed. He set to work on the salted caramel pumpkin cheesecake, another masterpiece that transported all who sampled it to a heavenly realm. Thank heaven for a mother who'd taught him to cook, despite the many other hats she'd worn. Only a saint of a lady would juggle two jobs in order to fund one child's nursing education and the other's culinary art pursuits. God knows their ne'er-do-well dad sure hadn't cared.

By mid-afternoon, Chuck grew antsy. Generally, Ida Mae traveled one of two ways to her home. One way took her past his house or in close enough proximity that he often noted her comings and goings. Not that he spied or anything. In a small town like Ruby, people's habits and patterns were easily observed and filed away for future reference. Maybe she'd gone the other way today, the two-block longer route, depending on her mood.

When another hour rolled by and five-o-clock approached with Ida Mae's vehicle nowhere in sight, he unplugged the slow cooker, finished mashing the potatoes, and wrapped the fresh baked biscuits in tin foil. He grabbed the cheesecake from the fridge and positioned it in a storage container. The entire meal fit nicely in the insulated bin he used during the holidays to transfer casseroles and various dishes between his house and Mom's and Voni's.

Realizing it was a risk to head over to Ida Mae's without knowing for certain she'd arrived home yet, Chuck pulled his cell phone from his pocket and barked out a command. "Hey, Siri...call Ida Mae's number."

Siri complied. One. Two. Three rings. No answer. What now? He paced the kitchen and contemplated options. He could wait a while. She might be driving. Or he could venture over to her house and hope she showed up soon. As if by divine appointment, a flash of bronze streaked past. Ida Mae's Malibu. Was that great timing or what?

Should he shoot her a text? Nope. He rather liked the essence of surprise. He hoped she did too. These days, her temperament varied. Maybe the same could be said for him. He didn't know why two grown adults who'd known each other most of their lives should suddenly develop moments of awkwardness. It wasn't always so. For years, their even-keeled relationship enjoyed a sense of continuity and sameness. In the past few months, their easy rapport had shifted. They read each other's moods with heightened awareness and weighed words and nuances with hopeful restraint. Again, he realized why. It didn't disturb him. It liberated him. Now, if only he could figure out this love thing that couples much younger than them seemed to master, life would be much smoother sailing.

He pondered it on his way over to Ida Mae's place and as he stood on her front porch, fingers poised at the doorbell. It struck him that maybe people who loved each other didn't have it all figured out. Maybe folks figured out love as they went along. Scripture guided. Mankind applied it. People loved according to the standard Christ set, yet sometimes, humanity messed up. So simple, and conversely, so hard. Or was it that mankind made it that way?

Courage be hanged. Balancing the container between his arms, he pressed the bell.

Chapter Eleven

What in the world? Through the peephole, she watched him gulp. What was he doing on her front porch? She jerked open the door and stared. "Chuck?"

"I know. You said 'see you Tuesday' but this will only take a minute. Please?"

He brought supper? Her brain tripped over his gesture. Part of her wanted to be annoyed at his assumption. The other part delighted in his kindness. Since when had anyone, besides her mother, made her a meal? The very thought drew goosebumps. The heavenly aroma of garlic, onions, and bay leaves wafted on the afternoon breeze and made her mouth water. Unless one was on the sick or homebound list at church, not that many men would be so thoughtful. Maybe her neighbors or the ladies' group, but rarely would a man cook an entire meal and present it to a woman on her doorstep.

"Okay." She was so absorbed in analyzing his intentions, she couldn't even string a proper sentence together. All she could do was step aside and motion for him to come in.

"May I take this into the kitchen?"

"Uh, sure. I was about to make a sandwich."

Chuck grinned. That lopsided smile of his made her heart pound. "I guarantee once you see what I've brought, a sandwich will pale in comparison."

He scooted past, leaving her to shut the door behind

him. She trailed after him to the kitchen, the food's delectable smell mingling with the woodsy scent of his aftershave. Since when did Chuck wear aftershave? That he did made her giddy.

He set the container down on the kitchen counter and began unpacking its contents. He produced a slow cooker, a covered casserole dish, something wrapped in a foil packet, and what looked to be dessert.

"I would've grabbed paper products, but it seems wrong to serve Beef Bourguignon in paper bowls. Hope you don't mind if I serve you in the real thing?"

Serve…her? Beef Bourguignon? She shook her head. "No, I don't mind. This is wonderful, actually."

"Great. Leave everything to me." He pulled out a chair for her. "I'll set you up and then get out of your hair. I realize you weren't expecting company."

"You mean you aren't staying?" She couldn't even hide her surprise.

"I know you'd intended to have time to yourself until tomorrow. I don't want to encroach on that."

"Don't be silly. You made all this. Of course, I want you to stay."

"Really?" His grin returned. "If you're sure you don't mind."

"I wouldn't say it merely to be nice. I am nice, but you know me. If I say I want you to stay, I mean it."

"Got it." He raised his fingers in a mock salute. He located forks, knives, and spoons, and reached for the red Fiesta dinnerware in the far cabinet, working quickly with the same skill and precision that he was known for at the diner.

Over generous mounds of mashed potatoes, he

spooned the bourguignon mixture. He arranged biscuits on the side plates along with creamy pats of what Ida Mae guessed were herbed butter.

"Oh. Would you like tea? I may have half a pitcher left in the fridge." She started to rise.

"Whoa. Allow me, remember?"

The giddiness wound around her heartstrings and tugged. Whatever was going on, she liked it. Maybe she should leave town more often. If this was Chuck's reaction after her being gone only one night, she wondered what a week might do.

He found the tea pitcher and poured two tumblers of iced tea, setting hers down first. After he seated himself, he extended a palm and proceeded to ask a blessing on their meal. The moment cemented itself in her memory.

Afterward, he watched as she took the first bite. *Oh. My. Word.* The utter lusciousness nearly took her breath away. The flavors burst on her tongue and lingered. That they referred to this as "stew" on the diner menu did Chuck a complete disservice. Beef Bourguignon never tasted so extraordinary.

"Mmm...sheer heaven." She scooped up another bite, detecting the ingredient that gave this dish its trademark flavor. "Did you add a splash of wine or more than?"

He laughed and winked. "I added the usual amount this recipe calls for."

"It's perfect. Thanks for doing all this. I know you worked for hours on this meal." Because of the prep time involved, when they served Billie Gail's Bust-My-Buttons Beef Stew at the Come and Get It, it was usually a daily special and made in copious quantities. She dabbed her mouth with a napkin and reached for a biscuit. "You're spoiling me."

"You're worth spoiling." His tone grew serious. "I'm sorry it's taken me so long to realize it."

An apology? An admission? What exactly was Chuck saying? She didn't want to read too much into this. She'd jumped to conclusions before and it had only come back to bite her in the behind. And yet, his countenance registered something different. His green eyes teemed with awareness. The slight scar above his left cheek—a remnant from recess when they were kids—appeared softer. Maybe because acknowledgement shone in his face rather than restraint.

"Wow. I should go away more often."

"I wasn't joking. You deserve to be spoiled. You deserve a lot of things."

He picked up his tea glass and sipped. His face relaxed, and he calmly studied her. What had happened in the past two days? He was the same guy she'd known since childhood, except he wasn't. It thrilled her and scared her, simultaneously.

She set down the biscuit she'd been about to butter. "Okay. What's going on? Please tell me you're not sick."

"No, ma'am. No worries there. Physically, I'm as healthy as a horse. For my age anyway."

"Mind clueing me in?"

He nodded. "I spoke with Edwin yesterday. Edwin Ramsey."

A wonderful man. A godly man. Everyone loved him. "Yes, the only Edwin in town. Is he doing well?"

"He seems to be. I visited with him at The Meadows. He invited me for coffee several weeks back and I finally took him up on the offer." Chuck dipped his spoon in the bourguignon. His hand remained poised above his bowl.

"I needed advice. His perspective, I guess you'd say."

"Well, Edwin's a wise man. Did talking with him help? Did you get clarity on whatever it was?" She didn't have to ask. She knew what they discussed. Her. *Them.* Possibly Chuck's past.

"You know, he certainly made me think. I have to admit, initially, his reasoning didn't mesh with mine. What he said took a while to soak in. I went home afterward and digested our conversation, and I realized most of his logic makes sense. I suppose I'll always be bitter about things I wish had been different, but I don't want to live in the past any longer. No telling what blessings I've missed along the way. I'm finally ready to see what else God has in store."

Her heart swelled with the knowledge of what he was trying to say. After all these years of hoping and dreaming that God would resurrect a future for them, was it now really possible? She proceeded with caution. "We all learn from the past. The beauty of that is choosing new paths and not allowing the old stuff to define us. It doesn't mean a few memories aren't going to hurt. We have to believe God's working in our favor to bring about good."

"I know you and I have a lot to sort out. I don't expect it to happen overnight." He touched her hand. Clasped it. Not like he had during the prayer. This was different. "I know I said it before, but I need to say it again. I'm so sorry I hurt you when we were kids. It sickens me when I think about it. Will you...can you forgive me?"

"I did, ages ago. I thought you knew that." This was her opportunity to ask for forgiveness, as well. God had forgiven her. Would Chuck? When he raised her palm to his lips, good judgment flew out the window. She could hardly breathe, much less form the words. *I made a mistake, a big one, and I paid dearly for it. I slept with Tyler, but I didn't love him. I loved you. I'm sorrier than you can imagine. Please forgive me too.* Her transgression beat his, hands down.

"Thank you. I needed to hear you say it. I hope this means we can start afresh?"

Tell him.

"I realize you've referenced something in the past. I want you to know, whatever it is, it absolutely doesn't matter. Everyone has crud. Let's agree to move forward from here. Can we do that?"

Oh, how she wanted to! Could they? If he said it didn't matter, did he even have to know? Why dredge up sins of the past if they were at last on the same footing?

"Ida Mae?"

"Yes, I want that too."

"Whew!" He pretended to swipe at his brow with the napkin. "I'm relieved to hear you say that. Now, I'd like to ask another question."

He shoved down his fear. "Would you like to go on a picnic next weekend? If the weather cooperates, that is?"

"Are you asking me on a date, Chuck Farrow?"

Aww, Ida Mae. He shouldn't be surprised by her reaction. The last several weeks—by golly, the last thirty years—had drained her reserves. If he spent the rest of their natural lives making things up to her, it would never be enough. With God's help, however, he'd try.

"I am." Granted, he wasn't very good at this sort of

thing. "Jaden Pond is pretty this time of year. There's some new picnic tables, compliments of the Chamber of Commerce."

Her eyes widened. Proof positive he stunk at this. "No, not Jaden Pond. How about Cusick Park? Gorgeous trees, rolling hills, nature trails. They have nice picnic areas too."

Cusick Park, named after philanthropist Lowell Cusick, one of Ruby's founding settlers. A beautiful spot, Chuck agreed, but not quite as secluded. "Sure, if that's where you'd like to go, that's where we'll go. Fried chicken and potato salad okay?"

"Perfect. I'll make a pie."

"Apple?"

"Don't you ever get tired of apple?"

"No, ma'am. Not yours." The sound of her laughter danced between them. How had he ever let her get away. Never again. Not if he could help it. "Sunday after church sound good—say around twelve-thirty? We can go home and change clothes first."

"Sure. We have a plan. A picnic, it is."

That plan sustained him during the next five days. Saturday evening, he grabbed the cooler from storage and set it in the kitchen. He made the potato salad and placed it on a shelf in the fridge. Sunday morning, he gathered a table cloth, napkins, plasticware, and paper cups and tossed everything in one of those recyclable bags Nora and Ned's Market now offered their customers. He fried the chicken and made a creamed corn casserole he knew Ida Mae liked and left both in the oven on warm during church.

Pastor Bill preached a shorter message that morning, and as Chuck walked out with Ida Mae, he noted more than a few stares. Why the sudden interest today? They often came and went together.

He leaned in close so others wouldn't hear. "What do you think?"

"You got me. I don't know either." Ida Mae shrugged her shoulders.

"I was afraid I had jelly on my face or a rip in my pants."

"Nope. No rip in your slacks and nothing on your face except that goofy grin." They made it to Ida Mae's car and Chuck opened the door and watched her slide behind the wheel. She waved to her parents as they visited with friends on the church lawn. "Guess everyone's curious. Mom and Dad sure are."

"Curious about what?"

"You. Me. Tongues have always wagged about us. Did you tell anyone about our picnic today?"

"No. Not that I care if anyone knows. The only time I've been anywhere other than work this week is the market when I bought picnic stuff that obviously wasn't for the diner."

"There you go." She waggled her fingers goodbye. "See you over at my house in a little while."

Ahh. Life in a small town. Amused, he whistled as he strode toward his vehicle. Wouldn't take long and folks would have 'em married by spring. They'd predicted that eons ago so theirs must be the longest running engagement in history. Naturally, it would be a shock if he ever did pop the question. Funny thing, that question. Where it once seemed most unlikely, now he mulled over the possibility on a daily basis. *Marriage.* The more he thought about it, the better he liked the idea.

He pondered it on the way home and as he changed into jeans and a sweatshirt. As he loaded the picnic things into the car, he considered how marriage might change the dynamic between two individuals who'd been lifelong friends, but now, more. Would it be awkward? Would it strain their friendship? A silly thing to contemplate, perhaps, but change happened. Look at some of the movie stars' marriages. Clearly, other factors played a part too, but numerous couples separated after only a few weeks because they found they made better friends than marriage partners.

There you go. Overthinking this. Not only that, but admittedly, thinking the worst.

A few more blocks. He drew in a deep breath. Expelled it. When he faced Ida Mae on her doorstep moments later, misgivings fled. Blonde waves piled high atop her head made her seem taller than her five-feet-two inches, and the red and white polka dot sweater and fashionably faded blue jeans she wore shaved at least six or seven years off her age. Except for the barest few laugh lines adjacent to stunning blue eyes, thirty-nine on this woman didn't wash. Thirty-one, thirty-two maybe, but almost forty? Nah. Surely not. When the edges of her mouth lifted into the most dazzling smile, words lodged in his throat and wouldn't come.

"What's the matter with you?" Laughter, feminine and full-bodied, rolled past lightly tinted lips and smacked him across the chest. "You expected the pink bathrobe again?"

"No...I...What you're wearing is perfect." *Oh, man.*

Stop ogling her. Good recovery, at least. "I don't think I've ever seen you wear that sweater before. It really compliments your...you." *Annnd...whop! You blew it.*

"It compliments my *me*?"

Great. Now, he'd made her self-conscious. "You're a beautiful woman, Ida Mae."

"Well, thank you." She stepped aside and motioned for him to come in. "Help me grab a few things and then we can be on our way."

"Sure. Happy to."

She bounded toward the kitchen, her floral-scented perfume trailing in her wake. As he followed after her, the fragrance tickled his nose and coaxed thoughts best shelved for the time being. "I didn't mean for you to go to a lot of trouble with the pie."

"No trouble. I made it last night so I wouldn't be rushed this morning." Thrusting a covered container toward him, she reached for a thermos and a plastic bag of cookies. "Sweet tea and snickerdoodles. I made these ahead too."

"Wow. Sounds great. I have fried chicken and creamed corn casserole in the car, along with potato salad and a few sodas and waters in the cooler. Oh, and I have plasticware and paper products and an old tablecloth."

"We're all set. We have plenty for us and half the town too."

The mirth in her voice skipped upon his heart and made it soar. Joy, and the subtle hint of something wondrous and bold, floated between them and expanded. Not easily given to nuance, he recognized a new twist in their relationship. He'd availed himself to new beginnings, which proved that God did, indeed, have a sense of humor. The feelings he'd held in check for three decades slammed into him with the force of a freight train. So, this was how it had been for Ida Mae? Love, raw and wild and uncontainable, stirred in his belly. Two people who loved each other. One accepted it and clung to it for thirty years. The other rejected it for as long, but today was tempted to move heaven and earth to claim it for the next thirty years and more. Irony bit him in the backside. Wasn't it like mankind to complicate the simplest things? He imagined God nodding a big, fat *yes*.

They arrived at Cusick Park that afternoon, expectant and hopeful. He read a dozen different emotions in Ida Mae's face—longing, elation, reticence—those, and others, his own surely mirrored. They chose a covered picnic table on the fringe of the park where sunlight met shadows in a seamless blending of memory and awe.

"I haven't been here in a long time." He glanced around, impressed with the park's quiet, ethereal beauty. "Don't know why. Guess picnicking is no fun by yourself."

"Before Mom and Dad bought the cabin down at the lake, I used to come here on Sundays with them. We'd bring picnic baskets stuffed with all kinds of goodies, and blankets to sprawl out on, and we'd spend the afternoon relaxing before the work week started. Sometimes, Mom would bring her camera and Dad would bring a book to read. Usually, it was a fishing tale. I'd thumb through old cookbooks of Grandma Ida's and get recipe ideas for the diner. I had a knack for choosing crowd favorites." A tinge of pink sprang to her cheeks.

"Sounds boring, I know, but those days with my parents count as my best memories."

"It doesn't sound boring at all. You know how I feel about the culinary world, and family's everything. My mom tried extra hard to give Voni and me the same advantages other kids had. She worked two jobs but managed to do things with us on the weekends. After Voni graduated nursing school and I got my culinary arts degree, Mom finally quit her second job down at the drug store. The past seventeen years or so, she's continued working at the school. She loves her secretarial work there, but I'm hoping she'll consider retirement one day."

"Liza's what now—early sixties?"

"Sixty-one. Had us young and says the school kids and Voni's two keep her that way." It was the truth. Those early years with an alcoholic husband hadn't been easy. Working two jobs while raising children hadn't been easy either, but they'd provided their family with a stable income, boosted his mother's confidence, and delayed the aging process. "Oh, and she still walks a mile three times a week down at the school."

"You definitely have her work ethic. She must be proud of you."

"Thanks. I think so. It goes both ways. I'm also proud of her." He spread the old, plaid tablecloth over the picnic table, and they began removing the cooler's and containers' contents. When they finished, Ida Mae slid onto the wooden bench across from where he stood.

"You have every right to be proud of your mother. Life isn't easy for single moms. In that era, it was even harder than it is today."

"That's the truth." Chuck seated himself, too. "Mom's

a self-made woman who's saved wisely and could afford to retire." When he'd surprised her by paying off her mortgage several years ago, he'd hoped she'd retire then, but she'd adamantly refused, saying she wasn't ready. If she'd had someone special in her life, she might have felt differently, but since Dad, there'd been no one else. In thirty years, she'd never so much as dated another man, much less entertained the possibility of remarriage. Not that he blamed her, but he didn't get it. More than once they'd discussed the matter, but the conversation always played out the same way.

"You can't possibly still love that no-account loser, Mom. Look what he did to us. To you. Left you practically penniless, saddled with a mortgage and in debt, not to mention with two kids to raise."

"Bitter doesn't make us better, son. Besides, everything isn't always what it seems. Lives and stories have many facets." She'd pat his arm and reassure him. "I'm happy. I'm fulfilled. I want that for you too. Don't base your views of marriage on mine and your father's and what you perceive marriage should or shouldn't be. People are fallible. They'll disappoint us. God never will. He's always working in our favor."

"Ahh, Mom. You're such a good woman. You have more faith than me."

"No, Son. I'm imperfect like everyone else. I'm simply not going to let a bad circumstance define me."

And his mother hadn't. Neither had his happily married sister, thank heaven. He'd taken that elephant on his own back for the three of them. It was the least he could do. But in the past few weeks, something had changed. Hope, maybe?

Restoration. The word tumbled across his mind, stopping him short. *Really? How, God? How can you put someone back together again when the experience shattered him?* When the actions of one he'd loved, one he'd trusted, dismantled all he believed? That word. *Love.*

But that didn't always solve everything, did it? In movies, maybe. Not in real life. But oh, how he wanted to believe. Here, now, with this woman, he almost could.

"Hey, are you okay?" Ida Mae's fingertips grazed his hand where he'd lain it on the table. "Still thinking about your mother?"

"Yeah. And the man she was married to for ten years."

"Your dad."

"I prefer to think of him in more of a generic sense rather than associate him with the actual word, but it is what it is." No amount of creative thinking or word wrangling would disguise facts. Sy Farrow, if he were still alive, was good ol' Dad. His father. "Sometimes, I wonder…"

"Wonder what? Go on."

"How the guy could have done it, you know. And too, if during the past thirty years, the family he discarded as easily as last night's trash ever crossed his mind."

"Oh, Chuck. You've never left his mind. Trust me."

"You say that like you know, but the truth is, you don't. You can't."

She scrutinized him, her face masking something unreadable and unsettling. "You're right. I'm not psychic, and I wasn't trying to minimize your pain, believe me. I was speaking more from intuition, is all." Her voice trembled for a second. She recovered, then brightened. "I meant that if your father had a chance to do things differently, I believe he would. I also bet if he could see the man you've become, he'd be extremely proud."

Though he questioned that, he hadn't meant to hurt her feelings or discount her encouragement. She'd tried to reassure him, and he'd snapped at her. *What a moron.* "Thank you. After all this time, you'd think the sting of abandonment would ease. I know it's stupid. I'm working on it. I'm sorry I was short."

"No apology necessary. Our feelings are our own. Until others have walked in our shoes, we tend to make assumptions."

He squeezed her hand, then linked his fingers through hers. "You're my silver-lining, you know that?"

If she said, "Prove it," he'd have no choice but to kiss her.

Chapter Twelve

"Flattery will get you everywhere. Thanks." But deep down, she'd hoped for more.

It pained her that she'd come across as condescending. Thinking with a mama's heart, from the perspective of a parent who'd placed her child for adoption, she'd wanted to give Chuck's father the benefit of the doubt. Though Sy Farrow would never win any "Father of the Year" awards, the word "abandonment" ratcheted up her emotions.

Granted, the way he left his family appeared to be self-serving and heartless, but wasn't there a part of her that always wondered if her own child felt the same way—abandoned by the birth mother who should have loved him...or her? Because her child hadn't yet bonded with her, though, circumstances were different. That was precisely why she'd done things the way she had. If she had kept the baby, she would have never, ever been able to walk away from him. To willingly abandon a ten-year-old without a word, a reason, or even a goodbye? *Lord, Lord.* Nope. She couldn't fathom it.

In her situation, she chose the path that would be best for her child. One where her baby would be loved by two parents who would provide advantages she couldn't.

A familiar ache pinched her heart. It was an ache that no over-the-counter pain reliever could lessen, and no magic wand could cure. Her only hope was that, one day, God would allow her to meet her child. Maybe the forms she'd signed all those years ago would find their way to her son's or daughter's hands.

She'd reviewed all the necessary documents. Agreed to certain specifics once the child turned eighteen. Maybe she'd meet her child. One day. The reality that boy or girl would now be twenty-one and still hadn't come looking was probably a bad sign. *Oh, boy.* Mustn't let her mind go there. She harnessed her thoughts and focused on the man before her. Her past didn't matter, he'd said. She had a feeling, though, if Chuck knew how closely their stories interwove, her past would matter a great deal. How could it not?

She waited for him to speak. His deep green eyes traced their linked hands and trekked upward toward her face...her mouth. Did he want to kiss her? Or had she misread those cues?

The picnic table between them acted as a barrier, but that could easily be remedied. What would it be like to kiss him, her friend? Not just a quick peck on the lips, but an actual kiss? Prior to that moment in the diner, the closest they'd ever come to locking lips was at their junior prom when the DJ played the crowd-pleaser by the Righteous Brothers. As the duo belted out the heartfelt lyrics in perfect harmony, she and Chuck melted into each other's arms as if the world was theirs for the taking. From that night on, she'd envisioned "Unchained Melody" as their song. Then Chuck retreated into himself and his own world again, and their future stalled.

But she'd never forgotten. She remembered what it was like when, for a while, he'd let down his guard and allowed her in. Could they ever make up for the ground they'd lost? God resurrected dreams, didn't he? Pastor Bill said that God wanted to grant His children the desires of their hearts. That is, when their hopes and dreams aligned with the Heavenly Father's will. If the desires of God's children coordinated with His best for them, nothing and no one could alter His plan.

Pining after another for thirty years—was that God's plan? She hardly thought so. Nevertheless, she recalled instances in the Bible where years, sometimes generations, passed before God redeemed what seemed lost.

The preacher's words spoken with such conviction, reassured her. "We can't know the whys and wherefores of God's timetable. It may take months, years, or decades to prepare hearts. But *wow-wee*, when we're receptive and ready? Look out! That's what I call a burning bush epiphany." Surely it must be so. *Help me believe.*

In the distance a dog barked. A cloudless, azure sky melded into infinity as golden-hued sunshine beat down on these Ozark hills, caressing the mottled, changing earth in fleeting warmth. In a few weeks, fall color would fade to sleepy browns, and barren limbs would wave goodbye to another earthly season. Some people welcomed change. Others accepted the inevitable. Some refused it only to have it happen anyway.

"We've made progress, haven't we?" His words, apt and oddly well-timed, broke the silence.

"I'd like to think so." How long would they sit there and hold hands? She liked holding his hand, but a woman could only take so much. Kiss or no kiss?

"I guess the fried chicken and creamed corn won't

stay warm forever. Would you like to eat and then relax under that red maple over there?" He pointed toward the tallest tree, ablaze in autumn color.

Okay. No kiss. She stuffed down her disappointment and nodded. "Sounds good."

The spread they brought covered most of the picnic table, and her stomach rumbled. As they ate, they talked about current events, town happenings, and the diner's transformation without slipping into the past. Chuck helped himself to another drumstick and tipped the plastic container toward her. "Please, have another piece."

"No, thanks. Everything's really delish, but I'm going to save room for a tiny sliver of pie and maybe a cookie."

"Me too." He laughed and bit into the chicken leg then followed the bite with a big swig of iced tea. "Right after I polish off this fellow. Willpower's not my strong suit today."

"Men like you don't have to worry about the middle age spread. All some women do is look at food and the calories immediately go to our hips." And other spots. For the one hundredth time, she wished she were a little less top-heavy. All her life, she'd been conscientious of the fact. That a naturally curvy gal should also own a down-home, country cookin' diner had to be one of life's cruel jokes. A skinny Minnie she'd never be.

"Your hips are perfect, as is everything else." Color flamed in Chuck's cheeks. "Not that I notice. Well, I notice. But I try not to." He grinned and shook his head. "Oh, boy. I'm bungling this, aren't I?"

Well, wonder of wonders. Was he blushing? That he should observe her figure and find her desirable made her giddy. Goosebumps pranced down her spine. "No. Not in the least. Actually, I was curious about that. I'm glad you told me."

His grin slipped. "You're kidding. You didn't know I found you attractive?"

"You have to admit, after high school, you didn't give much indication of that. Until our recent...understanding...that was one possibility I considered. A fashion model, I'm not."

"Are you kidding me?" He tossed the chicken leg bone on his plate and wiped his fingers on the paper napkin. "You really thought that? Look, besides being my friend, you're my employer. My boss. It's not exactly appropriate to compliment your boss's...er...attributes on the job or off. It's something that must be broached tactfully...tastefully. During the proper moment and all."

"I see." She almost snorted but caught herself before it scooted past her lips. "So, this was that moment?"

He didn't hesitate. "Yes, ma'am. It was. And let me state, for the record, you are mighty fine. Like raise-my-blood-pressure-a-notch kind of fine. Now, I think I'm ready for dessert, how about you?"

Pie and cookies? After this conversation?

"I thought we could have it under that maple. That okay?"

"Uh, sure." She suppressed her surprise. How could he possibly think of dessert? She grabbed the old blanket they brought and whisked up the pie container, bag of cookies, and paper plates. Chuck grabbed napkins and drinks.

Attempting nonchalance was no small feat. If this was his idea to romance her, Chuck had better learn the fine art of flirting. He'd dangled the carrot but failed to follow through. They plodded over to the maple tree and shook out the blanket, arranging it beneath an umbrella of red leaves. Except for a couple with kids at the south end of the park, they were the only ones here.

"Wow, I've never seen this place so deserted. Of course, I haven't been here in a while." Chuck glanced around as he took a spot on the blanket. "Guess with it being Sunday, most everyone's visiting family."

"What do you usually do on Sunday?" She sat down near him and began slicing the pie.

"Same thing." He redirected his gaze toward her and smiled. "Mom still enjoys doing Sunday dinners at her house and having Voni, Jim and the kids, and me over. She generally makes a roast or casserole and we provide the side dishes. Sometimes, we watch a movie or visit on the patio and play board games or cards. Our Sunday get-togethers are a family tradition."

"Sounds like fun. When Mom and Dad aren't down at the lake, we do Sunday dinners too. We alternate between my house and theirs." Ida Mae handed him a paper plate, laden with pie. The way his eyes lit up, one would think he'd never tasted plain, old apple pie before. Except he genuinely had a thing for hers. The mystery remained, though, if the adage *the way to a man's heart is through his stomach* were true, she'd be wearing a wedding band now on her finger instead of a freckle.

He took a huge bite and, clearly, savored it. "*Wow*. Fantastic, as always. Thanks for making my favorite."

Because of his professional training, the man's culinary skills could rival hers any day. Nevertheless, he did seem to appreciate her efforts, especially her apple pie, unrefined as it was.

"You're welcome. I got off easy with pie and cookies. You did all the hard work. Fried chicken, potato salad, creamed corn casserole. Picnic fare at its finest."

"Hey, your apple pie and snickerdoodles could cause a riot." His smile widened, deepening the laugh lines at various junctures of his face. Age certainly hadn't diminished his good looks or boyish charm. If anything, life had treated Chuck well. "I'm glad you enjoyed the food, but it wasn't much work. Cooking's my jam. We should have picnics more often."

"Now that we don't live at the diner twenty-four-seven, maybe we can."

"About that." He trailed his fingers across her hand. "Are you happy? About the changes?"

"You know, I really am. The diner's always been my life. Yours too. But I think having a life outside of the Come and Get It has been a good call. Everyone seems to have adjusted to the new hours, and we sure haven't lost any business. I kind of wish we'd done it sooner."

"I guess we got into a rut. Easy to grow complacent when we've done something the same way for so long."

"Yeah. And because that rut is what we love, we hardly recognize other things we sacrifice for the sake of routine."

His grin faltered. Did he understand the implication? He set down the paper plate and leaned in close. "I want to propose a plan."

Chuck cleared his throat. He'd wanted to say it for a long time. He'd danced around it enough. "Let's start fresh. I know we've said it before, and we can't roll back the clock, but from here we can forge ahead. We've talked about *us* for weeks. We're not children anymore, are we?"

"Maybe at heart." Ida Mae's eyes twinkled. She leaned toward him too, until their faces were mere inches apart.

"True. What I meant *is* I don't want to waste another minute without telling you...how I feel." His heart knocked in his chest. Happiness snuffed out fear. "Gosh, girl. Where do I start?"

She took his hands in hers. "From the beginning?"

"Good idea. Only one problem with that. We'd have to revisit the past for a bit." Her hands tensed. He shifted his palms and wrapped them around hers. How to reassure her? "I know I've said the past is the past, and I stand by that. I'm speaking more from my own perspective. You don't have to add anything...unless you're comfortable. Would that be okay?"

She released a breath and nodded. "Yes."

"Great. Here goes. You know a lot of my story. For that matter, the whole town knows the Farrow story. You can't live in a town the size of Ruby without knowing whose lights are on at midnight and who's doing what. But...sometimes, there are underlying layers to a story that people don't see or know." He paused, strangely at peace. He'd worried that sharing his innermost thoughts would be hard, but in Ida Mae's presence, reservations fled.

"I was ten when my father left. Voni, four. Dad's leaving affected each of us differently. Because she was much younger, Voni didn't understand all the dynamics at play. I, on the other hand, knew more than I wished. Sy's abandonment wounded each of us in different ways. For a while, Voni grew fearful and clingy. I became angry, hardened, and bitter. Mom, brokenhearted but resilient, rallied her little family and made the best of a bad situation. With time and lots of love and support from the community, my sister and I transitioned, and our emotions eased." It hadn't been easy. Far from. To simplify the story, he drilled down the details. "Thankfully, neither of us followed in our dad's footsteps. Despite our roots, we worked hard, made something of ourselves, and made our mother proud. You already know what a great example Mom is." He wanted to share his secret ambition, but that could wait.

"I do. Liza's the best. She'd do anything for anybody."

"I'm biased, naturally, but you're right. Now, I can't say my childhood didn't leave me completely unscathed. You know that. I know that. I have issues. And yet, in recent months, you've forced me to take a hard look at myself, and it's made me realize that without the tough things we wouldn't know what we're made of.

"While I detest aspects of who I used to be, you've made me believe that bad things don't have to forever hold us hostage. That only gives them power over the future and what we want to become."

Ida Mae lowered her gaze. "You give me far too much credit. I think, maybe, you've been on this journey for a while. With or without me, you would have eventually reached that conclusion."

"No. Without you, I'd be a mess. An utter mess." He captured her chin with his hand and gently nudged her cheek. "You undid me…and put me back together again."

"Since when did you become such a wordsmith?" Tears pooled beneath blonde lashes and spilled forth.

Her reaction squeezed his insides. He kissed away

each tear as it fell. "Aw, girl. Don't cry. Please don't cry."

Her tears tasted salty and sweet. Beneath his fingertips, her chin quivered. Slowly, he drew her into his arms. "I've been stupid. I know I've said it before, but I'm sorry. So sorry. I wish I hadn't taken my insecurities out on you. I wish I'd acted on instinct rather than reacted in fear. To see you with Fenston when we were kids... That crushed me, but I know I had it coming."

She trembled within his embrace. *Oh, no.* Had he said the wrong thing again? He wanted to convey what she meant to him, not throw darts. "Look, we won't talk about him or those days any more. Unless you want to, that is. Okay?"

Ida Mae sniffled. Tension eased from her body. "Okay."

He continued to hold her. He marveled at how perfectly she fit into his arms. Yesterdays' school events, musicals, and prom flitted across his memory. Life as a bachelor dimmed. Where once he could see only monotony and boredom, today he envisioned life repurposed. What to do about it?

"I'd like to court you." An archaic term, but certainly more romantic than "date." To him, "court" meant something intentional. Something special. With the desired outcome leading to the altar. Eventually, anyway.

Crazy? Yeah, probably. Why would Ida Mae even want a guy like him—one who'd snubbed and rejected her when she'd laid her heart bare? One whose sturdy façade and false bravado earned respect in the community's eyes, but anguish in hers? But he had to try. He realized this might be his last chance.

"Court?" With her face snuggled into his shoulder, the word came out muffled.

"Sure. As in see each other, and only each other, as we consider new possibilities." He brushed back strands of hair so he could see her profile. Mascara blotches decorated the cheek that was visible. "I'd like a chance to redeem myself. To be the man to you that I should have been before life got in the way. You deserve the best, and while I can't give you the moon, maybe we can lasso a few stars. What do you think?"

Ida Mae raised her head, the corners of her mouth tilting upward. "I think that's the smartest thing you've ever said, Chuck Farrow."

Forehead to forehead, their lips practically touched, and yet, he restrained himself from kissing her. Maybe because she expected it. Maybe because when they shared their first kiss, he wanted the moment to be spontaneous and joyful. Heavy moments didn't necessarily bode well for first kisses. Not that kissing was his expertise, but a couple's first kiss shouldn't hinge, in part, on memories and past regrets. He respected Ida Mae more than that. She deserved the best. The best of life. The best of him. He needed to prove himself worthy of her affection...of her love.

He shifted his weight, creating space between them. Ida Mae shivered as he did so. While the sun shone bright and warm, the breeze kicked up a chill. "Are you cold? I can get our jackets out of the car."

"No, I'm fine. As long as you're beside me, I'm great." She nestled into his arms again.

Whoa. If they continued sitting here like this, he wouldn't have to ponder spontaneity, first kisses or the cool breeze. None of that would matter a pig's snout because one more whiff of her honeysuckle-scented hair, and any attempt at creating the perfect moment would flitter away in the wind along with good judgment. Yet, kids, they weren't. *Aw, man.* But he didn't want to mess up with Ida Mae. He had to get this right, and timing was everything.

"How about we take a walk?" A few curls had escaped her mile-high bun, and he gave them a tug as he pulled her to her feet. "Does the spring still flow at the edge of the park over there?"

"Yes, it winds around what the locals have carved out as a nature trail of sorts. Ought to have lots of pretty foliage right about now." She shot him a curious glance. "Should we put away the picnic things first?"

"Nah, I don't think they're going anywhere, do you?"

"Guess not."

Chuck grasped her hand, and with palms linked, they made their way to the far corner of Cusick Park where the spring bubbled along in its narrow, zigzag pattern. Down the hillside it streamed, snaking past a leaf-covered path, partially hidden by a thick thatch of trees and underbrush.

The path eventually led into an open clearing that overlooked the south side of town. From that vantage point, Ruby's most prominent features were visible. Church steeples, tree-lined streets, and picket-fenced yards stood out among the rolling hills and meadows. Below the rise, down on Main Street and Elm, the Come and Get It, Hattie's Hair Care, and Nora and Ned's General Market, along with various other businesses, dotted the sleepy community. Framed in fall's royal robe, this tiny niche in the Ozarks revealed a glimpse of heaven. *Stunning.* Just as he remembered. He didn't know when he'd last visited this spot.

Yes, he did. Four or five autumns ago when he'd contemplated a life change. When the future looked as bleak and lonesome as the empty rooms in his house. When neighbors were getting married, having babies, and starting the families he fantasized about.

Fleetingly, he'd considered moving somewhere else. Somewhere far away from Ruby's memories, and opportunities that would never be. But he couldn't leave what family he had or this town or Ida Mae. Gradually, the melancholy passed, and life meandered on. Now, Chuck was glad he'd stayed. Glad he hadn't succumbed to his soul's grumblings.

Hope lit in his heart and renewed possibilities. *Why, God?* Why, after decades of yearning for the impossible, did his desires suddenly seem within reach? *Timing.* Once more, the word slapped him upside the head.

Hands entwined, he and Ida Mae stood in silence, scanning this land they'd forever called "home." Some acreage, one hillside over as the crow flew, had recently gone up for sale. That didn't happen often in these parts, though, when it did, someone quickly snatched it up. No one wanted to see these old Ozark hills and hollows razed in the name of progress for shopping centers, subdivisions, and the like. The locals lived by an unwritten honor code. Never sell to big business or to those who wanted to decimate the land solely for the sake of the almighty dollar. They'd seen that happen in too many areas, and the born-and-bred citizens in such places paid a steep price.

In this case, the twenty acres Marshall Realty listed last week belonged to a family who'd owned the land and the old home place for generations. Horace Sapp's grandparents had passed on in recent years, and it was all Horace could do to keep up his own house, much less his gram's and grandpa's, in addition to his law enforcement duties. While Deputy Sapp wouldn't sell to just anyone, Chuck knew the property upkeep drained him. The right buyer might very well motivate him to negotiate. A crazy notion fired in Chuck's head and set wheels turning.

"Gorgeous view, huh?" Ida Mae inclined her head toward the panorama before them. "I love my little house in town, but can you imagine waking up to this every morning? *Oh, my.*"

Yes. Yes, he could. Or he wanted to. The scenery would be an added bonus, of course. What would she say if he told her what he was thinking? Best to keep it to himself until he spoke with Jerry Marshall.

Chapter Thirteen

The Monday morning after their picnic, Ida Mae lingered in bed well after dawn. She'd dreamed of Chuck and the essence of that dream brought a smile to her lips.

Intangible, and yet, she could almost reach out and touch this place. Whatever "this place" was. The dream sparked a memory of something familiar. Something she yearned for, but didn't know why, because Ruby was home. Although she'd toyed with the idea, she'd never leave here. Mom and Dad were here. Chuck. The Come and Get It. Her friends. Everyone and everything that mattered to her, dwelled here.

Nevertheless, her dream evoked indescribable joy because Chuck was there with her, and she sensed this "place" was theirs. Together, they stood on the grassy knoll, wrapped in fall's red and gold palette, overlooking a sort of stone structure. A home, maybe? One with lots of bright, airy rooms imbued with color. The home seemed to belong to them. And then, she'd awakened.

Ahh. Could it be possible? Ida Mae stretched, relieved this was her day off. She wanted to hold this dream close for a while longer. Knowing Chuck, he was probably up with the birds and already gone for his morning jog. Thinking of him, of their day together yesterday, caused her pulse to race. Had God finally answered her prayer? Was there hope for them? Despite all the heartache, all the pain of the past, were things finally going in her favor?

If only the other pieces of her life puzzle would fit neatly together. While a reunion with her child seemed unlikely, it *could* happen, couldn't it? She and Chuck were a prime example. Lifelong friends to a "couple" within a month. That was the glossy version. The transition had been anything but smooth. In truth, their upgraded relationship status had been decades in the making.

She blew out a sigh and flung an arm across her face. What if her son or daughter found her? What then? How would she explain to Chuck? To Mom and Dad? *Like a reunion will ever happen.* That kind of thing was best left to reality TV shows and tell-all rags. But oh...how she dreamed to one day meet her baby! The baby who was no longer a child.

The recurring pain sliced through her. *Please, Lord. Let him or her be happy and healthy...wherever he or she is. Somehow, remind my child how very much his birth mama loves him.* Prayer didn't fix the past, but it helped connect her to a higher realm. It laid her deepest yearnings at God's feet.

Help me believe. She added the addendum to her prayer. Help her believe in what? In potential? In a bigger plan than she could foresee and certainly had no control over? If only people could realize how bad choices affected the future. How one devastating lapse in judgment could easily snowball into a lifetime of heartache and regret. She'd never be sorry that she chose life for her child, but if she hadn't willingly defied her dad and dated a guy who was completely unsuitable for her, then today might be so different.

Likely, she and Chuck would have found their way to

each other sooner. If she hadn't been pregnant and had hung around Ruby after high school instead of disappearing for four months, maybe he would have come to his senses and admitted his feelings. Maybe they'd have married, had a couple of kids, a dog, and the perfect place in paradise—in Ruby in these autumn-cloaked hills. Maybe they would have run the diner as husband and wife instead of employee and employer, as comfortable as that was. Maybe they'd be a normal family with mishaps and melodrama balanced with their fair share of successes and laughter too. Maybe.

Ida Mae consciously refocused her thoughts. Why ruin yesterday's perfectly good memory with what could have been? She shook off the covers and padded over to the window where sunlight filtered through the curtains. Off in the distance, the Ozark hills shimmered against a dewy skyline where remnants of last night's humidity remained. In her immediate eye-view, cars tootled along neighborhood streets carrying passengers to school, work, and errands. Seven-fifty a.m. and already Ruby burst at the seams with activity. For a tiny town, it rolled out the sidewalks early. Then, when dusk hit, it rolled them up with almost as much vigor.

If the Come and Get It wasn't closed on Mondays, it would be hopping by now. Usually excited to get back to work, she couldn't fib—today she was glad for the respite. Embarrassingly, her late thirties zapped more of her strength. Used to, she'd go like a freight train. Still did, but her caboose dragged a bit more these days. Hormones, probably. It happened with age she'd heard.

Get a grip, honey. You're not that old. You may feel like it sometimes because of what you've been through, but thirty-nine isn't over-the-hill. She had a career. One that she adored. She owned her own business and her own home. Though he hadn't said the actual words yet, she had a guy who loved her. The turn of events with Chuck demonstrated this. They might end up with their happily-ever-after before she hit forty. Now if the Lord would nudge the guy a few steps closer, she'd really appreciate it.

And who knew? Maybe they'd carve out their own slice of paradise somewhere in this town. Chuck's house was nice, but rather small. Her renovated bungalow offered more room, but she was ready for a change. A home with a view, perhaps, and one they could put their own stamp on, together. She enjoyed her quaint, friendly neighborhood and picturesque street, however, a rural abode appealed too. It was nice to daydream. For once, it seemed that this particular daydream wasn't that far beyond the horizon. Except in this daydream, cell phones didn't ring.

If it had been anyone else who called her this early on her day off, she might have ignored it, but she knew by the ring tone who it was, and she had no problem with the interruption.

"Hi. Did I wake you?" Chuck had waited as long as he could, but excitement drummed in his veins. He needed to hear her voice.

"No way. I've cleaned house, tossed in laundry, and baked up a batch of muffins."

"You're kidding."

The laughter on the other end of the line gave her

away. "Yep. I sure am. But no, you didn't wake me. You finished with your morning run?"

"Yes'm. Thought of you the entire time." He really had. Thinking of her put a new spring in his step. "I'm wondering how you'd feel about brunch?"

"Well, I'd feel real fine about it. You bringing, or am I making?"

"Neither. How about we go on a real date?"

"I thought yesterday was a real date."

"Sure was, and a great one at that." He cleared his throat, stuffing down the jitters. "Let me clarify and ask properly. Would you like to drive twenty minutes up the road to Sapphire and go to brunch? There's a new spot, an omelet and waffle café, I thought we might try. It can't compare to the Come and Get It, of course, but it wouldn't seem like a date if we went to the diner and made our own breakfast."

"Oh, I don't know about that. Could be fun." Her amusement resonated. "Can you give me about thirty minutes? Honestly, I'm in my sleep shirt and bunny slippers."

Oh boy. The picture that brought to mind. He gulped. "You bet. Take as long you need and text me when you're ready. Does that work?"

"Yes. Thanks. I'll touch base soon."

"Great. And Ida Mae…" He wanted to say it. Would she think he was crazy? He chickened out and said the next best thing. "Looking forward to it." Okay. Maybe not the next best thing, but all he had courage for at the moment.

He traipsed over to his clothes closet and thumbed through the meager selection there. Pitiful. His wardrobe stunk. He owned a few pairs of dress slacks and a couple of shirts, perfect for church. Other than that, he kept his attire simple. Blue jeans, tee shirts, and sweat shirts. Jogging shorts and sweats. He didn't own preppy clothes or anything that remotely qualified as dressy apparel. An extravagant dresser, he wasn't. Other than church, the only time he wore anything besides blue jeans was when he worked for that swanky restaurant after culinary school. Fancy white duds and a chef's toque were required at Settler's Haven, a posh blend of "uptown" and Ozarkian. "Where culture and heritage meet understated elegance" the menu slogan boasted. A first-rate tourist attraction...er...restaurant.

He'd enjoyed his stint there, but he'd jumped at Ida Mae's job offer when it came. Lord knew, it wasn't the money. There was no way she could compete with his previous salary. The reason he'd given his notice at Settler's Haven ten years ago was because he could contribute to the Come and Get It's legacy. That, and he also got to see Ida Mae every day. A win on both counts.

Finally, Chuck grabbed a long-sleeved, maroon-colored tee shirt and his nicest and least faded pair of jeans. Ida Mae would outdo him, hands-down, in the beauty and wardrobe department, but today, what he wore would have to do. When he had time, he'd go shopping. For now, he showered and shaved. He combed his hair. He opened brand new deodorant too, so there was that.

If the guy standing on her doorstep wore bib overalls and a flannel shirt with unicorns on it, it wouldn't have mattered. In fact, he'd blend right in with the area farmers. Well, except for the unicorns. Nevertheless, the man on her front porch couldn't have been more striking. Clean shaven, a recent haircut, and the color maroon definitely agreed with him. Laid back, casual, and smiling—they suited Chuck Farrow to a T.

"Hey, there." That smile of his melted the marrow in her bones. Always had. Even when they were kids. Playmates. Dance partners. Teenagers. Adults. As long as she lived, she'd never grow tired of it. "I need to grab a jacket, but come on in."

"It's chilly this morning. It'll warm up quickly once the sun's fully up." He stepped inside and waited as she rummaged through her coat closet.

"What do you think?" It was an older sweater, but one of her favorites. "Too ratty?"

"Nah. It's perfect. Blue looks pretty on you." He took the sweater from her and held it open as she poked her arms through the sleeve holes. "It complements your hair."

"Thank you. Mom and Dad gave it to me for Christmas a long time ago."

Chuck's hands lingered on her shoulders. "Your parents have good taste."

Yes. And they always hoped he'd be the one. Their future son-in-law. No sense in backtracking down that well-worn path. Today was a new day. She and Chuck had a fresh start.

Ida Mae turned to face him. "Ready?"

Was it her imagination or did his eyes flicker to her mouth? She couldn't be sure, and the moment passed.

On the drive into Sapphire, the bigger town that folks referred to as "the city," Chuck pointed out a flock of wild turkeys. Humongous and rather regal looking, they strutted alongside a stream that ran near a wooded embankment. "Real beauts, aren't they?"

"They sure are." She marveled at the birds, thankful to share the moment with someone like Chuck who appreciated life's wonders. How she would love to roam these old mountains and hillsides with this man by her side. No pretentiousness. No putting on airs. No need to be anything other than who they were. Being together, being themselves. Every day, it grew easier. Their banter came naturally without force or agendas. She gloried in the subtle, wonderful changes. Things between them were the same, and not. They'd grown beyond the constraints of expectation and anguish. They spoke frankly. The freedom in that, buoyed by sincerity and gentleness.

Chuck had said whatever happened in her past didn't matter. A check in her spirit revealed the truth. *Foundations* mattered. If trust were to be the cornerstone of anything to come, she knew what she must do. Eventually. The question was when? When to tell Chuck about Tyler? Her pregnancy? Certainly, not today. Not today as they stole away on this sun-glazed morn, side by side, eager to greet the day and make a new memory.

"Yoo-hoo. Earth to Ida Mae." Chuck squeezed her hand. "Mind sharing?"

"I was thinking."

"Okay. I'll refrain from the typical 'that could be dangerous' response." He glanced sideways at her, his mouth twitching. "Enlighten me, please."

She scrambled for something. "I was thinking how easy it is being with you." True. Not a fib. "How precious each moment together is and how thankful I am for our second chance." Also, true.

Without preamble, he lifted her palm to his lips, feathering a soft kiss there. "I've been dumb. So dumb. I wish I could go back and knock some sense into that teenage kid."

"Shh." In many ways, they both shared burden, guilt, and responsibility. High school seniors didn't have the best filters. Often, they simply weren't mature enough to act and react wisely to life-altering situations. At eighteen, Chuck rejected the idea of loving another because the potential for pain lingered. She, in turn, responded the way many young girls in love might. By seeking solace in the arms of one who flattered, however distorted and wrong that was. "I understood you were going through a lot. I shouldn't have pushed."

"No. No, Ida Mae. It wasn't you. It was so many things, really, but it sure wasn't you." He flipped on his turn signal and hung a left onto the main highway that would take them into Sapphire. "Trauma's a curious thing. We bust our backsides to move forward, determined not to revisit old wounds, then when we think we've healed, we allow our minds to play tricks. Our vision clouds. Old defense mechanisms kick in, and we end up causing ourselves more pain. I probably should have had counseling or something."

This was the first time he'd mentioned that. "It's not too late. A lot of people benefit from talking with professionals. There is absolutely no shame in that."

She'd probably benefit from the same thing. She'd bet Sunset Meadows' new social services director could refer them to a contact. Matt Enders' expertise and knowledge had garnered quite a reputation in Ruby. Though she didn't know him personally, he'd endeared himself to the locals, and word had it that he was a man of integrity.

"I agree. I'm glad the stigma surrounding mental health issues has eased. Back when we were kids, people sucked it up and went on. There wasn't as much information then, granted, but also, the era didn't lend itself to airing our dirty laundry as far as personal problems went. Discussing stuff like dads leaving, parents divorcing, and non-traditional families were seen as taboo territory." Chuck paused, as if remembering. "Ruby may have been the exception to that rule. Because we're a close-knit lot, our town rallied around those who'd been kicked to the curb. We cared for our own in our own way, but we didn't understand the importance of seeking outside resources. I'm thankful for our church community in the area. Some churches close a blind eye to the hurting in their midst because they're so focused on building 'numbers.' We're blessed ours wasn't one of those churches. Our church family helped Mom in countless ways when Dad left."

"Yes, Ruby may be about ten steps behind in many respects, but that's the culture here, which isn't necessarily a bad thing. Serving others and meeting needs are still a priority." In the back of her mind, Ida Mae wondered what life in Ruby would have been like for her child. No doubt he or she would have been loved, but would the circumstances surrounding her baby's birth follow their family? As well-meaning as people were, tongues wagged despite good intentions. Moot points now.

"You know, everyone's rooting for us." Chuck changed, or more like expanded, the subject. "The grapevine's flourished for a long time. It'll really thrive when folks realize we've…uh…gotten more serious. Are you ready for that?"

"Sure. I'll even supply the watering can."

"Should be fun then. Can't wait."

They arrived at The Hungry Hippo around nine. A small, quaint café painted gray with pink undertones and bookended by a pair of gold-leafed birch trees, the humorously named establishment embodied warmth and good cheer. Inside, the décor was trendy and colorful with the right mix of comfy and casual. There were a handful of booths and several tables, all occupied except for a few. A good sign.

A perky young hostess strolled toward them and greeted them with a smile. "Good morning. I'm Valerie. Welcome to The Hungry Hippo. Table for two?"

"Good morning, Valerie, and thanks. Yes, two would be correct." Chuck's hand rested on the small of Ida Mae's back. His touch caused goosebumps to raise on her arms.

Valerie led them to a small, round table over in the far corner of the café. She slapped down their menus and recited the brunch specials. "Hollis, your server, will be with you shortly."

"Hollis?" Ida Mae glanced at Chuck, then at Valerie.

"Yes. That's right. Do you know him?"

Chuck gave a short laugh. "No, ma'am. But Hollis is my middle name."

"Really? What are the chances of that?" Valerie cocked her head to one side and tapped her short red fingernails against the menus. "It's a pretty unique name. A good one though."

"Thanks. I'm kind of partial to it, too."

"Well, Hollis will bring your waters. Take your time looking over the menus." Their hostess bounced away leaving them to study the vast selections.

Friendly and efficient, minus the Come and Get It's distinctive, downhome atmosphere, the new café would probably fare well once it worked out a few kinks. Chiefly, some areas of the café weren't as well-lit as others, and a few of the tables could be repositioned to make a wider walkway for customers and staff. Knowing the restaurant business as she did, she had insight where others might not. Minor things weren't a deal-breaker. Fantastic food, great service, welcoming ambiance. Those were musts.

"What do you think?" Chuck whispered once Valerie was out of earshot.

"I like it. In a month or so, I bet they'll have improved some things, but overall, I think it's terrific. A nice addition to Sapphire."

"My thoughts too." He flipped open the menu. "Let's see, what are you in the mood for? The specials the hostess mentioned sound intriguing."

"Clever names. Not as clever as ours though. I'm thinking of going with the Eggs-tra-Ordinary Omelet or the Waist Not, Want Not. Eggs or waffles? Hmm..."

"Same dilemma here. Why don't we each order something different and we'll share?"

"You read my mind. Here comes Hollis, I think."

Hollis, being somewhere in the neighborhood of twenty and twenty-two, was an animated kid with a lot of pep in his step. He quickly set down two ice waters, the lemon wedges clinging for dear life to the glass rims. "Good morning, lovely lady and kind sir. I'm Hollis and I'll be serving you today. How are we this morning?"

It was all she could do to keep a straight face. A fellow free spirit. How grand. "Wonderful. How are you, Hollis?"

"I'm super, ma'am. This week's my fall break and I'm stoked. Not a lot of homework for a change. Thanks for asking."

"What are you studying, Hollis?"

"Well, sir, I'm pre-med. Can you believe it? As a little guy, blood and guts used to creep me out, but then my dad got sick and passed, and I decided I wanted to help people the way the doctors tried to help Dad. Even though the cancer spread, he sure had a bunch of people pulling for him. Sorry. This is probably TMI. Do you have any questions about our menu or brunch specials?"

In that instant, she knew this boy had won over Chuck. *Fatherless kid. A dreadful disease. Hard worker. Putting himself through school.* It all resonated. Empathy pooled in the man's eyes.

"Hollis, I'm deeply sorry about your dad." Chuck closed his menu and gave the kid his full attention. "Do you have any brothers or sisters?"

"No, sir. Only my mom and me. She works down at the bank and I pull as many hours as I can here. It's been ten years, but sometimes, it's kinda tough. I miss him, you know?" Hollis glanced down at his order pad and collected himself. "Geez. I never talk this much. I apologize. May I take your order?"

"No apology necessary, Hollis. I think you'll make a

tremendous physician." The young man beamed as Chuck continued. "I believe we'll have the Eggs-tra-Ordinary Omelet and the Waist Not, Want Not. Two coffees, fully loaded. And two orange juices, please."

"Awesome. I'll turn this in and bring your coffees. I'll serve your OJs with your brunch specials. Is that okay?"

"Perfect. Thank you."

"You bet, sir. Thank *you*. I've never told anyone here about my dad. You're the first. Dunno why."

As the boy bounded off toward the kitchen, for a few seconds, neither she nor Chuck said a word. Ida Mae finally broke the silence. "I've always found it uncanny how the Lord brings certain people into our path. We never know whose lives we might touch or how."

"What's the likelihood?" Chuck stared after the kid. "The likelihood that we'd get a waiter whose name is Hollis and that his life mirrors aspects of mine? What a kid."

What a man. Charles "Chuck" Hollis Farrow. The guy she loved and the waiter who'd never told anyone here about his father. Until today.

God thing or happenstance? Tears pricked the corners of her eyes. She knew the answer to that and the enormity of it jolted her. If God could orchestrate a meeting between a man and a kid who shared a name and a similar history, no telling what else God had up His sleeve.

A thousand butterflies lodged in her stomach.

Chapter Fourteen

Hollis unearthed emotions Chuck thought he'd buried. Compassion for the boy welled in his chest. After their meal, he plunked down cash with a generous tip and did something he'd never done before. On the back of the check, he scribbled an encouraging sentiment. *Brunch was incredible. Thanks, Hollis, for your attentive service. Cheering you on as you soar toward your dream and accomplish your life mission!*

He'd been in that kid's shoes once. Different scenario, similar situation. To know someone had rooted for him, believed in him, made him press a little harder. He reached higher and dreamed bigger when supporters had his back. Maybe on the discouraging days that were sure to come, Hollis would remember their encounter and realize that one bad event didn't determine the future.

"I really enjoyed that. Thank you." Ida Mae slipped her arm through Chuck's as they ambled toward his vehicle. "I think you made our waiter's day. I never knew a kid could talk so much."

"Yeah, I think he liked us." He pressed the key fob and unlocked the vehicle. He opened the door for Ida Mae, and she slid into the passenger seat. "People know the difference between platitudes and sincerity. Especially twenty-year-olds. They pick up on authenticity fast. That kid's going to succeed because he has what it takes. Intellect, work ethic, and relatability. All things that make an excellent physician."

"All the qualities you have too."

She said it with such honesty...such love. For them to have finally realized their readiness to commit to one another was nothing short of a miracle. If they'd been somewhere private instead of a café parking lot, he might have kissed her. Instead, he imagined that first kiss and how perfect he wanted the moment to be. The picture it brought to mind knocked the wind out of him. "Thanks. You've contributed to any success I've had. Even when we were kids, you believed in me."

"That was easy. You're an amazing person, Charles Hollis Farrow."

Whoa. Her smile curled his toes. If she kept this up, he wouldn't be responsible. He leaned down and feathered a light kiss on her temple. She wound her arms around his neck and embraced him. *Oh, Lord. She smells so good.* Her cheek was so soft and warm next to his. Honey-blonde curls tumbled past her shoulders and begged to be touched. Curves in all the right places made him swallow hard. His hands didn't stray, but his thoughts weren't particularly noble. He was a man. She was a woman. Since when did a forty-year-old man and a thirty-nine-year-old woman need anyone's permission to express affection? A simple kiss wasn't crossing the line. *No, but your thoughts are teetering mighty close.*

Chuck summoned his will power and disengaged himself from her arms. "Guess we better head back."

"Head...back?" Ida Mae scrunched her eyebrows together. "Already?"

Super. He'd hurt her feelings. Leave it to finesse and

timing. Specifically, his lack of it. "Would you like to take a drive?"

Her face brightened. "Sure. Where to?"

He had an idea. It would even serve a two-fold purpose. One, their date wouldn't end too soon. And two, he wanted to see her reaction. "It's a secret, okay?"

This better be good. Given their history with secrets, she wasn't very fond of them. They headed back toward Ruby. While Chuck drove, he attempted small talk, covering everything from weather, food, and flu shots to holidays and hometown happenings. They'd exhausted all the surface stuff when he turned onto a familiar country road that spiraled up a tree-lined hillside a few miles over the rise from Cusick Park. The steep incline rose farther and farther into a thatch of ember, orange, and cinnamon woods, yielding, at last, to open sky and scenic views that overlooked town.

Her breath caught. *Magnificent.* The word cartwheeled across her subconscious. The Sapps' old place? She knew from memory the general area, but it'd been years since she'd visited. She'd called on Horace's grandparents long before they'd passed. Brought them meals up until the end.

A twinge of sadness knotted in her chest. Knowing where they were now eased the poignancy of their passing, yet losing beloved souls like the Sapps sure pinched one's heart. Heaven gained two of Ruby's finest within a month apart.

After Horace's own mama and daddy passed away, Grandma and Grandpa Sapp were all Horace had left. Their two-story, century-old home, built entirely of native stone, remained here—empty, along with the twenty or so semi-wooded acres surrounding the property. Though Horace tended the homeplace as best he could, it needed a little TLC. Nothing major from what she could tell. Overgrown brush and weeds were the main culprits. Wonder if the inside of the house looked the same? She remembered it having big, spacious rooms, detailed woodwork, and glorious built-ins, perfect for knick-knacks and china.

Chuck parked and cut off the ignition. "Would you like to get out?"

"Do you think it's okay?"

"Positive."

They ventured from the vehicle and walked along the expanse of undeveloped land, unmarred by twenty-first century progress. He offered her his hand as they went, and she accepted, lacing her fingers through his.

"I'd forgotten how breathtaking it is here. You can almost see the entire town from this vantage point." She paused, mesmerized. "It's like a living, breathing painting, isn't it?"

"Yes, and you and I are part of it." He pointed toward Main street off in the distance. "We can see all our favorite places—the Come and Get It, Nora and Ned's General Market, Dander's Barbershop, and Hattie's Hair Care. Farther down, there's Pennies from Heaven, Ernie's Automotive, and Marshall Realty."

And beyond those were Sunset Meadows, the bank, schools, clinic, and churches that overlapped with quaint, cozy niches and tight-knit neighborhoods. Additional small businesses and points of interest peppered the hills and hollows adjacent to town. Picture-perfect, on the fringe of sublime, yet a few pockmarks remained. Most folks around here appreciated that because it conveyed a life well lived. Without a few blemishes, life stagnated. If people didn't recognize their faults and foibles, how were they to grow? Ruby, Missouri coaxed their own, and others, to gaze past the flaws and seek goodness in their slightly imperfect community that welcomed all with open arms. Even coddled troublemakers like Tyler Fenston. *Oh, no. Not going there.*

She resisted that bunny trail, and leaned into Chuck's shoulder, breathing in the heady scent of his aftershave. "Not Thomas Kinkade perfectville, but I'll take it. How about you?"

"Same. This is home. It's my future." He turned toward her, brushing fly-away curls from her face. "*You're* my future."

As a teenager, she'd wondered if he'd ever recognize that. As a woman, she knew. She sensed it. God was restoring what they'd almost lost. *Each other.* With razor sharp clarity, this day, this second, imprinted on her brain and begged for space there. Her heart thumped so hard against her chest, that surely, he could hear it. Could he? Conscientious, she grasped the folds of her sweater and pulled the fabric closed, as if the extra layer of material would act as a sound barrier.

Chuck's eyes didn't stray from her face. Her lips. Slowly, he leaned down, his mouth poised above hers. "You don't know how long I've wanted to do this."

"Why didn't you?"

"Good question. Clearly, I might have over-thought it."

He drew her into his arms and brushed her lips with a soft kiss. The kiss deepened, and she responded to his touch as she knew she would, unashamed and with abandon. In that instant, everything they were and everything they wanted to be absolved their past blunders.

Tenderly, he held her. He kissed away the dampness that moistened her cheeks, and once again, his mouth found hers. In their teenage years, this would be dangerous territory. As adults, they treaded lightly. Passion—such a powerful persuader—could hinder or enhance commitment. Left unchecked and to its own devices, it could wreck love's foundation. When Chuck stepped back, she sensed he realized this.

"I'm sorry." He shook his head, breathless, as if an apology were in order. "I thought this would be so easy."

She tried to make light of it. "Is kissing me hard?"

"No. That's the problem. Stopping is."

They remained motionless until their breathing slowed. Chuck's shoulders slumped, and for a second, he closed his eyes. Somehow, she'd known it would be like this. Intense. Thrilling. Powerful. Love, unbound.

He was right. Stopping mid-kiss made sense. No one knew that better than she did. With the right person, kissing was a natural form of affection. With the wrong person, it opened the door to heartache and regret. The first instance demanded responsibility coupled with good judgment and accountability. The latter did too, but unfortunately, the welfare of another rarely mattered when physical intimacy, alone, guided the relationship.

"I'm glad we stopped. The fact you're a man of integrity matters a lot." Ida Mae touched his cheek, absorbing the warmth of his skin through her palm. "I love you, Chuck Farrow. Like I did when we were kids. Teenagers. And now, as adults. Except more."

He didn't return the sentiment in quite the same way. Instead, he reached for her hand and kissed each fingertip, one by one. His mouth curved upward. "We think alike."

We think alike. Man, he must be crazy. Why couldn't he say it? He loved this woman. He wanted her and the whole world, for that matter, to know. Why the mental stumbling-block when it came to vocalizing it? He had no problem with saying it to Mom and Voni and the family. With Ida Mae, the words should roll off his tongue even easier. She was his soulmate.

Face it, bud. You're a chicken. A rookie. A complete greenhorn when it comes to romancing a woman. Fear pierced his cool-as-a-cucumber resolve. He'd rolled the words around on his tongue for a long time now. Yeah, but before, the possibility of rejection hadn't seemed so real. As long as the words weren't out there, less chance of something going wrong. A stupid thought he knew, but who said being irrational made sense?

He pondered how to put it. Maybe the straightforward approach was best. "Do you know why I wanted to bring you up here?"

The blue in Ida Mae's eyes pulled him into their depths. "To kiss me?"

"Besides that." Not that kissing her hadn't sent his blood pressure out the roof. In fact, it blew off the shingles and took the roof with it. And yet, another reason motivated this drive. "I wanted to get your impression."

"On what exactly?"

"About this property. What your thoughts are." The space between her eyebrows crinkled. He had the urge to press his lips there but refrained. "Do you like it here?"

"I'm sure you know the answer to that."

"Humor me."

"Of course, I like it here. Always have. When we hiked through the park yesterday, I visualized this land. I wondered if it was as pretty as I remembered." Ida Mae lifted her head to refocus on the copper-colored hills and sprawling acreage. She directed her gaze toward the Sapp home and sighed. Not an exasperated sort of sound, but a combination of yearning and admiration. "Lots of good living happened beyond those walls and where we now stand. I hope the new owners will pour as much love into it as Grandma and Grandpa Sapp did. This is where dreams come true."

Had she read his mind? Maybe his subtle innuendo was equally as effective as the clear-cut approach. She'd voiced the very thing he'd been thinking. After their picnic yesterday, he immediately drove home and phoned Jerry Marshall. Normally, he wouldn't have bothered Jerry on a Sunday to talk shop, but he was glad he had. They'd agreed to meet for a showing later this week. "Discretion's important, Jerry. I don't want the town chatterboxes to up and marry Ida Mae and me until I have the opportunity to at least pop the question. Don't know exactly when that'll be, but I'd like to take a gander at the Sapp residence and see if it'd suit."

"Understood, buddy. Mum's the word." Jerry had

whistled low under his breath. "I gotta say it. Do you know what a field day this town's going to have when you two lovebirds finally tie the knot? I mean that in the absolute best way. Congratulations, Chuck."

"Thanks. Let's not put the cart before the horse. She could say no."

"Not on your life, guy. God's a God of hopes, dreams, and divine appointments. You'll see."

Chuck refocused his attention on Ida Mae. "About that. What are your dreams?"

"The same as they've always been. They may have evolved a bit, but they haven't changed." She glanced skyward as a skein of geese honked overhead. "I dream of you and me bringing out the best in each other like those geese do. They work as a team. It isn't forced. It comes naturally."

"That's a great way to put it. That's my dream too." They watched the geese until they flew out of sight. Ida Mae's words cemented everything he hoped for their future. For ten years, they'd made a terrific duo at the diner. Their working relationship was one of mutual respect and high regard for the other's welfare. Marriage and the commitment that came with it would be no less. No doubt they'd experience some highs and lows. Didn't all couples? But one thing was certain. Their union would have what his parents' marriage had lacked. *Teamwork and communication.* Dedication in solving issues before bigger problems cropped up.

If only his father would have sought help before walking away, his family would have remained intact, rather than becoming a statistic. As it was, the only thing Sy Farrow communicated with was the opened end of a beer bottle. No amount of begging, pleading, or stern words from Mom made one iota of difference. The Farrow team died the day Sy Farrow skulked away while his family slept.

"Why did you ask me if I liked it here?" Ida Mae tugged the hem of his jacket, rousing him from memories of the past. Her face, so pure and sweet, carved a special place within his heart. A place where truth and goodness and light and loveliness, dwelled. He never fancied himself a wordsmith, but yes, she did bring out the poet in him.

"I wanted to know. It's good when a man and woman are on the same page about likes and dislikes. Each of us has always lived in town, and I wondered what your feelings were about moving."

"Well, I wouldn't want to move too far from the diner because of the convenience and all. But somewhere like this—only two miles away, overlooking town from the hillside here—would be perfect. *Heaven.*" She snuggled into his side and placed her palm along his ribcage. "Is there something I should know? Like a secret, maybe?"

The delight in her voice made him laugh. "I don't believe I'll tell you yet. Do you mind if I keep it a secret for a little while?"

"No, I guess not. But Ruby's an awful small town, remember? And it's well known that Marshall Realty recently listed this property. I heard Horace mull over the possibility with Sam Packard a while back. I kept it to myself, though, until it went on the market."

"Okay."

"Okay, what?"

"Then that part isn't a secret."

She giggled and stepped back. "But you aren't going to tell me the rest, right?"

"Right. I think life's more fun with a few surprises, don't you?"

"Oh, my goodness! I can't stand it. Tell me!" Her voice raised a notch and she clapped her hands. "What are you waiting for?"

"You said you didn't mind if I kept a secret for a while. Can you bear with me for a few days?"

He knew the listing price of the home and acreage, but he had yet to do a walk-through. The exterior of the home needed some minor attention. Would the interior, as well? According to what Jerry indicated, there were no major problems inside. A few cobwebs and maybe a leaky faucet or two. Nothing huge. Horace had tended his grandparents' abode with as much care and fastidiousness as he was able while working forty plus hours a week and managing his own place as well.

Still, Chuck wanted to see it before taking Ida Mae on a tour. The home may very well be what she envisioned in her mind...or it may not. It'd been years since he'd set foot inside Grandma and Grandpa Sapps' home. He remembered it being clean, tidy, and spacious. The interior boasted some updates, but the original woodwork and various other features remained intact. Knowing Ida Mae's penchant for vintage and nostalgia, he bet the bones of the house would be right up her alley.

But what about this courting thing? He wanted to properly date Ida Mae before they jumped into marriage. Because of their history, they knew each other better than most couples did starting out. It may have taken him a while to admit the depth of his feelings for her, but now that he had, why stretch out a long engagement? Why drag their heels? Maybe because the foundation for a lifetime commitment was best laid with care.

Emotional intimacy wasn't the same as physical chemistry. While those two worked in tandem, a healthy marriage also included a spiritual connection, an indisputable bond that neither good nor bad could fracture. Those things weren't issues as far as Chuck was concerned. He and Ida Mae had honed the emotional aspects and acknowledged physical boundaries, and it certainly seemed like God's hand guided their lost and found journey.

Nonetheless, Ida Mae deserved to be romanced. She deserved to be swept off her pretty, little feet and given the world. All these years, she'd waited for him when she could have chosen anyone. As it was, it grieved him that her childbearing years were almost behind her. She'd always wanted children. He'd read it in her face at church socials and even at the diner when couples like Sam and Charla Packard trouped in with their kiddos in tow.

Well, Chuck couldn't reverse God's earthly clock regarding kids, but maybe he could make her see how much he loved her. He'd pull out all stops. Mister Romance, he wasn't. Though, he could learn. Instead of flipping past the women's movie channels on television like he usually did, he mentally added a few to his list. In the name of research and all that was holy, he'd master this yet.

"You're stalling. I suppose I can handle waiting a few more days. Actually, I'm an expert at that." Her tone was lighthearted, however, the underlying truth of her words resonated.

"You are, and I'm more grateful about that than I can say. A mere *thank you* seems inadequate. Maybe this will help."

He'd intended to plant a swift peck on her forehead. One. Then she curled her arms around his neck and the scent of her hair teased his nostrils. He could no more plant one peck on the gal's forehead than he could eat only one bite of her apple pie. Both demanded his full attention.

Chapter Fifteen

"And then what happened?" Sugar's eyes widened. The grin that expanded across her face suggested she already knew. "After the kiss, that is."

"It isn't polite to kiss and tell. Some things are meant to be private." Ida Mae refilled her friend's coffee cup. They'd hit their slow period in the diner, and she joined Sugar at the far end of the counter out of Chuck's, and the other customers', earshot. "Suffice it to say, nothing occurred that we're ashamed of. He drove me home and we watched television. A fall movie marathon. Romances, actually. Can you believe it?"

"Chuck? Watched romance flicks?"

"He's trying to woo me."

"I thought he'd already done that."

"You're right. He captured my heart when we were kids, but now he's 'courting' me. His word even."

Sugar added some pumpkin spice creamer to her coffee. She stirred the brew and set down the spoon. "Well, my goodness gracious. The love bug finally bit Chuck Farrow. If that doesn't just curl your French fries. Good for him—and you!"

Ahh…friendship. What would she do without Sugar? Her true-blue friend since childhood. The friend who'd loved her through thick and thin without reservation or judgment. Ida Mae probably wouldn't be where she was today. Sugar had kept her sane when everything else during her high school years went crazy.

They chatted a while longer until business perked up. "Gotta get movin', darlin', looks like the five-o-clocks are trickling in. Don't want to leave little Ava to handle all the fun by herself."

Sugar nodded. "No problem. I can't stay long anyway. It's Lowell's early night and we have plans."

The wink said it all. "TMI, my friend."

"Hey, we're married. Besides, I only meant it's taco night."

"Then why the wink?"

"Hot stuff, baby. Tacos are Lowell's favorite and he likes 'em spicy. No inference intended. They do make him very happy, though, and he definitely shows his appreciation."

Snorting was so unladylike, but stifling it only made it worse. Thankfully, her customers weren't the judgmental kind. Snorts and giggles fit right in with belches, high-fives, and hiccups. "Well, on that note, want a to-go cup for the rest of your coffee?"

"Sure. Thanks, hon." Sugar accepted the paper cup, transferred the coffee, and stepped down from her stool. "See you later, girlfriend."

"You bet. Oh, and coffee's on the house. Your presence was payment enough."

"Wow. I love how I rate around here." Sugar leaned across the counter and gave her hand a quick squeeze. "Seriously, Ida Mae. I'm so happy for you both. If the guy wants to court you, then I say let him."

As Sugar made her way through the incoming patrons, a gentleman Ida Mae didn't recognize entered the diner. Casually dressed and not a regular customer, something about him seemed oddly familiar. Mid-sixties, clean shaven, and somewhat hesitant, the man ambled slowly toward a table at the back wall and sat down. Since Ava worked another table's order, Ida Mae filled a tumbler with water, grabbed a menu, and strolled over.

"Good evening, friend. Welcome to the Come and Get—" The words stuck on her tongue as the stranger glanced up, meeting her gaze. The water tumbler teetered in her hand. Could it really be him? *Could it?*

Hard living and excess marked the fine lines on his face. Forest-green eyes, no longer hazy, regarded her with a tenuous curiosity. "Ida Mae? Is it you, miss?"

Chuck tapped the bell. "Order up!"

Ava scurried over and handed off the next ticket. She began gathering the Tuesday specials, placing them on the nearby serving tray. "Looks like a busy one tonight, huh?"

"Busy is good. I'd rather have it busy than not," Chuck answered honestly. "Of course, you're the one doing the running."

"Aw, leg work is easy compared to what you do. I just deliver the goods after you've slaved away making 'em."

"Feeding hungry bellies is my gift. Nothing to it." He passed a basket of rolls through the window. "Here. Tell the Packards they're on the house. They go with the special."

"Will do." Ava positioned the basket on the tray as Dander Evans called to her from his spot at the counter.

"Say, those sure look good. May I have a few rolls when you get a minute, Miss Ava?"

"You bet. Let me serve the Packards first. I'll be right back, Mr. Evans."

Dander's request seemed to start the ball rolling, and soon, other patrons began calling out.

"I'd like some rolls!"

"Me, too, please!"

"Mind sending some our way?"

Ava giggled and shot Chuck a grin. "See what you started. Guess I'll be needing more rolls."

"And maybe roller skates," Chuck ribbed.

Their part-time waitress didn't appear fazed. She seemed to enjoy all the activity that went with rush hour. Good thing. As a college senior, Ava Kruse had a great career ahead of her when she finished school. If she could juggle this madhouse and grin, she'd certainly do well in the fast-paced world of marketing she planned for herself.

As he turned toward the grill, Chuck paused in mid-turn. Hmm. Who was the newcomer? They didn't get a lot of tourists at this hour during the month of October. Must be someone passing through town. Though, Ida Mae seemed to have struck up a conversation with the older gent, almost as if she knew him. Of course, that was Ida Mae. She could talk the leg off a table. That was one reason he loved her. The woman didn't know a stranger, be it an inanimate object or a real, live person. Didn't make a difference.

He flipped a couple of burgers, set baskets of fresh rolls under the warming lamps, and resumed other tasks. The craziness waned about fifty minutes later, and finally, Ida Mae stepped through the swinging door and into the kitchen.

"Ava got it covered?"

She nodded. "Her parents dropped in and she's

visiting with them for a few minutes. All other hungry palates accounted for and appeased."

"That's what I like to hear." He reached for her hand. "You okay? You look a little preoccupied." Her palm trembled within his. Color drained from her cheeks and a muscle twitched near her left eye. This couldn't be good. "Hey, girl…What is it? What's wrong?"

Chuck double-checked the order wheel. No new tickets. Good. He peered through the serving window. Customers chatted with one another over supper and sodas, and Ava remained observant of refills and various other needs. One of the bus crew delivered a tub of dirty dishes to Salty over in the east end of the kitchen, and then hung around for a second to give Salty a hand with some additional pans. Steady, as she went, the diner hummed along as traffic slowed.

"Looks like we've caught a break. Come on." He ushered Ida Mae into the office and closed the door. "What gives?"

"I don't know how…" Her voice came out in a tiny whisper. "That is, I'm not sure how to tell you this."

The incident from several weeks ago sprang to mind. The night she'd tossed her cookies on her front lawn. He had yet to learn what that was about. Was this a replay?

"Whatever it is, it'll be all right. Promise." He tilted her chin up with his forefinger and thumb. "This is more than work stuff, isn't it?"

She nodded. "I wanted to tell you earlier. When he came in. But we hit our busy period and I couldn't…until now. Until things slowed down."

"When who came in? The new fellow by the back wall—the guy who only ordered coffee? He's still here, isn't he?"

"Yes."

Had he flirted with her? Put the moves on her? The guy was much older, but these days, that didn't matter. The jerk. Irritation threatened to morph into red hot anger. Chuck attempted to count to ten. "What did he do, Ida Mae? Did the guy touch you? Make a foul comment? No worries, sweetheart. I'll show him the way out."

Ida Mae grabbed his arm. "No. It wasn't anything like that. The guy didn't make an off-color comment or say one unkind thing. He asked me something."

"Okay. What did he ask that upset you like this? Obviously, it rattled you."

"He asked if I'm Ida Mae. Then...he asked about you."

"Asked about me?" Chuck scratched his head. Granted, he'd only seen the guy from a distance, but as far as he could tell, he'd never met the man. "How does he know me? What's his name?"

Ida Mae's hand dropped to her side. She examined the ceiling. The floor. Her flamingo pink fingernails. Then she met his eyes and blew out a breath. "His name is *Sy*. Sy Farrow."

Ida Mae watched Chuck swallow. The cords in his neck tensed.

She repeated the name. "It's your father."

"I heard what you said the first time." He cleared his throat, stalling, perhaps, to absorb the shock. "I don't know what kind of cruel joke that fella is trying to pull, but I think we should escort him out. Sounds like a fruit loop."

"It's him, honey." She circled her arms around him and struggled to keep her voice from cracking. "It's him. And he'd like to talk with you after we close tonight." If only she'd been able to break it to him gently. But circumstances being what they were, it had been impossible.

"How can you even know it's him? It's been thirty years. *Thirty* years, Ida Mae. Sy Farrow was a mess when he walked out on us. A bleary-eyed, worn-out shell of a man who'd been on a binge for days. That guy out there is nothing like the man I remember. That guy's clean cut, fairly well dressed, and could pass for a respectable member of the community. He doesn't look like your typical town drunk." Chuck shifted his weight, causing her arms to loosen.

"That's because he isn't. Like many alcoholics aren't. He's a recovering addict who's maintained sobriety for twenty years. He's also a business owner—a small furniture store, I believe he said—and he lives a quiet life in the northern part of the state. He's older now. Rough around the edges. Gray hair. Lots of changes."

"Oh, boy. You swallowed his garbage?" Chuck laughed and shook his head. A vein bulged in his neck. "Even if I believed that man was my father, why in heaven's name would I put stock in anything that came out of that guy's mouth? A furniture store owner? Come on. The guy didn't have one red cent to his name when he skipped out on us. Well, maybe he did. Who knows? He sure knew how to scarf up money when it came to buying his beer."

"For the first ten years after he left, I guess he really struggled. In and out of homeless shelters and sobriety programs. Then he got serious about AA and turned his life around. Took small jobs and business courses, and he finally opened his own store several years ago. I know. I was skeptical too. But I think you should speak to him."

"Did he say anything about how easy it was to write off his wife and kids? Why he never once contacted us during the past *three* decades? How he let my mother slave away at two jobs while putting two kids through college?" He rubbed the back of his neck. His voice oozed resentment and hostility. "Huh? Did he clarify any of that?"

"Those are things you should ask." Ida Mae couldn't grasp Sy's mindset either. The man out there seemed different though. The fellow at that table seemed genuinely broken and remorseful over the past. Yet, there was also something else. Peace. A change. Some indefinable aspect she couldn't pinpoint. "Will you talk with him when we close in an hour? He said he'd wait."

"Bully for him." He turned toward the wall and cursed. "Sorry. I don't normally lose my temper."

"I know."

Again, he faced her. "Does anyone else know who he is? If this goes all over town before I have a chance to tell Mom, I'm not sure how she'll take it. She's a pretty tough, resilient woman, but this may crush her."

"She knows."

"What?"

"He can explain all this better than I can. I don't think any gums are flapping yet, though, you know it won't take long. We should get back to work."

"Yeah. You're right."

"What would you like me to tell him?"

Chuck frowned and shoved his hands in his blue jeans pockets. "After we close, I'll give him five minutes. That's it. Five minutes for thirty years of silence. A more than generous trade, don't you think?"

The sorrow that dripped from his words nearly broke her. The hurt smacked of the time when he was ten and Sy left. Now, the scenario flipped. The sorrow was because he'd returned. After thirty years gone, the wayward father had come home. Because of that, empty years of what could have been intersected with possibilities of those that remained. How to reconcile the two? She had no idea.

She looped her arm through Chuck's. She wished she could take away the pain, but how? *God, please help him.* "Will you make it until close?"

"Guess I'll have to. Probably good that I'll have an hour to regroup." He started to open the office door, then paused. "What will I say to him? He's a stranger. Sy Farrow hasn't been my father for thirty years."

He had a point. However, life unfolded according to God's plan and timing. They didn't always understand His ways, but His ways were higher than their own. When circumstances seemed bleak and out of control, the Lord worked behind the scenes on His children's behalf. Hadn't Pastor Bill often preached this?

Chuck resumed his work in the kitchen and Ida Mae strode back into the main hub of the diner. The crowd had thinned out, and Ava rang up a few more customers at the register. The young woman worked efficiently and without prompting. She took initiative and Ida Mae appreciated that.

Later, patrons' chatter waxed and waned, and eventually, it died down altogether. Besides Sy who sat alone, only a handful of customers lingered. Chuck's father toyed with his coffee cup and Ida Mate watched as he continued to eye the serving window for any glimpse of the son he'd once walked away from.

His Adam's apple bobbed as Ida Mae approached the table. "Chuck agreed to see you after we close."

A rush of air whooshed past Sy's lips and his fingers stilled around the coffee cup. "Thank you, Ida Mae. I appreciate you letting me know."

"I meant to tell you earlier. I got sidetracked." She wanted to despise Chuck's father, but part of her softened. She'd like to think that her own child would give her a few seconds of his time if God were to ever open that door. Besides, the fellow who sat in her midst now hardly resembled the guy she remembered from childhood. Knowing the man he'd been, one couldn't help but channel some empathy for him. Would Chuck feel the same way?

"Looks like the Come and Get It's still a crowd pleaser. Always was a favorite of mine." Sy scanned the diner with appreciative eyes, his vision no longer clouded by an alcoholic haze. "Your mama and daddy retired several years ago, I understand."

"Uh, yes. That's right." Ida Mae scratched her head. How'd Sy know?

As if reading her thoughts, he pointed to the menu. "You're listed as owner beneath the diner logo. And to be honest, I've kept tabs on the area for many years. There was a big write-up in the paper when Emory and Selma stepped down from the business. You've certainly done your parents proud."

"Thank you." Had Sy followed his own children's successes, as well? Did he know his son trained as an accomplished chef and that he'd received many accolades in his field? That all of Ruby adored him? That Chuck was a man of honor, talent, and skill? "Chuck's done very well too. He's helped me take the Come and Get It to the next level. Together we've made a great thing even better."

"I've tracked his and Voni's careers," Sy murmured. A wistful expression crept across his face. "Liza did an exemplary job in raising them."

That was it? No admittance of guilt...or a show of remorse? *Don't point fingers, Ida Mae.* She had no right. Instead, she asked a question. "About Liza. Earlier when we first spoke, you indicated you'd talked with her. I guess it's none of my business, but how did she react to..."

"My homecoming?"

An odd way to phrase it, but yes. After thirty years, Sy's reappearance had to be nothing less than a shock. Ida Mae nodded.

"No rudeness intended, but I think I'd best discuss that with my son...er...Chuck. Forgive me, please?"

"Certainly, Mr. Farrow. No forgiveness necessary." *At least from me.*

"Thanks, and please—it's simply 'Sy.' Never was much for formalities."

Ida Mae held up the half-full coffee carafe. "Almost closing time. Would you like a reheat?"

"Yes, I believe I would. Thank you."

Ida Mae poured another round of the strong, hot brew and tried not to think about the inevitable showdown between father and son.

Chuck watched as the last of the customers paid at the register and ambled out into the star-filled night. As he peered through the serving window, he noted Ida Mae's usual routine. She flipped the sign on the door to "Closed," tugged down all the window blinds, and checked napkin dispensers and salt and pepper shakers. She then scurried toward the kitchen and Chuck finished wiping down the grill. He had the wildest urge to grab Ida Mae's hand and steal away with the rest of the patrons, leaving the one who remained to wait until infinity as he'd once done to his ten-year-old kid. It'd serve the old man right. Instead, Chuck completed his task and tabled those thoughts. He wouldn't take the coward's way out, but he sure as shootin' wanted to.

"Except for janitorial, I told the rest of the crew to scram," Ida Mae whispered. "Whatever needs doing I'll take care of while you speak with your...with Sy."

"Thank you, sweetheart. No need to whisper. I'm not about to put on airs for Sy Farrow." Chuck yanked off his apron and tossed it on the stainless-steel countertop. He raked a hand through mussed hair and straightened the collar of his work shirt. He wouldn't "put on airs," but smoothing out a few rough spots hardly seemed extravagant. A well-ordered appearance conveyed confidence. Never mind the fact that he probably smelled like today's special—chicken fried steak and peach cobbler. He wasn't about to change into one of his clean shirts he kept on hand in the office. His old man didn't merit that much effort.

"Hey." Ida Mae squeezed his arm. "Have I told you lately how much I love you?"

Chuck caught her hand in his and brought it to his lips. "Yes. But I'll never tire of hearing you say it. Do you know I feel the same way?"

"Yeah. But a woman sure likes to hear those three words."

In a diner? Not the most romantic place, and certainly not like this. Not smack dab in the middle of conflict. Professing his love to Ida Mae as he was about to face down the father who'd deserted him and his family thirty years ago didn't seem to gel with his current frame of mind. He wanted to tell her. He would tell her. But not here and not anywhere near Sy Farrow. To do so would only sour what should be a sweet memory.

"You deserve to hear those words when we can revel in the moment, which I'm afraid isn't now. No worries though. This little chat with dear ol' Dad won't take long, and then we'll resume our discussion. Sound good?" Chuck attempted a smile and Ida Mae returned the effort.

"I'll take care of a few things here in the kitchen, and when I'm done, I'll wait for you in the office." Ida Mae's breath caught, almost as if she were about to cry.

Oh, boy. Him and his idiot reasoning. "Sweetheart, come here." He slid his arms around her and kissed the top of her head. She quivered and he mentally kicked himself. So much for the proper place and time to profess his love. Loving others and telling them so shouldn't require a detailed instruction booklet. If he'd learned anything, it was this. Missed opportunities came with consequences, often negative ones. He wanted to rectify that. Would she even believe him? He continued to hold her tight. "I love you. I have forever."

"I don't want to push you into saying it," she faltered, her voice barely a whisper.

Aw, super. He'd hurt her—again. She had every right to nudge, though he didn't consider a prompt unreasonable. "You're not pushing. I've been a stupid coward. Kinda hard for a guy like me to admit, but there you have it. And part of the reason why is sitting out there at that table. I know I have to assume partial responsibility, but a lot of emotional baggage we carry as adults is traced back to our parents."

Ida Mae flexed her palms against his back, allowing them to rest flat upon his shoulder blades. "Not always. Sometimes, we make choices that don't have anything to do with our parents."

All right. Did she want to debate this now, for heaven's sake? Chuck inched back a little, and with his arms around her, he studied her. Her face mirrored frustration and...sorrow? Great. That his dad should still affect present day, rankled him. How dare the guy show up now, after three decades, and suddenly want to chat. Well, he wasn't having it. "We can revisit this in the future. Meanwhile, let me go see what the guy wants."

"Would you like me to come with you?"

"No thanks. I'll be fine. I'm not going to lose my temper or anything. He's not worth it."

"Don't say that, okay?" Ida Mae stepped away, her mouth sliding downward in a frown. "I'm not excusing what your father did, but people make mistakes. Everyone's worth something to God."

Huh? Well, of course, he believed that too. But that didn't mean jerks didn't have to pay for their transgressions. Since when did Ida Mae feel sorry for the ne'er-do-well dud that masqueraded as a reformed businessman? Chuck didn't understand this sudden allegiance toward his father. Ida Mae's regard for humanity spoke highly of her character. Even when the obvious presented itself, she always found a kernel of goodness to offset the horrible.

"I know, but I'm not God." Chuck left it at that and walked through the swinging doors.

Across the room, his father's gray head snapped up. Slowly, the man rose to his feet. He turned toward Chuck and extended a palm, the moment forever cementing itself in Chuck's memory.

For the briefest instant, he recalled a long-limbed boy given to laughter, yet mature for his youth. That kid, an early bird and also a deep thinker guessed the truth even before Mom told him, but he wouldn't believe it. His mind rejected the notion.

"Daddy? Daddy, where are you?" He tore through the house that brisk fall morn. "I have the answer to yesterday's riddle!" They always made a game of it. Every day, Dad related a nugget of wisdom in the form of a question. A clue to the answer would often be in the question itself. If Chuck didn't immediately guess the correct answer, he pondered it overnight and reported back to Dad the next morning.

"If woolly worms have thicker black bands in the fall, it means we're gonna have a long winter. Twelve black bands mean twelve weeks of winter!"

"Darling, Dad isn't here." His mother clutched a single bill in her hand. Money? *One hundred dollars?* Something in her voice caused Chuck to stop in his tracks. Was Mom crying? "Dad...has gone away for a while."

"What do you mean *gone away*, Mom?"

"To get better, honey. Your dad isn't well. He's left to get the help he needs."

"Huh? I don't understand, Mom. They have doctors here. Dad wouldn't leave us." Chuck dashed around their small home in his pajamas and searched for his father, the truth sinking in, along with panic and pain, as he ran from room to room. "Daddy! Daa-deeeee!"

When he'd examined every nook and cranny, dazed, Chuck found his way back to the kitchen where four-year-old Voni, wide-eyed and on the verge of tears like Mom, whimpered and clung to their mother's legs. "There, there, precious. It'll be okay. Your daddy left to sort through some things. He'll be back when he's done that." Mom patted his little sister's back and reached for Chuck too. "The day can only go up from here. We have each other, and I love you both very much."

Hell must really be an awful place because Chuck couldn't have fathomed anything worse. Only difference was he hadn't died yet. At least physically.

Life meandered on. Without Sy Farrow. While three hearts broke, grieved, and attempted to mend, their father never returned. Until now. What in blazes had Mom said when she found out he was back?

Surreal, like an oddly placed scene in a grade B movie, Chuck's face-off with his father unfolded. The hand that paused in midair held its position as if the film stopped and begged attention. A face, familiar and wreathed in wrinkles, brightened. "Son, it's good to see you."

Good to see you? Chuck's feet refused to move. His legs turned to lead. There the guy stood—about fourteen feet away—no longer a figment of memory and longing, but flesh and bone proof, an ache awkwardly appeased, in the present. The once young father with cloudy vision and a wobbly air, now an older version of clear-minded resilience and thoughtful composure, waited...and hoped? For what? What sort of reaction did dear ol' Dad expect after his thirty-year absence?

Chuck balanced his adult perspective alongside the weight of childhood anguish. Tonight's here and now compared to yesteryear's loss. None of the emotions suited. He couldn't, wouldn't offer his hand in a conciliatory greeting or perfunctory acknowledgement. Why should he?

He harnessed some resolve, however, and forced his feet to carry him forward. Instead of thrusting out a hand, he poked one in his pants pocket, and purposely kept the other positioned at his side. He drew in a breath to steady his nerves.

"I wondered if you were dead. What brings you back?" Probably not the heartfelt response his father envisioned, but under the circumstances, the best Chuck could muster.

His father retracted his hand and motioned toward the table. "Could we talk, son?"

What was this "son" business? Chuck stopped being Sy Farrow's son the minute his father walked out on them. Talk about guts. He guessed the guy had found some. "Thirty years of silence and now you want to talk? Wow. That's rich." Bile rose in his throat. His belly churned. Never in his life had Chuck spoken to another human being with as much venom. The sensation immobilized him.

"I realize I deserve that." His father's countenance fell. His shoulders drooped and the light in his old hazel eyes dimmed. "But there are some things I want to tell you. Things I want you to know. Please?"

Oh, Lord. The plea, a prayer, expanded. *Father, I don't want to do this. Don't make me do this. Don't make me listen to this jerk. Help me walk away from him like he walked away from me.*

So now he prayed that his Heavenly Father would help him spurn his earthly dad? Was that like asking God to help him sin? To completely contradict His loving, sinless nature? Ludicrous. *Chuck, you dummy.* However, a paragon of virtue, he wasn't. He hated his dad. Or, at least, he strongly, strongly disliked the man. He choked back a sob. Grown men didn't cry.

"I'll give you five minutes." Chuck snatched out a chair and sat down. He glanced at his Fitbit. "Countdown's on." Why did the words and his tone wrench his insides? He wasn't at fault here. Sy Farrow was. Their entire life story was based on this one man's thirty-year-old decision.

"Fair enough." His father slid into the chair from where he'd risen. His lips curled upward in a slight smile. "You still have your mother's hair—the color of sun-drenched hay, and you have my eyes except, naturally, yours outshine your old man's."

Naturally. Who was Chuck to argue?

"I'm proud of you, Son. I'm proud of Voni too. Your skills, your expertise in the culinary arts. Your sister and her nursing career."

So, was he supposed to be impressed that his dad knew something of their success? Had he heard the details from Mom? Voni? Had he tracked Chuck's professional career? Well, his old man couldn't know about his secret ambition. No one but him knew about that project. The one that came in at roughly three hundred and fifty-nine pages and contained palate pleasing, vintage-themed recipes, kitchen hacks, and Ozarkian slice-of-life vignettes. The project he'd nurtured for years now. The computer file that Chuck hoped would one day become his first published cookbook. He hadn't even told Ida Mae about it. But a guy could dream.

Best to steer this conversation around to the obvious subject. "Pardon my bluntness. What is it you want? Money?"

His father swallowed, resting his hands on the shiny tabletop. "No, Son. My visit has nothing to do with money. I'll be blunt also. I'm selling my furniture store up north and I'm coming back home. To Ruby, Missouri. To your mother...if she'll have me."

Chapter Sixteen

Ida Mae imagined every possible scenario, her ears attuned to any raised voices or outbursts. Neither happened. Only the low hum of steady conversation pierced the semi-silence. Would Chuck's long repressed hostility toward his father build to an emotional crescendo? *Oh, my.* What if something terrible happened? She traipsed back and forth, circling the kitchen, imagining the worst. If only she could do something. Anything. But what? She strode to the office to wait...and pray.

"You're coming back *home*?" If someone stuck a pin in him, he'd burst. Chuck forced himself to exhale. Have mercy, that's all he needed—to drop like a rock in a dead faint. He stared, open-mouthed, at his father, willing away the black spots that burst before his eyes.

"Here." His dad slid a glass of water across the table. "Miss Ida Mae brought an extra one when she topped off my coffee. "Drink, Son."

Who was he to tell Chuck to do anything? Still, Chuck obliged. The water cooled his throat and tamped down the lightheadedness. Slowly, the spots disappated.

Dad leaned forward and touched his arm. "Better?"

Yeah. But he wasn't going to acknowledge it with a thank you. Instead, he gave a curt nod. His dad withdrew his hand and settled back in his chair.

Finally, Chuck spoke. "You had to have known how this homecoming of yours would affect Mom and Voni and me. Why'd you handle it this way?"

The old guy's eyes flashed with surprise. "What way? You mean why didn't I contact you rather than simply show up?"

"No. Why didn't you hire a pilot to skywrite *Sy Farrow's come home*?" Chuck snapped. He flattened his palms on the table and counted to ten. "Of course I mean why didn't you contact us first. After being gone thirty years, didn't you think showing up without so much as a word might seem kinda crazy, not to mention, cruel?"

"I can understand why it might seem that way. But honestly, my homecoming has been a long time in the making, and being cruel is the farthest thing from my mind."

"Guess that remains to be seen. Regardless, please don't call me that again."

"Call you what? Son?"

"Don't look so shocked."

"But...you *are* my son." His father's voice remained calm. Gentle. "No matter what I've done, no matter where I've strayed, nothing negates that fact. "You have my blood pumping through your veins. You have my build—or the one I used to have—and even some of my temperament. You share my eyes. My genes. Some of my memories. I'm your earthly dad. You are my son and I love you."

I love you. What was he supposed to do with that? Sidle up to the old guy and forgive and forget? No way. Believing Dad had changed was like wishing on a star. Imaginary daydreams. Both of 'em. Still, the way his father said it made him wonder. Could it be true? *Did Dad love him?* A very small sliver of Chuck's heart softened. The "earthly dad" reference stirred something even deeper. Had Dad found religion? God?

"I see the invisible wheels turning." A slow smile spread across his father's face.

Chuck scratched his head. Took another sip of water. Prolonged the moment. "You're different."

"You mean sober?"

"Well, yes. For starters. But it's something else. Something I cant't quite place. It's almost like..."

"Like what?" The man across from him beamed. Hope anew lit in his face. "Ask me."

"Like you're someone else. A different person." Warmth surged through Chuck's body. Every nerve ending tingled. He drew himself upright and blinked. "After all these years...have you made a profession of faith?"

"I have. Well, actually, I made that decision a long time ago—sitting in a homeless shelter with nothing but five bucks, the clothes on my back, and a bottle to my name. It's just that it's taken me a while to fully grasp the gift of salvation and the freedom that comes with that. Nothing like a slow learner." His dad paused, looking him straight in the eye. "I won't sugarcoat it. As you know, life isn't perfect. On this old earth, it never will be. Nothing can erase the wrong I've done, the lives I've wrecked. But through Christ, your old man became a *new man*. I've wanted, for years, to prove it to you and your sister and your mama. I finally got the courage to do that. The time's right. My question to you, Son, *is* will you let me?"

Whoa. Not what Chuck expected. Not what he expected at all. *Will you let me?* His tongue lodged near the roof of his mouth as words failed him. The verbal bashing he'd intended to unleash, never made it past the tears.

Five minutes of Sy's visit had stretched into one hour. Eventually, Ida Mae slipped from the diner office and into the kitchen where she lingered out of sight beside the serving window. She didn't intend to eavesdrop. She only wanted to make sure everything was okay. From her vantage point, she observed Sy tip his head, as if nodding goodbye.

Chuck walked his father to the front door and Sy strode away into the darkness, presumably to his car. The rumble of an engine confirmed Ida Mae's assumption, and soon after, gravel crunching beneath tires indicated he'd gone.

What had they talked about for an hour? Should she give Chuck some space? Ida Mae paced the kitchen, her stomach in knots. As long as she lived, she'd never forget the look on Chuck's face when she told him that his father was here. Could there be anything more stressful than to tell the man she loved that the father who'd abandoned him as a child had returned? No, she didn't think so. Then, of course, another memory barreled to the forefront.

What would it do to him when, one day, she told him about the baby? Her baby. The one that others had loved and raised as their own because she'd abandoned her child too? *Not abandoned*, Ida Mae corrected herself. The term the adoption agency used was *placed*. She'd allowed her baby to be *placed* for adoption. Huge difference between what Sy Farrow did and the choice she made. His was cowardly and self-serving. Hers was sacrificial and selfless. Though, in Sy's defense, maybe he had valid reasons for deserting Chuck and his family. No one knew the whole story yet.

"I thought maybe you'd gone." Chuck's voice startled her. "I certainly didn't expect you to stay when this thing with my dad morphed into an hour."

Ida Mae spun around and folded herself into his arms. "Where else would I be? I wouldn't leave you."

"You should have gone home. You've been here since daybreak."

"I'm fine. Ever since the new schedule, I have a lot more energy at the end of the day. Besides, you've been here as long as I have." She reached up and touched his cheek, tracing the lines of exhaustion there with her fingertips. "Would you like to talk about it? How your visit went?"

"Yeah, but I need to think a bit. Why don't I follow you home and we can talk there?"

"Sure. That's fine. Are you okay though?"

Chuck hugged her. "If you mean am I okay to drive, sure, I'm good. Somewhat on overload, but nothing that'll make me wreck my car between here and the few blocks back to your house."

Leave it to him to downplay the evening's events. Or maybe it wasn't that at all. Shock manifested differently in people. "If you're positive."

"I'm positive. Let's lock up and I'll head out behind you."

He didn't offer to have her ride with him as he often

did now, and Ida Mae didn't suggest it. The short ride alone would give him an opportunity to regroup and clear his head. She should clear hers too.

As always, here of late when he entered Ida Mae's home, he wished they didn't have to worry about "hers" or "his." He wanted a home that would be "theirs."

"Come on in the kitchen and I'll make some hot chocolate. How does that sound?" Ida Mae tossed her jacket and purse on the sofa and laced her fingers through his.

Her touch made him want to hold her and never let go. He didn't want to waste another single minute pondering past mistakes or considering proper ways to court her. He supposed he should thank his dad for that life lesson. His father blew it with Mom and tossed thirty years down the drain when wrongs should have been rectified. *Oh Lord, please don't let that be me. Us.* "Hot chocolate's perfect."

They made it together. Not the stuff out of the packet, but one of their favorite recipes from the diner. As Ida Mae whisked together the cocoa, milk, and brown sugar, Chuck added the chocolate chips and vanilla extract. The trick was to stir often so the milk wouldn't scorch. When the hot chocolate was ready, Chuck ladled the decadent mixture into two generous-sized mugs, and Ida Mae spooned marshmallow cream on top, followed by more chocolate chips.

"Now this is what I call hot chocolate." Ida Mae sipped carefully. When she drew the mug back from her lips, some of the marshmallow cream remained. "Have you ever tasted anything so delicious?"

"I sure have. Our first kiss." The memory prompted a grin. Despite the evening's somber events, this woman could lighten his cares with the bat of an eyelash...or a sip of hot chocolate. He couldn't get enough of her. How he'd once managed to deny his feelings for Ida Mae seemed alien to him now.

"Why, Chuck Farrow, the gleam in your eye suggests you're flirting." She grinned too and smacked her lips. "I have marshmallow cream on my mouth, huh?"

"Yep. Here, let me take care of that." He slid the hot chocolate mug from her hand and set it down, along with his, on the kitchen counter. "Don't want any burns."

"We most certainly do not." Her laughter pulled him into the past to the carefree years of their youth.

She'd been the one to draw him out of his funk after Dad left. Because of her, he'd retained some semblance of wit. He sorely needed some of that wit now, ironically, because his father had returned. "This will only take a sec."

He snatched a paper napkin from the basket on the table and brought it to her lips as if to dab her mouth with it, but at the last second, he hoodwinked her. Instead of dabbing her mouth, he kissed it. A few light pecks at the corners of her lips to erase the marshmallow cream residue, except it didn't quite remedy the problem. If only she hadn't put her arms around his neck and pulled him closer. It would be impolite not to kiss her back.

How had they lived without this? They'd gone from winter coats to short sleeves in the turn of a season. The chemistry between them could fry an egg. An honest analogy that called for discretion.

Chuck gave himself a mental shake. Man, what he'd put her through. He sure didn't want to blow it now. He'd almost exhausted Ida Mae's patience and who could blame her? Only a saint of a woman would wait for a man the length of time Ida Mae had. A saint and someone in love. She wore both well. He didn't deserve her devotion, but so help him, if God allowed them to continue down this path, he'd never take her for granted again. The light pecks sparked passion and yearning, and a protectiveness too. As much as he itched to kiss her with abandon, he respected Ida Mae. When he covered her mouth with his, he held himself in check, but fully communicated his intent. He wanted her in every sense of the word—within the holy bonds of marriage—and he wouldn't compromise the progress they'd made. He ended the kiss with the promise there'd be more. Then he dabbed the corners of her mouth with the napkin and erased the marshmallow residue as he'd first intended.

"You surprise me," Ida Mae whispered, resting a palm at the nape of his neck.

How tragic was that? Was she surprised by his love or that he showed it? She should hear it too. At least a dozen times a day. "I love you, Ida Mae. *I love you.*"

"I know."

That settled it. He could talk about Dad now and what transpired between them. As long as he had Ida Mae by his side, Chuck could conquer anything. Old doubts and new ones.

She could almost see the invisible wheels turn inside his head. He'd never kissed her like that before. This time, something new ignited. A switch flipped. It was more than his candor and attentiveness. More than his declaration of love. The change, an intrinsic need to be together, forever, came full circle. As kids, they'd laid the foundation for friendship. As adults, they prepared for something more. The framework for a lasting future finally seemed within their grasp.

Oh, Lord, is it really so? Ida Mae knew they needed to talk about tonight. If this was their appointed season, she prayed that God would continue opening doors to better understanding. They both had to be honest. Regardless what Chuck said before about the past being the past, she would tell him about the baby. Maybe not now, but soon.

She didn't know if he wanted to talk yet, but she'd try. "Would you like to take our hot chocolate in the living room?"

"Sure. I wanted to suggest that, but I thought you might be too tired."

"Of course not. I want to hear everything. Or whatever you'd like to share."

He nodded and gathered their mugs. In the living room, Ida Mae placed a tray on the ottoman so they could set their drinks down between sips. As they made themselves comfortable on the sofa, Chuck slipped an arm around her. "Guess I won't mince words. You know I've despised Sy Farrow since I was ten. From the second he left, I blamed him for every harsh thing life doled out, and I convinced myself that he was the source of delayed dreams and doomed relationships. I can't lie. I think his leaving affected my family and me in ways that'll always be with us. I bet any mental health professional would agree." He ran a palm over his thigh, letting it rest there.

"Tonight, though, my perspective's changed. Who I remember as my father—the aimless guy with boozy breath and a beer in his hand—conflicts with the confident, clear-eyed fellow I met earlier. I'm pretty good at reading fakes, and I was prepared to write off my dad's act. What I wasn't prepared for was his one-eighty. I'm not talking about the physical changes one might expect. I'm speaking more about his demeanor. The man I knew as a kid had a loving nature. He may have been a drunk and had lots of problems, but up until the point he left us, he was a kindhearted guy. In other words, he wasn't a mean drunk."

"Did he say something cruel to you earlier?" Ida Mae couldn't reconcile that with the Sy Farrow she talked to. "Or do you mean your father's changed for the better?"

"Yes, that. And no, not cruel. He radiated goodwill and spoke with such gentleness and compassion that I forgot everything, every abrasive word I'd planned to say. He wasn't only kind. He was...transformed. I don't know how to describe it." Chuck shifted positions. He gazed at her with an odd expression. "I wanted to be mad. Furious. But man, I couldn't. After I initially railed against him and sat down, the anger I'd bottled up for so long faded. Not totally, don't get me wrong. But a lot of it. And then we started to talk.

"I can't explain it. I want to stay mad. I have every right to. When I try to summon the strength for it though, I can't. It's the craziest thing."

Goosebumps rose on Ida Mae's arms. She'd waited on Edwin Ramsey at the diner today, a few hours before Sy wandered in. When she rang up his meal at the register before he left, he'd said something curious. "Tell Chuck I've been praying. I've asked the good Lord to reveal Himself in a mighty way. Tell him life's about to throw him a zinger, but it's all good."

At the time, Edwin's comment unnerved her, but business picked up shortly afterward and she'd forgotten to tell Chuck about the encounter. "Maybe it's not as crazy as you think." Ida Mae grasped Chuck's hand. "I forgot to tell you something." She relayed Edwin's words, verbatim.

"Are you certain that's what he said?" Chuck sat up a little straighter. His hand curled tightly around Ida Mae's. "Do you think he knew Dad had come back?"

She shook her head. "No. I didn't get that impression." Everyone in town recognized Edwin as a devout man of faith. He had a unique handle on spiritual matters and a reputation for being a prayer warrior. Folks claimed he had the gift of discernment. "I think God uses certain people as His conduits. We may not understand that, but I believe it." There'd been talk that was how Charla Packard came to the Ozarks. She'd been Charla Winston then, and Edwin Ramsey prayed that God would send Sam Packard, his former son-in-law and a widower, a wife.

"Well, if Dad is the 'zinger' Edwin was referring to, I guess he certainly pegged it right. About the 'It's all good' part, all I can say is what happened to Dad, and my reaction to my father this evening, isn't typical. It's like…something miraculous. I've carried such animosity toward the guy for so long that this feels weird. Almost otherworldly." Chuck stared at her, his face a mix of surprise and elation. "It's like I've cracked open the mental suitcase of crud I've carted around for so long, and suddenly, it's not near as full or as heavy as I thought. I don't know why or how that is, but I like the way it feels."

The twinkle in his eyes made her heart soar. This was a side of him she'd never seen, and she liked it. "You can't know how happy I am for you." Ida Mae wondered, though, what Sy Farrow had done for the past thirty years? If he'd straightened out his life, why hadn't he contacted his family? Why hadn't he come home? She didn't want to be the wet blanket, but these were things Chuck had pondered too. Gently, she asked, "What did he say? Did he answer some of your questions?"

"Well, as he told you, the first ten or so years after Dad left, he struggled. He did stints in and out of homeless shelters and sobriety programs. He landed up north around St. Louis, and a church there introduced him to a local Alcoholics Anonymous chapter. We didn't get into specifics, but his sponsor encouraged him in additional areas. Dad said he started attending church services. He got his life on track, scheduled business courses, and eventually, opened a furniture store that turns a good profit. Of course, I'd be lying if I said I took his word for it. Mom called my cell while Dad and I were talking. She corroborated his story.

"Not only that. She said my father has sent her money every month for a long while now...to try and make up for some of the past. Initially, he swore her to secrecy because he didn't want or expect a pat on the back. He finally wanted to step up to the plate and be the husband and father he should have been years ago— even if he was late to the game. And my mother being the honorable woman she is, God love her, remained true to her promise. She never said a word about the additional resources." Chuck exhaled and continued. "Mom has a comfortable nest egg, but the reason she still works at the school is because she genuinely loves her job, which I already knew. That's not the kicker though." Chuck took a deep breath and slowly released it. "All these years Voni and I wondered why Mom never remarried. It's because she and Dad never divorced. They're still husband and wife."

What? She couldn't wrap her mind around it. *Still married?* Why would Liza not tell anyone—especially her children? Chuck must be in shock. Or denial. That was the only way to explain his calm rendering of the facts. Ida Mae squeezed his hand. "What now?"

"Dad has a buyer for the store. He's coming back home."

"Coming back home? As in here—to Ruby?"

"Yes. To this town…and to Mom if she'll have him, he said."

"Do you think she'll take him back?" The possible scenarios kickstarted a firestorm of reservations. How on earth would Liza and her children deal with this? Ida Mae's hands trembled, and Chuck rubbed them reassuringly between his. Funny in a way, because he was the one dealing with this, but she ached on his and the Farrows' behalf.

"I have an idea she might. Despite everything our family endured because of my dad leaving, Mom never stopped loving him. Deep down, I always suspected that. Now, I know. Mom's a wonderful woman. A loving, goodhearted soul who trusts God without question.

Apparently, she maintained some contact with Dad, especially in the last five years. I think by doing that, it was her way of leaving the door open for reconciliation.

"Am I apprehensive about it? You bet. But I also know Mom well enough that she wouldn't let Sy sashay back into her life without proof he'd changed. Of course, I'll talk to Voni and get her thoughts. She was only four when Dad left so she doesn't remember him much. Other than what she heard from me, Mom shielded her from the more painful stuff. Voni isn't naïve though. I'm sure she'll have a lot of questions for Dad like I did and still do. We're going to meet this week, all of us, and talk."

Talking was good. Who'd dispute that? She leaned into the warmth of Chuck's arms as he wrapped them around her. She couldn't explain why tears sprang to her eyes except that Sy Farrow's return did, indeed, seem like an answer to prayer. Hadn't she asked God to help Chuck? To realize that God heard her gave her hope.

If Chuck was able to forgive the father who'd abandoned him, would he find it in his heart to forgive her too? She'd know soon, because she was going to tell him about the baby. No more secrets. She'd already decided.

November ushered in a nice run of seventy-degree days. In a rare move, Ida Mae decided to close the diner for a week. Said it was high time they rested and recharged longer than a weekend. They'd need the extra energy to gear up for Thanksgiving later in the month. The Come and Get It would close again for the big day, but the busyness right before the holiday always zapped their strength. A small vacation before would renew them physically and mentally, a move Chuck applauded.

He completed the last round of revisions for *Heart and Soul: Homespun How-To for the Non-Cook Cook*, the working title of his nostalgia-themed cookbook, and one afternoon, he e-mailed his first round of query letters. Now, to wait. According to his research, he realized it could take anywhere from several weeks to many months for a literary agent to respond. And in some cases, the agent might not respond at all. But at least he'd pursued a lifelong goal and now he'd start his next project. He already had ideas for his second cookbook, one in a similar vein with witty anecdotes from the diner.

In the meantime, he and Mom and Voni met with a family therapist in Sapphire. Dad joined them in the sessions, and while things went well, Chuck admitted he struggled with issues of mistrust concerning his father. "Understandable and something we'll work on," the counselor assured him.

Moving forward, his parents also scheduled marital counseling. Naturally, a joint living arrangement wouldn't be resumed immediately so Dad rented a small duplex not far from the family home. Still married or not, living together again after a thirty-year separation wouldn't come without tremendous effort. In his mind, people didn't go from married to separated to married again without an adjustment period and counseling. Or at least they shouldn't. Chuck's mother and father opted to do the sensible thing and go slowly.

"I'm glad you're proceeding with caution, Mom," Chuck told his mother. "It's obvious Dad's different, but he's still basically a stranger. You may have been married and lived under the same roof for ten years, but a lifetime's passed since then."

"I agree," Voni added. "I hardly remember Daddy. While I'm excited to get to know him, our first priority is you, Mama. Please be careful."

"Don't you two worry." Mom smiled knowingly. Her words reminded Chuck of when they were kids. It was something she'd often say to him and his sister to reassure them. Today she added something. "I'm sixty-one. I'm not senile or inept...yet." And then she winked. At least their mother's quick wit remained intact.

What the future held was anyone's guess. His father had asked their forgiveness, but how did a person forgive someone in the throes of alcoholism—someone who ultimately chose to drink again and again, despite the consequences? Someone who'd inflicted so much pain, however unintended? Alcoholism was a disease, yes, but ultimately, we all made choices. Only God could help Chuck work through his reservations.

He absorbed his father's homecoming slowly, day by day, moment by moment. Short of divine intervention, he and his dad would never be best buds, but maybe they'd be friends. Maybe.

Chuck placed those thoughts on hold and wheeled the new thermal tote, containing lunchtime goodies, up to Ida Mae's front door. Was someone singing? He craned his neck and listened. The very distinct soprano he knew well from church drifted from within and captured his attention. The door kind of muffled it, but the sound twirled a figure-eight around his chest and gave it a squeeze. "Unchained Melody." Their song. At least the one he'd always thought of as theirs. Not a church hymn, but it could, no doubt, spirit him away to a higher place. With Ida Mae singing it, that place had to be heaven.

Chills shuffled down his spine. Would it be considered eavesdropping if he were to stay there and listen? What if eagle-eyed neighbors were watching? Oh, well. He guessed they could call law enforcement. If Horace Sapp showed up, they'd make a mighty fine trio. A soprano, a baritone, and a bass. Perfect. The thought made Chuck grin.

He waited until Ida Mae finished the song, then he reluctantly rang the doorbell.

"Coming, good lookin'!" Her laughter bounced around on the opposite side of the door and expanded, and she flung open the door as if expecting a Hollywood heartthrob, which he certainly didn't qualify as, but her enthusiasm buoyed his confidence.

"Wow. I like this reception." He leaned forward and kissed her cheek. She smelled of apples and cinnamon. "I hardly think I'm 'good lookin', but I'll take it."

"Well, come on in. The movie's cued up. We'll arrange our lap trays and eat in the living room. What's for lunch in that fancy thing?" Ida Mae pointed toward the tote.

"Homemade chicken and dumplings, bacon mac and cheese, and green beans almondine. The basics. You have pie?"

"Does an orchard have apples?"

"We're in business then." He chuckled and rolled the tote past her. "Really, I was kidding. When I invited myself over to lunch, I didn't expect you to cook. That defeats the purpose of what we're trying to do here. Rest and relax."

"Are you telling me you rested when you whipped up this feast?"

"Ahh. See that's the thing. I find cooking relaxing."

He'd mentioned that in his cookbook manuscript and offered tips and insights for today's twenty-first century cook. The one who found cooking anything but relaxing. The trick, he explained, was to make the meal prep and menus work for *the person* rather than the other way around. He wheeled the tote toward the kitchen as Ida Mae closed the front door. "So, what movie are we watching?"

"*You've Got Mail.* I know you've probably seen it a hundred times like me, but a classic never grows old, right?"

"That's what I tell myself after my morning jog. That I'm not old. I'm a classic."

"Ha! Good one." She linked her arm through his. "So, you've seen *You've Got Mail*, right?"

"Actually, no. I've heard of it though." He'd seen almost everything else with Tom Hanks. Surprisingly, not this one.

Ida Mae stopped in mid-step. "You're kidding. You've never seen *You've Got Mail*, one of *the* most romantic movies ever? Meg Ryan, Tom Hanks. Business owners who butt heads and he... Well, I won't say anything else except this. You will love it!"

"I don't doubt it. If it's as great as the bliss on your face, I'm a goner."

Arm in arm, they laughed all the way into the kitchen. There they worked together, spooning the chicken and dumplings into bowls, and the green beans and creamy mac and cheese into small side dishes. They arranged their iced tea tumblers with their other dishes on the wooden lap trays, and Ida Mae nodded toward the homemade apple pie, which cooled on the counter.

"When we're through with all this, if you still have room, that's for you."

If he still had room? Who was she kidding? "Good gracious, girl. You do know the way to my heart." He'd always have room for her apple pie. He hoped—no, he prayed—that Ida Mae still had room in her heart for *him*. He'd worked up the courage to ask her the most important question a man could ask a woman. Now, he only had to time it right.

"Well," Ida Mae said between sniffles. "What did you think? You loved it, right?"

Judging by his happy smirk, Chuck had enjoyed *You've Got Mail.* She snuggled close to him, dinner trays long abandoned. Was that his heartbeat she heard or the drumming of her own blood rushing to her ears?

"I never thought I'd be a chick-flick fan, but you've won me over. You're right. I loved it." He wrapped her in his embrace. "I enjoyed the growth of the characters and the message that, sometimes, there's more depth to people than what we initially perceive."

"I agree. What strikes me about this movie, though, is how quick we are to judge others' faults and mess-ups...before we fully examine the true motives behind their shortcomings." Deep inside, Ida Mae began to quake. Was it time? Time to unpack the past and air her soiled laundry? *How can I? Telling him about the baby could ruin everything.* Even so, she drew in a breath and plodded on. She'd always known this moment would come. Too bad it had to be now, but she didn't know when there'd be a better opportunity. Crud was crud, no matter when or how one dispensed it. "I think what I love best about Hanks's character, Joe Fox, is his change of heart. He made a great business decision, at least for his bookstore, but he also conveyed that our best intentions can often result in a domino effect of bad consequences regardless of our goal. He chose the best thing for his company, but he regretted placing Meg, Kathleen Kelly, in a bad position."

Ida Mae sensed Chuck smile by the upturn of his mouth against her forehead. "Yes. And ultimately his decision, even though he regretted having to make it, made Kathleen examine her own ambitions. It forced her out of her comfort zone and prompted her down a new path toward something new and wonderful." Chuck nudged her chin upward with his fingertips. "*You've Got Mail* is an awesome movie. You know, this romance stuff isn't half-bad, huh?"

"Half-bad? I'll have you know, Chuck Farrow, romance is fantastic. Combined with love, it's *everything*." The familiar scent of him, a subtle mingling of earth and woods and good food, warmed her to her core. Why ruin this moment? They could stay like this forever. Couldn't they? But what started as a tremor in her stomach, swelled to a full-blown earthquake. It was now or never. "That's why I have to tell you something."

Chapter Seventeen

"Tell me what, sweetheart?" Was it him or did something in Ida Mae's voice change? He eased away from her so he could see her face. On her lower lashes, tears collected. Not puny ones. Big ol' crocodile tears like she'd peeled a boatload of onions. "What's wrong?"

"I love this movie. I do." She sniffled. "But part of why I wanted us to watch it was what we talked about. Its message. The way Kathleen and Joe fall in love before they really know everything there is to know about each other. Then, when they do know everything, they realize what they thought was so terrible wasn't something worth sacrificing their love for. They acknowledged the pain but grew past it."

Alarm bells pinged. Chuck's pulse raced. Why did it feel as if a big shoe were about to drop? He disengaged from the embrace and clutched both of her hands in his. "Yes, I liked the way the movie nailed that aspect. But we aren't talking about the movie now, are we?"

She shook her head. "No."

"Can you elaborate?" How did they go from hearts and flowers to tears and secrets? Whatever the mystery, it had to be bad. Nevertheless, it wouldn't make him stop loving her. Not now. Not ever. "Nothing you say will change how we feel. I've sensed for months there's something you wanted to discuss. Take a deep breath."

Ida Mae obliged.

"Exhale, sweetheart." Again, she complied. "Now, tell me. It'll be all right." He seized a paper napkin from the extras on one of the dinner trays and gently blotted the tears that trailed down her cheeks. "Take your time. I'm not going anywhere."

"You've said before the past is the past, and we didn't need to talk about when I went away."

"When you went away after high school?"

She bobbed her head. "Yes."

"You don't have to tell me. I still mean that." Of course, he wondered, but he had meant what he said, hadn't he? What could be so awful that twenty-one years later it continued to trouble her?

"I've always loved you. From the time we were kids to those crazy, angst-filled teen years to adulthood...and now. Granted, ours hasn't been the typical storybook romance, but true life rarely mirrors the romantic love we read about in fairy tales." Ida Mae hiccupped and paused. She took the paper napkin from his hand and, again, wiped her eyes.

She wasn't telling Chuck stuff he didn't already know. "I agree. Romantic love and enduring love are similar, yet different. To survive, romantic love often has to overcome obstacles. That's what leads to the enduring part. Go on, sweetheart. It's okay."

After a while, she continued. "In high school when I tried to tell you how much I loved you, I didn't fully grasp how your father's leaving impacted you. I knew it did, obviously, but at seventeen, I believed I could love you past that. I thought we had something special. I thought I could make you see how worthy you were to love, and that your dad's mistakes didn't reflect who you were or who you'd become. I wanted you to understand I'd never hurt you or abandon you the way he had. That's how teenagers think. At that age, we rationalize differently."

Some of this seemed a rehash of previous conversations. Chuck summoned patience and stroked her hand with his fingertips. "Yes. I wish I could rewind the past. I wish I could recant every dumb, harsh thing I said. I was a stupid, clueless jerk."

"No, you weren't. I'm not looking for that. High school's an awkward season." Ida Mae scooted away and glanced down. "You're not the only one who wishes we could rewind the past."

When she met his gaze, what he saw etched on her face haunted him. It propelled him back to their senior year. "I think I know what you're referring to."

"You do?"

"Sure, sweetheart." He'd rejected her, her declaration of love, and next thing he knew, Ida Mae had taken up with Tyler Fenston, the wild, mouthy newbie with an ax to grind and something to prove. It grated on Chuck to see Tyler's arms draped over Ida Mae's shoulders in the high school hall. While girls oohed and aahed over his charm and good looks, Chuck called it as he saw it. A manipulative deceiver with a fondness for fast cars, loud music, and pretty females. Emory Hoscutt nixed his daughter from dating the narcissistic newcomer. "I surmised a long time ago that Tyler Fenston's somehow connected to whatever 'this' is. Am I right?"

After her daddy's decree, Ida Mae emotionally retreated. For a while, she paid him and others no mind. Other than that friendly fake wave as she drove out of town following graduation, communication between them ceased for several months. He couldn't even wheedle anything out of Sugar Perkins either. Maybe Emory and Selma chalked up their daughter's trip as nothing more than a fun summer jaunt, but something about it stymied Chuck. Always had. He waited for her to answer.

"I wish I could deny that. But yes, you're right. I needed to put some space between this town and me, Tyler, you. Everything."

He didn't want to be crass and state the obvious. However, when Tyler wrapped his car around a tree after graduation, Chuck silently thanked God that Ida Mae hadn't been in that vehicle with him. He hated that the boy died, and he prayed he was a believer. It didn't seem likely, but one's poor judgment didn't always mirror his heart.

"It surprised me when you didn't return from your summer trip to attend Tyler's funeral. I know you only dated for a few weeks, but I thought you might come home when you heard the news."

Ida Mae fidgeted with the napkin in her hand. "Actually, we dated longer than a few weeks."

"Excuse me?"

That didn't make sense. Emory Hoscutt had disapproved of Tyler from the start. Despite his charm and slick ways, Fenston hadn't fooled Ida Mae's dad for a second. When the kid's true colors emerged, according to Ruby's get-up-and-go grapevine, diner customers overheard Emory's emotionally charged ultimatum. "Young lady, I don't want you to have anything to do with that boy again. One of God's children or not, until Tyler Fenston tames that wild driving, drinking, and swearing, you're not to see him. Understood?"

It pleased Chuck immensely when he'd heard the scuttlebutt about town. If Emory hadn't issued a directive, he might've had to take that kid in hand himself.

Ida Mae cleared her throat and jerked Chuck back to the present. "Tyler and I dated in secret for another month or so after Dad forbade it. Up until then, I never disobeyed my parents. I don't know why I did it. I came up with a million excuses why I should be able to make my own decisions."

Chuck's mouth went dry. All the while he thought she'd ditched that creep, and they secretly dated? Impossible. How did no one find out? Where'd they go? What did they...do? Various memories fired in rapid succession. Questions congealed in his brain. "I never saw you and Tyler together after your dad told you not to date him."

"We were careful. We went to places where no one would see us." Ida Mae rose from the sofa and paced the length of the living room. With her back to him, she continued. "I convinced myself that you didn't love me and never would. Tyler said so many right things. All lies, of course. I wised up, but it took a while. By that time, I'd made terrible choices."

A full-blown dustbowl warred in Chuck's mouth. Nausea roiled in his belly. He stood too and walked the twelve or so steps to Ida Mae. He placed his hands on her shoulders. "You slept with him, didn't you?" *Oh, God, let her say no.*

"Yes."

The gravity of the word nearly dropped him to his knees. In that instant, her answer wounded him more than anything his own father could have said or done. Worse. He'd always known what Dad was. Who he didn't know was this stranger who stood before him.

"How many times?"

"What?" She whirled around and faced him. Chuck's arms fell to his sides while her features colored with shame and embarrassment.

"How many times did you sleep with him, Ida Mae?"

"You want…details?"

"I think I deserve to know, don't you?" He steeled himself for the next blow. Somehow, he knew there was more.

"Twice. We had sex twice. And I never regretted anything more in my life."

He that is without sin among you, let him first cast a stone at her. The scripture from the eighth chapter of John, verse seven, jumped to mind. They were the very words of Jesus, in reference to an adulterous woman. That day, Jesus taught forgiveness and modeled it, as He continued to do throughout His thirty-three years on Earth. And because of His ultimate sacrifice on the cross, today everyone could access that same forgiveness.

But I'm not you, Lord. I'm human and I'm fallible. This hurts. Chuck tried to imagine how Ida Mae felt. He wanted to channel compassion because, after all, this lapse in judgment happened twenty-one years ago. Twenty-one years. As an almost eighteen-year-old girl. If Ida Mae were truly sorry and had asked God for forgiveness, couldn't he muster some forgiveness, too? God didn't color code sin according to deed and degree of sin. Everyone sinned. The healing came when people repented and turned from their sin. Lord knew, he'd erred plenty. Sometimes, unintentionally. Sometimes voluntarily. Like when he spoke cruel words to Ida Mae and started this chain reaction. Yeah, she made a bad choice, but he'd hastened the process. Some of the blame rested squarely on his shoulders.

"Is there anything else I should know?" They remained at arm's length, their breathing labored and laden with weariness.

"There is. There's a lot more you should know." Ida Mae wobbled back to the sofa and sat down. Her tears had ceased, though her face grew pale and drawn. "Eventually, Tyler and I did break up. After graduation, the reason I left town wasn't because I wanted to travel. I left Ruby because I was almost five months pregnant with Tyler's baby."

The room swayed. Chuck staggered to the chair opposite the sofa and sank into its cushiony depths. *Lord Almighty.* This had to be a bad dream.

"I told Sugar and swore her to secrecy. Tyler never knew and I never told Mom and Dad. I had a baby that September, in the northern part of the state, before coming home." She spoke in a monotone now, recounting the story in rote-like fashion. "I worked with a respected adoption agency and pinpointed qualities I wanted in the adoptive parents. It wasn't considered an open adoption, but I did sign forms allowing records to be unsealed when the child became of age."

Chuck's temples throbbed with a dull headache. What started as a small thud, picked up steam and beat a rat-a-tat-tat around his eye sockets. Ida Mae and Fenston? Ida Mae *pregnant?* Surely, he'd heard wrong. The rat-a-tat-tat became a bongo drum.

"I don't know whether the baby was a boy or a girl. I

asked the nurses and doctors not to tell me. I didn't even hold my child. My choice. I knew if I did, I could never do what I needed to, which was allow him or her to be placed for adoption." Ida Mae hesitated. "In some ways, it's like it never happened. Other than the weight gain around that time, I never came home with a baby or anything to show for the experience. Nothing but the emotional scars, that is. And as you know, those can remain with us a long, long time."

It all made sense now. Ida Mae's demeanor when she returned home that September. The additional pounds she eventually lost. Her reluctance to talk about her trip. The secretiveness. A grown-up persona far beyond her eighteen years. Emotional baggage she'd carried for two decades.

When he didn't say anything, she resumed talking. "Like I said, I signed a bunch of forms and legal documents with the adoption agency that placed my baby. In that paperwork, I gave permission releasing my name and other pertinent details when my baby turned eighteen. I always hoped he or she might try to find me, but so far, zilch. No phone calls, contacts, nothing. What with all the resources at our disposal, I could try searching, but if I haven't been contacted by now, that's pretty telling. I don't think my child wants to find me." She stared at Chuck. "Aren't you going to say something? I know you want to."

A numbness settled in his bones so debilitating he wondered if he were having a stroke. He stretched his fingers and then relaxed them. He did the same with his toes inside his shoes. What could he say? He'd bet their future on the solidity of their foundation, except that foundation was a lie.

Somehow, he mustered the strength to tug himself up out of the chair. "I'm not sure where to begin, Ida Mae." *Oh, God, help me.* Her blonde curls bounced on her shoulders as she started to sob. He wanted to sob too. What now? He should sit with her. Comfort her. But he couldn't. He'd promised to stay, but he had to break his word. He had to get out of there. If he didn't, he might say things he'd later regret, and he didn't want that.

Chuck leaned down and cupped her chin within his palm. "I love you, Ida Mae, but I need to go."

"Will...you..." Her tears started to fall once more, wetting her cheeks. "Will you be back?"

"I don't know."

What she'd seen in Chuck's eyes confirmed her worst fears.

What repulsed him more? That she'd slept with Tyler or that she'd had his baby? Or was it that she'd allowed the baby to be adopted—even though she was unmarried with a very limited income? Maybe all three disgusted him. Yeah, this time he may have said he loved her, but when he walked out that door, his reaction grieved her more than anything he'd ever said or done as an immature kid.

Rising from the sofa, Ida Mae swiped at her face with a handful of napkins. So much for their happily-ever-after. Joe and Kathleen may have found theirs in *You've Got Mail*, but for her and Chuck, it would take a miracle for them to survive this.

She juggled the dinner trays in her arms and carried them to the kitchen. Like a robot, she went through the motions and rinsed glasses, dishes, and silverware, and arranged everything in the dishwasher. Next, she wiped off the trays and set them on the table to dry. Finally, she rolled Chuck's tote out of the way, deciding she'd take it, along with his washed containers, to the diner when they reopened next week. More than likely, he wouldn't return here for it.

Next order of business? Pie. The splendid, Instagram-worthy apple pie, Chuck's favorite, with its ultra-fancy latticework and twin heart cut-outs, remained untouched on the counter. She'd intended to serve dessert after the movie, but then she'd felt the nudge to share what she'd bottled up inside for so long. *Crazy.* And yet, she wasn't sorry. Chuck deserved to know everything, and now he knew. It may have tanked their future, but keeping secrets killed futures too.

Ida Mae averted her eyes. She'd never make another apple pie as long as she lived, much less eat one. In fact, maybe she'd ax apple pie from the Come and Get It's menu. She supposed Chuck could make it, but the diner pies were her department.

The tears started afresh. She didn't doubt that she deserved what life doled out, but at some point, she'd always hoped for something better. *I'm spent. Used up. I don't even have the strength to pray.* Often, Pastor Bill spoke about the Holy Spirit interceding on our behalf when words failed. Well, that's what she needed now. Divine intervention dropped on her doorstep.

For the first fifteen minutes, Chuck simply drove. Didn't matter where. Anywhere except home. Because home no longer felt like home. He slept there, ate there. That about covered it. Home to him meant wherever Ida Mae was.

He drove past his street. The church. The market. The Come and Get It. Finally, Chuck circled back around and lumbered up the familiar driveway—his own. He didn't want to. Hadn't expected to. But going back to Ida Mae's was out of the question. At least for now.

He cut off the ignition and sat there. He gripped the steering wheel and lowered his head. He'd never been one to bawl, but as the barrage of images taunted him and the grief sliced him like a Thanksgiving turkey, moisture seeped from his eyes and dripped down his cheeks.

So. Ida Mae slept with Tyler, had his baby, and kept it a secret for twenty-one years. Have mercy. He could hardly fathom it. Over and over, he ticked off the events and wondered how she'd done it. How she'd worn the façade of the bubbly, well-adjusted businesswoman when, deep down, the memories must have mocked her too. Had she somehow walled off those hurts so she could function? Knowing Ida Mae as he did, or thought he did, she wouldn't merely dismiss them. They would have constantly preyed on her mind. So would the shame and guilt and loss. Suddenly, things that Chuck hadn't comprehended made sense now. Things she'd fretted about and alluded to.

And what had he done? Heaped on more guilt. Walked out on her. Instead of rising to the occasion, he had sunk to a new low. No matter the shock, no matter the pain, no matter the secrets, he should have stayed. He promised he wouldn't leave, and he had. Chuck dragged a handkerchief from his back pocket and swiped at his face. Yeah, this hurt. It muddled things in his mind. But his pain and bewilderment couldn't compare to Ida Mae's agony. She'd bared her soul and he'd crushed her spirit. What kind of man did that? Shame sidled up beside him and slapped him in the face. He had to make this right. But he couldn't tonight.

Ida Mae climbed into bed and buried herself beneath Grandma Ida's hand-me-down quilt. The darkness enveloped her and she willed herself to sleep, yet it refused to comply. Even with her eyes closed, she couldn't shake the revulsion and suffering she'd seen on Chuck's face. She wasn't surprised that he hadn't returned. But she was disappointed.

When sleep finally did come, it came in fits and starts, as did the self-recriminations. When Ida Mae woke for the dozenth time, she gave in to the insomnia and padded to the living room. Where to land next? The couch? It seemed like the perfect spot for her next crying jag.

Morning. Chuck eased himself out of bed like an old man. He hadn't slept a wink. The twisted bedcovers gave testament to the fact, along with a pounding headache and burning eyelids.

Oh, God... Had it all been a nightmare? For a moment, he held hope. Then memories of Ida Mae's confession came flooding back. Yeah. It was a nightmare, all right. A real one.

Nausea bubbled in his belly as he made his way to the bathroom to douse his face in cold water. As awful as the truth was, he could only imagine how it must be for Ida Mae. She'd shared the secret that had haunted her for decades, only to have him add to her misery. *Jerk. You could have forgiven her on the spot...and didn't. Are you so lily white that forgiveness is now beneath you?*

He spun the faucet to "on" and watched the water stream forth as he pondered what to do next. He couldn't hide his feelings from God, nor did he try. *I can't see Ida Mae today, Lord. Or tonight, tomorrow, or even the next day. Gotta be honest. I don't know if we can get past this. Ida Mae had dozens of opportunities over the years to tell me the truth...and didn't. Even if we weren't seriously committed at that point, we shared a history. We were friends. Or so I thought.* Hurt squeezed his chest, and resentment took root.

Chuck splashed cold water on his face, strangely comforted by the water's icy sting. At least, for a moment, something else besides Ida Mae occupied his thoughts. But when he dried his face, again, the woman he thought he knew, bounced to the forefront of his brain. Images of Ida Mae with Tyler fired in rapid succession. Why hadn't he surmised the truth before? That she'd been pregnant when leaving town immediately after high school? He'd never bought into the travel bug idea. Not really. So, why? Why hadn't his mind gone there?

Because, by then, Tyler and Ida Mae had long since quit dating. Or so he'd thought. Plus, he wouldn't have believed Ida Mae to be capable of such deception. Boy, how stupid he'd been.

Chuck slung the hand towel on the counter. This would get him nowhere. Revisiting history and analyzing whys would only add to his anguish, which was precisely why the break from work couldn't have happened at a better time. The remainder of the week he'd hibernate. Maybe run. Write. Watch sports. Anything to fill his days and head with something other than what—who—mattered most.

Funny how one defaulted to autopilot when faced with heartbreak. Instead of languishing in bed as she was tempted to do, Ida Mae rose from her spot on the couch that morning, calmed by the semblance of a routine. She may not have to ready herself for work, but still, she made her bed, dressed, dolled up, and drank two cups of coffee as she listened to the morning news. Grief and shame trailed her at her every turn, but she couldn't remain in their clutches forever. Life went on, and so would she. Since Chuck hadn't called or returned, she could only assume that he'd made his decision regarding their future. They were history.

Even if Chuck did return now, Ida Mae didn't know how'd she'd react. She realized her news had rocked his world, but she'd paid dearly for past transgressions. God had forgiven her, and if Chuck couldn't, then he'd have to reconcile that on his own. She'd done everything she knew to do. *Yeah. Right.* Well...it sounded good anyway.

A need for fresh air sent Ida Mae scurrying for a jacket. Maybe a walk would clear her head and loosen the weight on her heart. Later in the week, she planned to visit Mom and Dad, but not today. Today, solitude claimed her.

As Ida Mae left the house, bright, warm sunshine engulfed her. She lifted her face toward the sky, thankful for pretty weather and mild temperatures. In the Ozarks, seasons could change on a dime, especially on lazy, fall days primed for winter. Rain would have suited her mood except God hadn't allowed it. Maybe He wanted to prove a point. That He was, after all, still in control, despite her inner turmoil.

Unbuttoning her jacket, Ida Mae rounded the street corner and stopped short. Blood pounded in her ears. She hadn't considered they might cross paths this way, and Chuck paused in mid-run when he saw her. Should she wave? Call out to him?

He made her decision an easy one. Save for a quick, curt nod, he immediately turned around and jogged in the opposite direction. Ida Mae's hands never left her sides. His reaction conveyed what she didn't want to believe. He'd steeled his heart against her.

She began walking again, and a couple of crows cawed from nearby treetops, as if to taunt her. *Oh, hush. I know.* She and Chuck might be done, but she still loved the man. Behind her tinted sunglasses, fresh tears pricked her eyes.

Tuesday melded into Wednesday. Wednesday into Thursday. By Friday, Chuck's tiny home started to wear on him. It'd been four days since Ida Mae told him the truth. Three since he'd last laid eyes on her. In the interim, he'd accomplished nothing. He'd forgone his morning runs. He hadn't opened his laptop. Television didn't appeal.

Why hadn't he heard from her? After their brief encounter on Tuesday, he'd imagined she'd at least text him. But what had he expected? He'd rebuffed her that day on his morning run. He'd punished her by refusing to wave or speak, and by turning around, and literally, running in the opposite direction.

Reeling with misery and hurt, Chuck had retaliated toward Ida Mae in an uncharitable manner. In a manner unbecoming of the man his mother had raised him to be, not to mention the man who God intended.

Chuck paced the living room and stewed. He had to fix this. Or at least try to. Things might seem like a mess, but God crafted masterpieces from messes—as the Bible proved.

Grabbing his car keys off an end table, he sprinted out the front door. A few minutes later, he pulled up to the curb in front of Ida Mae's, unlatched his seatbelt, and slipped from his vehicle. He straightened his clothing without really knowing why, and ran a hand through his hair, realizing he'd failed to comb it. He imagined the neighbors enjoyed watching his antics. Nora and Ned Brewster were probably at the market, but he suspected others were home and glued to their windows. One couldn't pass gas in this town without a kind soul offering an antacid. Well, whatever. Let 'em watch.

Chuck pressed the doorbell and waited. Nothing. He rapped the door with two solid knocks. Silence. Was she still asleep? Had Ida Mae gone somewhere? Hopefully not. He turned and traipsed toward the back of the house. It wasn't like her not to answer the doorbell or even a couple knocks. Chuck spied her car in the garage, and the breath he hadn't realized he'd been holding, whooshed out.

He tapped the back door. "Ida Mae?"

Why were the window blinds still drawn? It was almost eight-thirty in the morning. He tapped again. Still, she didn't answer. He tried the doorknob, and to his surprise, met no resistance as he twisted. *Oh, Lord.* Was it considered trespassing or breaking and entering if a door wasn't locked and a person entered a home? He thought he knew the answer to that but decided not to dwell on it.

Slowly, he nudged open the door. Scents of apple and cinnamon tickled his nose, and a sharp pang of regret poked him in the chest as he remembered the apple pie she'd baked on Monday. Chuck's picnic tote stood beside the door, and his dishes he brought were washed and on the sink counter. The trays they'd used for lunch were stacked, neat as a pin, on the kitchen table. Why hadn't she put them away?

Chuck closed the door but remained there. He didn't want to wander through the house as if he had every right. "Ida Mae? It's me. Chuck." Muted cries carved through silence.

Blast it. Propriety be hanged. He strode through the kitchen and into the living room where he found Ida Mae curled up on the sofa, wrapped in a fuzzy blue blanket, with a box of tissues nearby. Mascara blotches covered her cheeks, and traces of red bordered the rims of her eyes. She sat up when he approached. "What are you doing here?"

"Why didn't you answer the door when I rang the bell or called?" He lowered himself beside her and gently fingered the curls away from her face. He hadn't processed everything yet or come to terms with the hurt, but one thing he knew as sure as the sun would rise again tomorrow. He loved this woman. Nothing in the past, present, or future would change that. The fact remained.

"I don't know. I couldn't seem to find the words." She rolled her shoulders and sighed. "How'd you get in anyway?"

"You left the back door unlocked. *All night.* Which, by the way, I know Ruby's a safe, close-knit community, but don't do that anymore, please."

"I must have forgotten to lock it when I went to bed last night. I put your storage tote by the door, and I washed the dishes you brought the food in. They've been there since Monday."

"Thank you, but that's the least of my worries. I didn't come back for that stuff. I came back because I wanted to apologize." A lump formed in his throat. He didn't want to bawl in front of her. "I reacted badly and I'm sorry."

"Sorry? Honestly, except for that cold shoulder treatment on your jog this week, you handled the truth better than I expected." She hiccupped on a sob. "I know it changed things between us."

"You're right," he answered. "To a degree. It's made me wonder if keeping secrets will be our default when tough seasons come. It's changed my perspective about relationships. How honesty in all aspects is crucial, even if speaking the truth hurts. What hasn't changed is that I love you."

"I tried to tell you. I came close so often. At the last second, I'd always chicken out. When you said whatever was in the past didn't matter, I knew it did—this did—but I convinced myself otherwise." Ida Mae's voice grew soft. "I'm sorry too. I'm sorry for all of it except I'm not sorry for having the baby. Me getting pregnant wasn't an innocent child's fault. Life is precious. Sacred. I couldn't snuff it out. I think God used my poor choice and reconciled it for others' good. Like for the couple who'd tried for seven years to get pregnant and desperately wanted a little one to love. I only wish I'd shared this with you sooner."

"Yes. I wish you'd told me." What if she had? Would it have made a difference in him loving her? Nope. The knowledge would have decked him, but eventually, he'd have dealt with it. Circumstances and events were far easier to process in the now versus decades later when more was at stake. "I understand why you didn't feel like you could, and I take responsibility for that. I'm sad and I'm sorry."

"So you'll know, I never loved Tyler. I sought comfort and validation in someone who ultimately devalued me in every sense of the word. I asked God to forgive me, and I believe He has, but I wonder if you can?"

He didn't know how to say it. Maybe the direct way was best. "Ida Mae. I'm not a saint. I'm selfish and fallible. You've thrown a lot at me, but if we can manage to extend grace to each other, then all this stuff isn't the end of the world. We'll trudge through it—together—like we committed to do, weeks ago. The thing is there *is* someone else who needs to forgive you."

"Mom and Dad? I know. I plan to talk with them tomorrow. It'll be hard."

"I'll come with you, if you like. But they're not who I mean."

"I'm not sure who else there is."

He drew an invisible heart in the center of her chest, over her own. "Sweetheart, it's you. You need to forgive *you*."

Chapter Eighteen

The inevitable happened the next day. Ida Mae straightened and approached the front door of her childhood home. She'd come alone, as she knew she must. Not that she didn't want Chuck's support, but one had to tackle some things alone. This being one of the them.

Ida Mae jabbed her key into the ancient lock and nudged open the door. "Mom? Dad?" She'd stepped away from the diner for a bit, arriving at lunchtime, and the aroma of celery, onion, and chicken stock scented the air. "Yoo-hoo...it's me!"

"In here, Daughter!" Dad called.

Ida Mae found them in the kitchen, working together, preparing lunch. They grinned as she entered the room.

"My goodness, dear, you startled us." Mom stepped over and kissed her cheek. "You never come at lunchtime. Everything okay?"

Not really. But this is something I should have done a long time ago. "The diner is still closed for a few days. Can we...talk?"

Dad's eyebrows crinkled together, and Mom set the soup ladle in the spoon rest. Their faces registered mutual curiosity. Or was it concern? Whatever it was, she wished she didn't have to tell them this way—right before lunch. But when would be a good time?

"Of course, we can talk, sweetheart. We're always

happy to have you join us." Dad motioned toward the kitchen table. "Have a seat. Let me pour you some of your mother's fresh, hot brew."

"No thanks, Dad. I don't really feel like coffee. I appreciate the offer though."

"No coffee?" Mom wiped her hands on her apron. "What is it, Ida Mae? You don't seem like yourself."

"I'm not, Mom. And I'm sorry. Really sorry for what I'm about to tell you..."

They cried when she shared her story. Even Ida Mae's tough-as-nails daddy shed tears into opened palms calloused from years of labor and grit.

"We wish you had come to us, dear." Her mother dabbed at her nose with the embroidered pink and white hanky that Ida Mae gave her one year for Christmas. "We would have worked through this. To think you faced pregnancy and childbirth alone...is overwhelming." Mom swallowed hard and struggled for composure. "And then, believing you had to give the child—our grandchild— away. Never would we have issued an ultimatum like that."

"Placed for adoption, Mom." She relived it all over again as her parents digested the news. The story stung. One couldn't sugarcoat it. They deserved to grieve, and she needed to allow them that. Ida Mae sniffled and choked back fresh emotion. "Again, I'm so sorry. I never wanted to hurt you or Dad or bring shame on the Hoscutt name. I wish I could have a do-over. You don't know how much I wish that."

"Honey, people make mistakes." Dad leaned toward her, looped his arms over her shoulders, and hugged her close. "I sensed that Tyler was a loose cannon. I prayed for the boy, but I realized he needed to get his life in order. I think Pastor Bill even counseled him for a while. While we may never know the condition of his heart, maybe the preacher planted some seeds. Your mother's right. We wouldn't have turned you away. Ever."

"Do we know...Is there a way we can find out whether our grandchild was a boy or girl? Where he or she lives? Anything?" Mom clinched the hanky, twisting it back and forth between her hands.

"I signed some forms granting access to certain records when my baby turned eighteen, but now he'd be twenty-one, and nothing's come of it. There are also genetic testing companies that offer DNA insights and information. Many are legitimate, but they don't provide all the answers one might hope." Would her son or daughter ever look for her? It seemed like a long shot, but God specialized in long shots, didn't He?

"Yes, I've seen those ancestry sites advertised on television. Heard them mentioned on the radio too. Never thought much about 'em." Dad stepped aside and attempted a smile. "Until now. Maybe this young person is looking for his birth mama right this very minute. Maybe he's searched the birth records and we're one heartbeat away from meeting him."

It seemed curious the way Dad also defaulted to he and him. They didn't know the child's gender, but perhaps it was her father's way of personalizing his grandchild. The one he might never meet. Ida Mae agreed that it seemed less generic that way. Almost like speaking life into a disembodied figment of one's imagination and acknowledging the child existed.

"Yes, dear. Extraordinary things happen." Her

mother linked hands with Dad, and she spoke with a forced bravado, but Ida Mae admired Mom's effort. "Now, something else. You haven't mentioned Chuck. How's he handling this?"

She expected they'd come around to that. It was only natural her parents would wonder. "It's been hard, Mom. Before this, we were talking about a future. Today? I'm not sure where things stand. He says he loves me, and he offered to be here with me when I told you. That counts for something, right?"

"It certainly does, and he best do something about it."

"Oh, Mom. You say that like we're running out of time."

"No, dear. I'm speaking as your mother, or rather, woman to woman. Don't disregard your worth or underestimate your value. If Chuck can't figure out what he wants by now, maybe you should reassess things."

"Now, Selma," Dad intervened. "Ida Mae has a good head on her shoulders. She'll figure things out with Chuck without any interference from us."

For the first time in days, Ida Mae smiled. Mom and Dad believed in her. Each, in their own way, wanted her to move beyond mistakes of the past. Their words were meant to encourage, not blame. No longer that teenage girl who'd made a bad choice, but a woman old enough, and certainly wise enough, to make mature, enlightened decisions.

"Thank you, both. I appreciate your votes of confidence." She'd already decided that she wouldn't live in limbo anymore. She loved Chuck. Always would. Having told him about the baby, though, unearthed new feelings. It changed the landscape. Everything was out there now. No more secrets. Chains of the past fell away. "I'm going to nurture myself for a while. If Chuck and I are meant to be, I suppose it'll work out. If not, I'll know it's time to finally let go."

Dad nodded. "Chuck's a good man. You're a good woman. We'll give it to God and let Him sort it out."

When tears and talk were spent, they reconvened around the family table, the source of much love and contentment during Ida Mae's growing years. Dad prayed and they dined on Mom's homemade chicken noodle soup and buttermilk biscuits. Even for a woman pushing forty, she still found solace in her parents' presence.

If Ida Mae initiated a search for her baby, word would eventually make its way around town, as it had about Sy Farrow's homecoming, but how folks reacted was out of Ida Mae's hands. In twenty-one years, almost everyone who lived here, except for a few newcomers, were still the same ones who'd lived here all their lives. Most people would remember Tyler Fenston. He'd been one of the rare kids who'd died a tragic death in the past fifty years. His fatality led to new signage along Halo Hill, the same dangerous incline where Angie Packard, Sam Packard's first wife, lost control of her vehicle and crashed down an ice-laden embankment. Difference was Angie died during a winter blizzard. Tyler lost his life on a mild May evening, the day after their high school graduation. According to the police report, his blood alcohol level far surpassed the legal limit.

Yes, folks remembered Tyler, all right. They also remembered Ida Mae's daddy dressing him down at the diner and ordering him to never set foot near his daughter again. Tyler had been that troubled soul who folks prayed up a blue streak for, but "the kid had a penchant for trouble" as one old farmer put it after Tyler passed. Yes. Yes, Tyler had.

Dad scooted the jar of blackberry jam across the table. "Nothing like your mother's homemade jam to ease what ails us, honey. The good Lord's plan is already in motion even as we sit here and partake of this wonderful meal. You can trust Him to work out the kinks between you and Chuck, as well as guide you in other areas too."

"Thanks, Dad. I want to believe that."

"You can, dear." Her mother's eyes shimmered with moisture, but she held fresh tears in check. "We're weak, but He's strong. Our faith doesn't mature without trials."

Lord, Lord. Well, she'd certainly had enough of those. Was it really necessary to experience more hardship to grow her faith? She hoped not. God had a plan like Dad said, right? *Help me believe.*

Perhaps, at another table, a young person sat with his parents. Parents of the heart, who loved their child as much as Ida Mae's mom and dad loved her. And perhaps, that child would someday know his biological mother loved him too.

Ida Mae carried that thought home with her and hugged it close to her heart well into the night as sleep and dreams found her. On the periphery of her subconscious, a new day floated. One that held promise and answered prayers. She woke briefly and wondered if God really did reveal truth in dreams.

Memories of the past seven days weighed heavily on Chuck. He hadn't been able to sleep again. No surprise there. This morning, he threw off the covers and padded to the bathroom. Who was that man in the mirror? The one who stared back with raccoon eyes and a five o'clock shadow?

In the past week, he'd dissected the many facets of Ida Mae—or who he believed she was—and he realized something. His love for her remained unchanged. The human side of him ached. A hard fact. The thought of another man, a boy like Tyler Fenston, putting his hands on her all those years ago, set his blood afire. *If you'd responded with kindness instead of cruelty, Ida Mae wouldn't have made the choices she did.* Chuck shook his head trying to free the agonizing images. The enemy loved to strike at folks' hearts and heads. He knew their weak points, who they loved, and went for them, full throttle. What to do next? Chuck needed to think.

He traipsed over to the closet and tugged out his running gear. The weather had shifted for worse, but thirty-six degrees or not, he'd grab his morning run and then return for a shower and get ready for church. With the diner still closed another two days, he wouldn't be so rushed. He'd have plenty of time to get his thoughts in order. Was Ida Mae doing the same thing? He'd given her some breathing space yesterday since that was the day she visited with Emory and Selma, but he was eager to find out how that went. When he called her last night, she'd seemed exhausted and subdued. He hoped that wasn't an indicator that things had gone poorly.

Once suited up, Chuck braced himself for the cold front that moved through overnight. When the frigid air smacked him in the face, he almost caved and went back inside. Normally, he jogged in all sorts of elements, but today the bitter chill and the promise of rain made him think twice. Typical Ozark weather. Seventies one day, thirties the next. He should get a treadmill. Or buy property with acreage where he could run and be done with it. No more running street blocks for exercise. He toyed with the idea of calling Jerry Marshall later. Then he shelved the thought as he contemplated other things. Like whether or not he could move forward, given facts of the past.

Despite his cold weather gear, cold was cold. Not even winter yet, he wondered if the almanacs would be right this year about the season being a rough one. Chuck jogged about a mile before the rain hit. At first it splattered the ground in a smattering of small droplets. Then the real fun started. A big, old cloud cut loose, and the rain whooshed down hard. Puddles formed on the sidewalks as he ran. Why hadn't he heeded his weather app notifications? *Moron.*

As he did an about-face, preparing to circle back toward home, a newer model Chevy Equinox eased alongside him. The driver slowed and came to a full stop at the curb near Chuck. Dad? His father motioned for him to get in. What was he doing out at seven a.m.?

He tried to shake off the rivulets of water the best he could as he hopped in the vehicle, but the rain still managed to soak the interior door and dampen the passenger side seat. "Thanks. Sorry about the mess."

"No worries, Son. It's only a thing and it'll dry." His father pressed a button and toasty, blessed warmth circulated around Chuck's legs and feet. "Mighty brisk day for a run."

"Yeah, I know. I'd hoped to beat the rain." It was the

first time in thirty years he'd ridden with his dad. Mighty nice vehicle. According to Mom, Dad's business had done well. He'd built a healthy nest egg for retirement over the years, and unbeknownst to him and Voni, funded part of their education when he began to get his life in order. Chuck guessed, in Dad's mind, money could right wrongs. It didn't do much in the way of making up for his absence. Their counselor said that alcoholics navigated recovery in various steps and stages. While their behavior might seem irrational to others, to them, it seemed logical. For a long while, Dad thought his returning home would do more harm than good.

"I'd planned an early breakfast at the diner, but I forgot you're closed on Sundays. I also saw the sign on the door that said you'd closed down for a bit of a break." His father paused an extra minute at the intersection. "How about a cup of coffee and donuts at the gas station? My treat."

Hmm. Should he accept? He'd like to, but he didn't want to be too quick with his answer. "I can do you one better than that. How about breakfast at my house?" It struck him how clean cut and put together his dad appeared. Older, certainly, than he'd been thirty years ago, but other than the fine lines that creased his mouth, forehead, and eyes, he tidied up well. Maybe Chuck overlooked it in the counseling sessions because he focused more on the intrinsic changes.

"Well, that sounds like an offer I can't refuse."

Thanks to small-town life and a far-reaching grapevine, his dad knew where he lived, but it would be his first time in Chuck's home. He hadn't invited him over until today. "You can pull in behind my car. I guess we'll have to make a dash for it. Are you good with that?" He didn't think of mid-sixties as ancient, but then he had another thought. "Tell you what, Dad, let me go get an umbrella and I'll run back out. You wait here, okay?"

"Nonsense. I'm not a jogger like you, but I can move at a pretty good clip for an old guy. Lead the way."

"You sure?"

His dad secured the top button of his jacket and flipped up his collar. They dashed around to the side entrance of the house where Chuck hurriedly jabbed the key into the lock and flung open the door. He motioned his father inside and followed behind him as the rain picked up pace. If the temperature held steady, the rain would remain as rain. If not, the stuff would freeze and turn the roads into a slick mess. That was the thing about living here. The Ozarks always kept life interesting. They wiped off their shoes in the tiny, tiled mudroom and hung their dripping jackets on the brass wall pegs.

"This is a dandy place. It has character." His father scanned the room and trailed after Chuck into the kitchen. "I remember when the preacher and the missus used to live here. They invited your mother and me over on many occasions. Sadly, we always had to give them a rain check—no pun intended. Back in the day, I couldn't put down the bottle long enough to do much socializing, although I suspect the real reason the parson wanted us to drop by was to encourage us and advise. Good people, Pastor Bill and Sister Sharon."

"Yes, they are, and they're still going strong," Chuck agreed. "Older, like the rest of us, but still doing the Lord's work, and if their involvement in the church and community's any indication, loving every minute of it."

Would Pastor Bill have been able to help his dad then? Doubtful. He hadn't hit bottom yet. Though, Chuck appreciated that snippet of information and gratitude warmed him. "Make yourself comfortable. I'll change into dry clothes and be right back. Bathroom's down the hall and to the right if you'd like to towel off."

"Aw, I'm good, but thanks. My coat kept me mostly covered, and the top of my head won't take long to dry. Hair's a little thinner these days, you know."

When Chuck returned, he found his father at the kitchen counter, hovering over two coffee mugs, pouring hot brew and humming a classic hymn he knew well. "Blessed Assurance." They sang it often at church. While other churches had foregone the old songs in favor of praise and worship music, theirs maintained the traditional order of worship, and the congregation liked it that way.

"I hope you don't mind that I took the liberty." Dad pointed to the mugs. "I reheated what you had left in the coffee decanter."

"Of course not. I'm glad you saw it." Funny how something so small could mean so much. Not necessarily a father-son bonding moment, but an act of kindness, nevertheless. "I'll make more if you'd like."

"Oh, this will do fine. Thanks."

Chuck rubbed his hands together and made his way to the stove. "I can whip up omelets, waffles, pancakes, French toast, you name it. What's your pleasure?"

A smile inched across his father's face. "Surprise me."

"That could be dangerous." He dragged out mixing bowls and gathered ingredients from the fridge and went to work. "Feel free to have a seat here at the table or in the living room. This won't take long."

"What can I do to help?" his dad asked. "You may not believe it, but I do know my way around a kitchen. I've done a fair bit of cooking for myself over the years."

"Really? That's great. Everyone should know the basics. What are some of your favorite recipes?"

"Oh, let's see. I do a lot of interesting combos in the slow cooker. Mainly easy things, but filling and delish. As far as breakfast goes, to be honest, I usually have toast and fruit with some coffee and OJ."

"Well then. You're in for a treat." Chuck began cracking eggs into a glass bowl. "I suppose you could set the table if you want, and if you'd like to pour drinks, there's apple juice in the fridge. I killed off the orange juice a few days ago. Sorry."

"Not a problem. I can drink anything."

Was that a joke? He waited for his dad to add something, but he didn't. They worked together in comfortable silence. Every now and again, his father would hum a stanza of another hymn. Where a few weeks ago, Chuck's interactions with his dad would have been tense and reserved, unbelievably, today he enjoyed the companionship. Extending mercy and grace freed him in incredible ways. It hadn't happened overnight. It was an ongoing process, and he definitely wasn't perfect at it. Forging ahead with Dad might always take restraint in some areas and effort in others. But still, it was a start.

Surprisingly God had reshaped his thoughts. Once, he'd held nothing but contempt for the miserable failure of a father who'd walked away from his wife and kids.

Now, he regarded the man with awe and compassion as the one who'd returned, admitting mistakes and seeking forgiveness. He marveled at the odd awareness that the love he thought that died simply splintered into a thousand different pieces. Those pieces lodged in his heart, mind, and soul—all the places that mattered—and places where God had been working.

Chuck flipped one of the Southwestern omelets, garnished it with green onions, black olives, and avocado slices, plated it on his best dinnerware, and set it before his father. He repeated the process with his own omelet. "I hope this isn't too rich for you this early in the morning."

His father whistled. "My, oh, my. Are you kidding? This is fit for a king." He extended his palm. "Mind if we pray first?"

To accept his father's hand or not? To rebuff his dad's gesture wouldn't seem right. "I'd like that."

They bowed their heads and his dad began to pray.

"Almighty Father, you are so gracious. Thank you for this time with my son. Thank you for opening doors, forgiving debts, and refurbishing dreams. We praise you for that. Thank you for this mouthwatering bounty, and we humbly ask that you would bless this food to the nourishment of our earthly bodies. We love you, Lord. Amen."

"Amen." Chuck echoed. He'd never heard his father pray before. Not that he could remember anyway. Who was this guy? A new man? *Exactly.* Tears moistened his eyes. Oh boy. He hoped he didn't start blubbering. It wasn't like him to be so emotional. It almost happened at Ida Mae's the other day when she told him about Tyler and the baby. All the jumbled and up and down feelings he'd experienced for decades suddenly aligned and coalesced, clarifying what mattered. *Love.* Life battered everyone, for sure. Christ's love sustained them. Why had it taken thirty of his forty years for him to fully get that?

"We're never too old to learn." Dad's voice penetrated his thoughts.

Had he spoken aloud? He didn't think so. "Pardon?"

"Long ago, as I started the recovery process, the fog began to lift. I grew in my faith. I realized, though I'd failed at a lot of things, God wasn't done with me yet. He could still use me." His father slipped his hand into his back pants pocket and drew out his wallet and opened it. Scripture cards, a slip of paper with AA resources and phone numbers, and various old photos. He pointed to the pictures. "Not many people carry pictures around anymore other than what's on their cell phones, but thirty years ago, this was all I had."

In one of the photos, he and Voni were cuddled next to Mom as she read them a bedtime story. Voni looked to be a toddler and Chuck about seven. Dad must have taken the picture.

"Every day of my life, that's the one I looked at. It kept me going. To be the man who God intended, I vowed to get better. With His help and AA's, I did. I wanted to come home—I kept tabs on your mother and you children—but I'd convinced myself I'd inflicted so much harm that you were far better off without me."

"What made you change your mind? Why did you finally come home?"

"My friend continued praying for me. The one who

never gave up on me and refused to take no for an answer. Well, besides the Lord, of course, and your mother."

"A friend?"

"Yes. A dear, dear friend. Edwin Ramsey."

Edwin? Chuck recalled their visit at The Meadows. It seemed like ages ago, but he well remembered their conversation. Something the older gentleman said resonated. *Reserve judgment. As you know, there are reasons people do what they do. They may not make sense to us. They may be self-serving and sinful. Or they may reveal additional truths and transparencies. Some bad. Some good. God's hand is always at work.*

"Ruby, Missouri's very own prayer warrior. I won't share our private conversations because those are between God, Edwin, and me, but let me tell you, Son, over the years without Edwin praying and nudging me in the right direction, I'd have floundered." His father picked up his fork and knife. "We'd best sample this deliciousness, huh? Don't want it to get cold."

"Wait, Dad. You mean Edwin was instrumental in you coming back?"

"You really don't know?"

"No. I don't."

"Edwin was an initial investor in the furniture store. He backed me financially until the business became solvent."

Chuck's stomach somersaulted into his chest cavity. "He what?"

"I tried to repay him so many times, but that old bugger tore up my checks. Said the only way he'd ever accept payment was if I personally handed him a check when I returned home. For good. Well, I have and I did." His dad cut into the omelet and stabbed a bite. "Know what the stinker did, though?"

At this point, Chuck couldn't hazard a guess. He knew Edwin was well off financially. He knew he was a good man and an intercessor. He knew, most assuredly, friends and family meant the world to him. But good gracious, to sacrifice his resources and do something of that magnitude for his father—a recovering alcoholic— when so much could have gone wrong? Man, oh, man. The tears he'd held at bay threatened again.

"What? What did he do?" Something bigger was coming and he braced for it.

"Edwin tore up that check too. Said my debt to him had been canceled. He asked me to pay the blessing forward. Oh, and he made me agree to checkers and coffee every Friday. And there's the matter of a wedding he's asked me to coordinate."

"But...you and Mom are technically still married."

"Not ours, Son. Yours and Miss Ida Mae's."

The wind blew hard, and dark clouds hung low in the sky, but blessedly, the rain tapered off around noon without turning into a wintry mix. Ida Mae had skipped church and had no inclination to go out. With her precarious emotions, she decided it best to stay home and lounge around in her pink sweats and bunny slippers. While she'd missed the hum of the diner, and church today, she liked holing up in her cozy home. She planned to binge-watch her entire stash of rom-coms and bake cookies. There would be no apple pie for a while. It reminded her too much of Monday.

The truth was out in the open now, but the memory of Chuck leaving when she'd initially told him the story was still too fresh. She understood his reaction. Expected it. But it stung. Yes, days later, he'd come back, but when he first walked out, it shredded her self-confidence all over again. She loved Chuck and he loved her. Was it enough? If they were to have a future together, would Tyler and the baby continue to come between them, or could he honestly let go of the past? If only she could be sure.

She finished her grilled cheese sandwich and tomato soup and perched on the sofa beneath the warm Sherpa blanket. A huge Doris Day fan, Mom loved this old movie. In the same vein as *Yours, Mine, and Ours*, *With Six You Get Eggroll* came with laughter, romance, mix-ups and mayhem. It was the perfect antidote for an emotionally spent gal on a dreary afternoon.

Ida Mae sank into the strategically placed pillows and pressed the remote to start the DVD. She never skipped the opening credits because she enjoyed the intro and the upbeat music. The nostalgia surrounding the time period reeled her in and made her wish for simpler days. Besides the romantic plotline, there was a fun balance of chaos and comedy. She didn't need more disorder in her life, but she could sure use a good laugh.

Nothing like a good ol' dose of escapism. She settled back, already lighter, enjoying the interplay between Doris Day's character, Abby McClure, and her kids. At first, she almost didn't hear the familiar ringtone because she'd turned down the volume on her cell to immerse herself in the movie. Chuck? She hit "pause" on the remote. "Hi."

"Hi. Missed you at church today. Got a minute?" Chuck's voice drifted over her, reaching that special spot reserved only for him.

"Sure. How are you?"

"Cold. Mind opening the door?"

He was outside? She threw off the blanket and padded to the door. The peephole made his head appear disproportionate to his body, but sure enough, there he stood in jeans and coat, holding a gigantic stuffed bear and a long, white box. Flowers? Whatever for?

She threw open the door and cold air whooshed in. "I didn't know you were coming, or I would have waited to eat. I could make some more soup and a grilled cheese sandwich if you like." Ida Mae ushered him in, noting a new light in his eyes. Judging by his hair's shimmery glow, he'd tried to tame his unruly waves by adding styling gel, and was that a new cologne she smelled?

"No thanks. I appreciate that offer, but I'm still full from breakfast." He held out the teddy bear and box. "These are for you."

"It's not my birthday. That was almost two months ago. Remember?"

"I know. Is there a law that says a guy can't give his girl presents at other times too?"

"No, not that I know of. Thank you." She accepted the gifts and walked over to the sofa to set down the adorable bear and open the box. What had gotten into him? The past week had been far from celebratory. She guessed it was his attempt to perk up her spirits. Nice. It was working.

Ida Mae removed the pretty pink ribbon that secured the box and slowly raised the lid. Pink roses, a dozen of them, lay swathed in baby's breath and tissue paper. "Oh, my goodness. These are gorgeous!" She inhaled deeply. The flowers probably cost Chuck a pretty penny, but they truly were the prettiest roses she'd ever seen. "Thank you. I don't know why you did this, but I love them, and I love the bear too." She raised on her tiptoes and kissed his cheek.

"I know this week hasn't been easy, and I thought these might cheer you up."

"They do." Obviously, he'd shopped earlier.

"Another thing." Chuck grasped her hand. "I know we've experienced a lot in our lives. Me with my dad, and you with...the baby. We can't undo that heartache. We can't pretend it doesn't exist. All I know is with Christ at the helm, I believe we can handle anything that life throws at us now. It's all out there. We don't have to run from the truth or hide it under a rock. We can talk about it and try our best to work through it—as long as we have each other." He let go of her hand and dropped to one knee.

Oh, my. He *wasn't* proposing?

He pulled a small velvet box from his inside shirt pocket and flipped open the lid. For a second, all Ida Mae could do was stare. The solitaire sparkled in the living room light.

"I'd planned to do this earlier in the week, but it didn't go as I'd hoped. Actually, I had the ring with me when we watched *You've Got Mail*."

She wished she could put that episode out of her mind forever. It had definitely not been the day to propose.

"From the time we were kids, you're the one who

centered me and kept me on course. As we grew older and made mistakes, I realized that those mistakes and tough times cost us a lot, but they also developed our mettle. We wouldn't have arrived at this place without that stuff. I don't want to go through life alone. It's not so much fun. I want us to spend forever together. I love you, and I'm hoping you feel the same way." Chuck reached inside the box and slipped out the ring. He smiled and held the ring next to her left hand. "Sweetheart, would you do me the honor of becoming my wife? Will you marry me?"

Chapter Nineteen

"You know I love you."

Chuck's heart hammered against his chest. She was turning him down? It hadn't occurred to him that she'd say no.

"All my life, I've dreamed of this moment." Ida Mae curled her fingers around his. "But circumstances change. People change. You've recently faced a lot. Your dad coming home. Me...and the baby. Marriage is a huge step. A lifetime commitment."

"Whoa. This isn't a rash decision. I've had this ring for weeks." He stood up, still holding the ring between his fingers. "Yes, it's been a lot to absorb, but I'm not so emotionally fragile that I don't realize what I'm doing, what I'm asking."

"I know you think you're ready."

"Trust me, I've never been more ready. If I don't know what I want by now, I'll never know. I'm forty-years-old, Ida Mae. Old enough to realize I don't want to regret what could have been. I'm not asking you to marry me out of guilt. I'm asking you to be my wife because I love you. I'm asking because I hate being without you. I miss you when we're apart. Being with you at the diner isn't enough anymore. I want us to go home together. Wake up together. Brush our teeth together. Live this adventure we know as *life* together."

Couldn't she see that he loved her? His rationale

wasn't so skewed that it affected his judgment regarding a wife. He leaned down and grazed her lips with his. The kiss started slow and sweet. Then, tiptoeing near silent boundaries, he took her in his arms and conveyed how much he loved her. Finally, he pulled back and refrained from kissing her once more. "That's my thought on the matter. If you feel we should table the proposal, we will."

Ida Mae's cheeks bloomed with color. "You expressed your thoughts very well."

"And? Or is it but?"

"Neither. I'm saying give it a while. Then ask me again."

"Hmm. How long is 'a while'?"

"I'll leave that to your discretion. You'll know when it feels right, and I'll know when to give you my answer."

Way to keep him guessing. Well, no one could say that Ida Mae didn't add zest to life. And what a beautiful, zesty life it was. He wouldn't take her deliberation on the matter as a *no* then. He'd take it under advisement and ask when she least expected it. Maybe soon. Maybe not so soon. He'd work on the wow factor too. She liked the bear and roses, but why stop there? What he had in mind would top those, hands-down.

The Come and Get It reopened on Monday, three days before Thanksgiving. Because Ida Mae planned to close the diner for the holiday and the Friday after, they'd have another break soon. She'd planned it that way.

Patrons teased her about Cupid calling on her and Chuck. Funny, folks had paired them together for years, but now since they openly displayed their affection, the banter went full tilt. Today was no exception. Ida Mae played along, and neither confirmed or denied when Dander Evans and Zeke Ledbetter asked if they should buy tuxes for a wedding.

"Well, boys, if you plan to wear penguin suits to a wedding in this town, you best ditch that chocolate pie you're having because it's fully loaded. There are enough calories to guarantee you won't fit in anything for a month, including the church doors."

"Ooh. Burn!" Horace Sapp sauntered in and heard their exchange. "She gave it to you good, fellas."

The men laughed and slapped each other's backs, immersing themselves in town chatter and second helpings of pie. Women diners stared at the men and dismissed them with a shake of their heads. While the guys teased in good fun, the ladies in the crowd genuinely wanted to help. If nuptials were on the horizon for one of Ruby's own, it usually turned into a full-scale event. Ann Marshall offered to make the cake, and Charla Packard said that her bakery, Pennies from Heaven, would supply cookies and that she'd make them in the likeness of Betsy, the diner's infamous cowbell. Widower Delia Scroggins and her sister Dorothy would decorate the church.

"We have candelabras and those white arches from Charla and Sam's wedding, and Dorothy's still a whiz at floral displays, aren't you, sister?"

"I certainly am. I'm on the mend since last year's gall bladder surgery and complications. I'll be glad to help. Oh, and if you like, Delia and I can provide the music too. Can't go wrong with "I Love You Truly.""

"You gals have my vote. If there's a wedding, feel free to coordinate." Ida Mae gave them the A-Ok sign.

Traffic in the diner continued to pick up, as was common before a holiday. All support staff reported in and worked extra hours until January, and no one complained. Ava flew around the diner, from customer to customer, taking orders, delivering food, and refilling waters and coffees. She was one of the best temps Ida Mae had, and she'd be sad to see her go in May when she graduated college. Ava's parents said she wanted to work in brand development and social media, which she'd be great at. With her engaging personality, Ava wouldn't want for job offers. An advertising or marketing firm would snap up the girl in no time.

Today, as Ida Mae surveyed the crowd, she watched with interest as Miss Melinda Brewer bebopped in and grabbed a spot at the far end of the counter. As activity director for Sunset Meadows, the young woman had boundless energy and moved at a frenetic pace. Her bubbly personality and kindness endeared her to everyone. Too bad she and The Meadows new social services director clashed. Matt Enders seemed like a good guy, but for some reason when those two interacted, fireworks flew, and not necessarily the Fourth of July kind.

When Matt ambled in and seated himself one stool down from Melinda, he tipped his head toward her, and she in turn, responded with an eyeroll. *Ahh.* A love connection. Ida Mae pegged it. She had a knack. Would Cupid's arrow hit its mark? If Matt's kooky grin were any indication, it appeared it already had.

More patrons came and went. Some ordered meals to go. The usuals stayed and visited. Such were the daily goings-on at the Come and Get It. Lives intertwined and paths intersected. There were the regulars one could set a clock by. There were the occasional patrons who stopped in for a meal and good company. Then there were the visitors who passed through town and sometimes returned. Each day brought something different, and Ida Mae liked that.

Later as closing time approached, she circled the diner and delivered tickets, to-go drinks, and good-nights as she normally did. Chuck and Salty and the rest of the crew put things to order in back, and when the last customer paid at the register, Ava flipped the sign on the door to "Closed" and fiddled with the blinds. The way she tossed her blonde ponytail aside as she tried to adjust one of the slats reminded Ida Mae of her own youth. As always, something about the girl's mannerisms tickled her. Not prone to ill talk or impatience, Ava pinched the slat and tugged.

"Come on. Work with me here, you stubborn bugger." She laughed and continued finagling with the slat. "Quit trying to be difficult. You're a piece of plastic. I'm a college graduate. Well, almost."

Ida Mae didn't know what was funnier—Ava trying to cajole a window blind slat or her fully appreciating the humor of the situation.

"Need some help?"

The girl swung around in a fit of giggles. "Oh, Miss Ida Mae. I thought you went to the office. How long have you...um...been standing there?"

"Long enough."

They both dissolved in laughter as Ida Mae attempted to draw the blinds and release them again. It almost worked. "Hon, you hold the slat and keep it straight as I pull the cord."

"Got it." Ava wrapped her fingers around the slat. It continued to hang, and she used her other hand to jiggle it.

"You aren't kidding. This is a cranky devil." They worked in tandem, until finally, the slat came free. "Gracious sakes. Guess that's a sign I need to replace these old things."

"Yeah, but we did it! We are women. Hear us roar!" Ava fist-pumped the air. A red, splotchy area on the young woman's left hand winked under the fluorescent lights.

In that instant, time stopped.

When Chuck got the call, he let it go to voicemail because he was still wiping down the grill. Who did he know in New York anyway? Probably a telemarketer. Maybe a scammer. This time of year, they seemed to crawl out of the woodwork. Then again, could it be? *Nah.* He wouldn't hear anything this soon from a literary agent. He'd heard they took the entire month off from November through December. Still, he hurried through his nighttime routine and went to the office to access the message in private.

The blood rushed to Ida Mae's ears. She hung on to a booth for support. "Did you burn yourself?"

"No."

"It's a birthmark?"

Ava's eyes clouded, then cleared, as if suddenly understanding. "You know…about…the birthmark?"

"A lot of people have birthmarks. It's nothing to be

self-conscious about." Her reaction must have frightened the girl. How could she even explain? "I knew someone…who had a birthmark similar to yours."

"I know."

"How? How do you know that?"

Ava blinked. Slowly, her smile returned. "I'm that someone."

What was she saying? Ida Mae couldn't focus. She heard the girl's words, but she couldn't wrap her mind around them. Instead of twenty-one-year-old Ava Kruse, she saw another child's face. A tiny, beautiful infant with a perfect, upturned nose, a sweet mouth, and crystal blue eyes with flecks of gold. A head covered in soft down. A hand—the baby's left—with a strawberry birthmark that nearly covered it.

"The birthmark doesn't bother me, but when I started working here, I used makeup to cover it. For obvious reasons. Today I didn't use as much, and between the hand sanitizer and soap, the makeup all washed off." Ava touched Ida Mae's arm. "The doctors said the birthmark would eventually fade, but it never did. Then they suggested laser surgery, but Mama and Daddy said it was up to me, and I decided not to do it. I wanted to leave it as is. I know it probably sounds weird, but I felt like it connected me to…you."

"What are you saying?" The room spun. Her knees shook. Ava Kruse was her child? *Her baby?*

Ava gently guided her into the booth and sat down across from her. "As soon as Mama and Daddy gave me their blessing, I searched all the available records and they led me here. Since you'd signed all the documents, it wasn't hard. Then I got an apartment in Sapphire and enrolled in college. At first, my parents didn't want me to move so far away, but I'm pretty mature for my age. They drive down to see me often, and I go back home when I can." The girl paused and rested her hands on the table. "I had this plan. If my birth mom was a terrible person, I'd walk away and never look back. I applied for part-time work at the diner to be near you—the mom who gave me life. I wanted to get to know you better. I envisioned this perfect scenario in my head of how I was going to tell you. I figured if you'd signed all the forms, you must have hoped to, one day, meet me too. By the way, now I know you're an awesome person and a selfless human being."

Oh, Lord, Lord. Was it really true? Tears welled in Ida Mae's eyes. How could she not have guessed? She'd hired Ava months ago. She'd even met the Kruses, her parents. When they were in town, they often came into the diner. Sometimes, they'd have dinner and wait for Ava until her shift ended. And all this while, Ida Mae had been clueless.

"Your parents know too?" *Your parents.* The word rolled around on her tongue, gathering steam, and tugging her heart. Yet, that's who they were, and gratitude for the couple who'd adopted her child and loved her as their own, settled deep in Ida Mae's bones.

"Yes." Ava nodded. "Before my parents gave me their blessing to move to the area, they did their own research. A *massive* amount of research. They could write a book on who's who in Ruby, Missouri. They found out that everyone in this town adores you. And so do I."

Ida Mae couldn't stop the onslaught of tears even if she'd wanted to. The words she'd uttered like a broken record marched across her memory. *Help me believe.* This prayer, along with so many others, God answered, not by merely answering, but by knocking it completely out of the park. When she thought she knew best, He blew her away by doing one bigger and better.

"This isn't how I pictured our reunion." Ava's voice grew soft.

Oh no. She'd disappointed her. She couldn't bear it.

The girl started to cry. "The real thing is so much better."

They slipped from their respective booths and fell together, mother and child, embracing for the very first time in twenty-one-years. Before, when she'd pondered a moment such as this, Ida Mae manufactured the perfect things she'd say if her child ever found her. All those perfect words, however, evaporated, and she could only think of the three that mattered. "I love you."

"I love you too, Miss Ida Mae." Ava hooked her arms around Ida Mae and squeeze hard. "I'm so happy you're happy."

"Oh, honey. This calls for a five-dollar word. The word's *ecstatic*. I'm plum ecstatic." She returned the young woman's hug, drinking in the feel of her child in her arms. "Add to that another word. One that's priceless. *Blessed.*"

"Ladies?" Chuck cleared his throat. "Everything okay out here? The crew and I heard what sounded like some waterworks."

Ida Mae glanced toward the swinging doors where Chuck stood, grinning. She laughed and cried at the same time. "You'll never guess how okay everything is."

"Try me."

As Ida Mae explained, Chuck nearly dropped the pan of leftover lasagna. Ava, Ida Mae's daughter? His ears must be plugged. He couldn't have heard her right. But as he studied the two women, his breath caught. Hadn't there always been something familiar about the girl? Something reminiscent of Ida Mae? He hadn't had any inkling it could be her daughter, but the revelation thrilled him. What would Emory and Selma think? No doubt, there'd be tears all over again. But now for a different reason. It wasn't every day folks suddenly became grandparents.

"Aw, sweetheart." Chuck slid the pan on the nearby countertop and looped his arms around Ida Mae. "God knocked it out of the park, didn't He?"

"He sure did."

Ava laughed and flung her arms around them. "I *love* love!"

"Will seeing Ava at the diner every day be hard for you?" Ida Mae asked him a few days later as they ventured out for a drive. "Because she'll continue working there until she graduates next spring."

"Of course not. When I see Ava, I see you. I don't see poor choices or bad decisions. I see her as the beautiful blessing God restored to you."

"Did anyone ever tell you how eloquent you are?" Ida Mae ran her fingertips over his jawline.

"Well, folks have told me a lot of things. Probably called me some things too, but I don't believe that's one of them." He circled her palm with his and drove onward.

A late November snow fell, already coating the hills and valleys. Joy, bold and consuming, nipped their coattails.

Chuck guided the vehicle to the special spot he had in mind and cut off the ignition. "Wait here." He had to get this right. He stepped out and came around to the passenger side and opened the door. Offering her his hand, she clasped it and followed alongside him to the incline overlooking Ruby. "Magnificent, isn't it? I wanted you to see town from this vantage point, all covered in snow. The last time I brought you here, it was a kaleidoscope of color. Today, pristine white. Each season's different. Some are marked with trial and error, while others burst with promise and new possibilities."

"Yes. Sometimes, we have to endure hundreds of snows to arrive at our spring."

"True."

They stood for several minutes overlooking the community that had known all seasons. Heartache balanced with hope. Hardship weighted with mercy. Sometimes, God revealed his love in ways Chuck dared not dream. Like Scripture said, His ways weren't our ways. His ways were higher than our ways. God cleared dead ends to make way for new beginnings.

Chuck released Ida Mae's hand and retrieved the box from his coat pocket. He kneeled and tried to say the words he'd rehearsed, but they wouldn't come. He could only speak from his heart. "I want to experience every season with you, Ida Mae, for the rest of our lives. Right here on top of this hill, in the home behind us, overlooking the town where it all began."

"The rest...of our lives... In the home behind us?" Ida Mae squealed. "What do you mean 'in the home behind us'?"

"I've made an offer on Horace's grandparents' place. I'm hoping you still feel the same way about it...and me."

"I do. You know I do. I wanted you to be sure."

He drew out the ring and slipped it on her left hand, fourth finger. "I didn't bring a bear or roses this time. Will a house and twenty acres seal the deal?"

Ida Mae threw her arms around him and laughed. "Gosh, I don't know. Is that all?"

"Well, it could be more. Don't know yet. There's a little matter of a cookbook I've penned. I have a literary agent interested."

"You're writing again? That's wonderful!"

"Life could get crazy."

"We'll work through it. Didn't we just do that?"

Their laughter echoed on the November wind.

Epilogue

She imagined it would be a quiet, simple affair, but weddings in Ruby were rarely quiet or simple. As expected, the Hoscutt-Farrow nuptials turned into a full-scale, four-alarm, summer event.

In keeping with Ida Mae's blush pink and cornflower blue themed wedding, Grace Fellowship's decorating committee pulled out all stops. From the coordinating pink and blue balloons that festooned the church property to the pretty floral sprays, pew embellishments, and candles that adorned the sanctuary to the fittingly bedecked fellowship hall, clearly, this day shouted "celebration."

"I don't know. Do you think it's too much?" Ida Mae turned from the floor-length mirror and faced Sugar. Yards of tulle and lace billowed around her legs, forming a sea of blue fabric. She'd always dreamed of a gown like this—magnificent, yet non-traditional, with a vintage flair. The sheer blue gloves with tiny pink ribbons were a last-minute decision, and the rhinestone and pearl tiara, a complete splurge but fitting, according to the very nice salesclerk. "Is this dress too over-the-top?"

Sugar shook her finger. "Do you think Cinderella asked such a question?"

"But I'm not a princess."

"Not a princess? Doll, every woman's a princess on her wedding day." Her friend adjusted the blusher veil over her face. "You're stunning. Trust me, your Prince Charming and all your friends will think so too."

Sugar didn't lie. As Ida Mae took the arm of her father and strode down the aisle, collective breaths caught, and eyes misted. All stood and joined in a holy moment of solidarity. Years fell away as Ida Mae stepped toward a new future with the man she'd loved since her youth.

Outside, July's heat baked the Ozarks in typical mid-summer fashion, and humidity hung low over the hills. Indoors, no one seemed to notice. Thanks to Sy Farrow's generous monetary donation, the church's newly installed air-conditioning units worked more efficiently than the ancient system of twenty years ago, and wedding guests appreciated the luxury.

As she approached her groom, Ida Mae smiled at those in attendance. Many she'd known all her life. Some, like Shep and Juanita Kruse, she'd bonded with more recently, yet the relationship cemented itself within her heart as if she'd known them forever, because in a way, she had.

When Ida Mae glanced their way, the Kruses beamed. Shep gave her a thumbs-up sign, and Juanita blew her a kiss. The child they shared in common since birth, nodded, and returned Ida Mae's smile. *I love you.* Ava mouthed the words as Ida Mae glided closer, and Ida Mae reached out to squeeze her daughter's hand. In that moment, Ava's parents reached out too, and covered the pair's hands with their own. Music continued to play as the foursome exchanged private whispers.

"You'll always be family to us." Juanita leaned forward and pressed her cheek to Ida Mae's. "From my mama-heart to yours, thank you for our Ava."

"Thank you for loving her," Ida Mae replied, trying desperately to hold any tears in check. "I'm so grateful God chose you as her parents."

There was no judgment or condemnation from those in the congregation—only the warmest regard and love.

God had answered prayers and revealed Himself in ways Ida Mae couldn't have planned, dreamed, or expected. The past eight months earmarked reunions, first meetings, healing, and hope. None of it easy. All of it, good.

At the altar stood Ida Mae's future husband. Chuck waited, smiling and handsome in his simple black suit. He trained his gaze on Ida Mae and swallowed, as if checking his emotions. Was he about to cry? *Oh, mercy.* If he started that, heaven help her. She couldn't possibly contain herself then, and there was no way Grandma Ida's vintage-era hanky would stand up to more than a few tears, let alone a full dousing.

Ida Mae inhaled. Exhaled. She could do this. Tears, albeit happy ones, might cause a flood. Unless she wanted her mascara to smear, weeping best wait. With a firm grip on her father's arm, her resolve strengthened. She winked at Chuck, and the simple, unspoken acknowledgment made him smile.

The pianist's fingers stilled over the piano and Pastor Bill cleared his throat. "Who giveth this woman to be wed?"

They'd practiced this moment last night during rehearsal. It seemed easy at the time. "Her mother and I." Her father's voice plucked at her heartstrings. He leaned forward and kissed her cheek and whispered, "Be happy, Daughter. Your ol' dad loves you."

Hold it together, gal. Focus on this moment. On answered prayers and new beginnings. "I love you, too, Dad. Always."

Dad then placed her hand in Chuck's. "You're getting a jewel, son."

"Yes, sir. I know."

They exchanged wedding vows in the company of friends and family—cheerleaders of the past and present. Together, Chuck and Ida Mae lit the unity candle as Zeke Ledbetter, Grace Fellowship's most notable tenor, stepped forward to sing "Unchained Melody." When Pastor Bill pronounced them "man and wife," folks rose from their seats and cheered.

Above the din, Pastor Bill added one last thing. "Chuck, you may kiss your bride."

"Don't mind if I do."

In a grand production, Chuck lifted Ida Mae's veil, swept her in his arms, and tipped her backward, kissing her flush on the mouth. Several ladies squealed. A few fanned themselves. Some of the men fist-pumped the air. Not the typical wedding decorum, but appropriate, everything considered. Love birds together, at last.

"Been a long time comin'!" Horace Sapp called before Hattie jabbed his side.

Instead of the traditional postlude, the wedding ceremony culminated with the church choir singing "There's a Sweet, Sweet Spirit in This Place."

Arm in arm, they made their way down the aisle. Before they exited the sanctuary, a thought struck Ida Mae. "I'll give it less than a year."

Chuck laughed. "Care to enlighten me, Mrs. Farrow? I'm not following."

"Those two." She gazed at the couple who barely regarded each other without so much as a blink. It hardly seemed fair that she should peg it before they even knew.

"Enders and Miss Melinda? Less than a year for what?"

"Until Matthew proposes."

Author Note

Beloved friend, in many ways *His Love Revealed* tested my mettle. Ida Mae's valleys and mountaintops mirrored my own as I wrote this story during a time of intense heartache and struggle. My precious daddy—my biggest cheerleader—continued his downward spiral into the lonely abyss we know as Alzheimer's Disease, and the journey challenged and changed me.

Though my characters' trek through the figurative wilderness differs from my own, Ida Mae's and Chuck's belief in better things ahead symbolizes the hope and healing that's possible when we place our faith and trust in Christ. This truth is what makes tough circumstances bearable. The here and now is temporary, but eternity with Him is forever.

Perhaps, your life has taken an unplanned detour. Maybe you've faced hurt, made a poor choice, or suffered loss. Maybe you've experienced a health crisis, an estrangement, or a bitter setback. Please know you're not alone. Hardships, when shared with those who've trudged a similar path, encourage us to press forward in victory. We draw strength in each other as we overcome life's delays and diversions. When we seek higher ground together, it immobilizes fear and bolsters our resolve.

Today, like Ida Mae and Chuck, may you cling to those who uplift and inspire. May you sense our Heavenly Father's presence as He walks beside you in your travels. May you laugh. May you smile. May you know *you are loved*.

God bless you.

And he said, "The things which are impossible with men are possible with God." Luke 18:27 (KJV)

If you enjoyed ***His Love Revealed***, would you please consider posting a review on Amazon and additional major book sites? Readers' reviews help spread the news about an author's books and significantly help authors increase book sales. Also, please share your thoughts with family and friends, as this generates buzz about my novels. Please encourage your local library to add ***Her Hope Discovered*** and ***His Love Revealed*** to their bookshelves. Consider joining my **Fabulous Readers'** group on Facebook where we share grins, giggles, and encouragement, and where we have in-depth discussions about my upcoming books. You can also find me at my online home **authorcynthiaherron.com**, **Instagram**, **Twitter, and Pinterest**. Speaking of Pinterest, check out ***His Love Revealed***, one of my newest Pinterest boards, and immerse yourself in fictional Ruby, Missouri. Come feel the love!

About the Author:

As an avid encourager and lover of the underdog, Cynthia writes Heartfelt, Homespun Fiction from the beautiful Ozark Mountains.

"Cindy" has a degree in psychology and a background in social work. She is a member of ACFW, ACFW MozArks, and RWA. She is a 2020 Selah Award Double-Finalist, a 2017 ACFW Genesis Finalist, a 2016 ACFW Genesis Double-Finalist, and a 2015 ACFW First Impressions Winner. Her work is represented by Sarah Freese @ WordServe Literary.

Besides writing, Cindy has a fondness for gingerbread men, miniature teapots, and all things apple. She also adores a great cup of coffee and she never met a sticky note she didn't like.

Cindy loves to connect with friends at the following places:

Her online home: authorcynthiaherron.com
Twitter: twitter.com/C_Herronauthor
Facebook: www.facebook.com/AuthorCynthiaHerron
Facebook Readers' Group:
www.facebook.com/groups/195462117765130
Instagram: www.instagram.com/authorcynthiaherron
Pinterest: www.pinterest.com/cynthia_herron

Sign up for her monthly e-NEWSLETTER at
authorcynthiaherron.com

Welcome to the family!

Again, if you enjoyed ***His Love Revealed***, please take a minute or two and post a review. A book review needn't be a long, drawn-out missive. Without revealing spoilers, simply sharing a few thoughts why you enjoyed the book and why you'd recommend it to others is such a blessing to authors *and* readers. Thank you so much for your support!

Book Club Questions

1. When our story opens, we find Ida Mae considering a menu overhaul at the Come and Get It. Have you ever been reluctant to shift gears and go in a new direction, but you did so anyway? What was the deciding factor? How did the change make you feel?

2. As Chuck slides into the booth across from Ida Mae, it's apparent there's some history between them. Do you think when friends share a history, it's easier or harder to share what's on their hearts? Why?

3. What do you like best about friends-to-more stories? Have you experienced this dynamic in a personal relationship? In your opinion, are there more or fewer obstacles for couples who've first been friends?

4. As we dive deeper into the story, it's apparent that Ida Mae carries a decades-old secret that she believes will be a detriment if it's revealed. Talk about a time in your life that involved secrecy and how it affected your decisions. Did keeping the secret come with a cost?

5. Has a friend ever shared a secret with you that called for discretion? Was it something that affected your feelings for your friend? How did keeping this confidence make you feel? Did you counsel your friend to share her secret? Why/Why not?

6. Speaking of friends, what qualities do you appreciate most in a friend? Are there any characteristics that turn you off? Other than your spouse, what's the length of your longest friendship? How are you different? Similar?

7. When Chuck and Ida Mae begin to explore their feelings for one another, what are some things that prevent their relationship from moving forward? Consider a relationship in your life. How did God reveal His will? Can you think of examples from your own life where God's will was immediately apparent? What about examples where there wasn't a swift answer?

8. During the course of the story, an important figure from Chuck's past re-enters his life. How did this reunion make you feel? Why are reunions sometimes bittersweet? Have you experienced a reunion as a result of an estrangement? How did it go? Was reunification possible? If so, what steps did you take to reopen the line of communication?

9. In what scene do you sense the softening of Chuck's heart for Ida Mae? What's your favorite interaction between the two? What ups the ante in their relationship? Consider a time, after a season of trial and testing, when your heart softened toward a loved one. How did you reach a mutual understanding? What finally tipped the scale with regard to moving forward? What positive things have come from your decision?

10. After Ida Mae's secret is revealed, how does God reveal His love for Ida Mae? For Chuck? Have you faced a season of heartache only to realize that God allowed this season for a reason? In what ways did you grow during this time? What do you like best about *His Love Revealed*?

Now, a Sneak Peek at Book Three
Coming January 1, 2022

Her Faith Restored

Chapter One

Wrapped in Autumn's gold curtain and nestled deep within the Ozark foothills, Ruby, Missouri shone like a beacon. A close-knit community reminiscent of old ways while cognizant of new seasons, the little town glimmered in the lazy morning sunshine. The good Lord must smile on days such as this—days His timing was impeccable and His plan, perfect...even if, in our humanity, we sometimes wondered.

Why today of all days? Hadn't they maintained civility up to this point?

"He didn't mean it, Mel."

"Yes, he did." Melinda Brewer paced to the window of her office and back again. She met her friend's wide-eyed gaze with equal emotion. "Matthew Enders meant every measured word. In fact, he's been full of words since he came here six months ago."

To his credit, Enders' vocabulary rivaled Webster's. His favorite word, though, was a simple one. *Change.* When Mel considered the many changes that the new social worker had implemented at Sunset Meadows, it set her teeth on edge. She might have less clout than Enders, but she did have seniority. And as the facility's activity director she wasn't about to let him run roughshod over her plans and programs.

"If he thinks I'm going to step aside and watch him undermine everything I've accomplished in the past five years, then I have news for him. But I'll break it to him in a Christian kind of way, of course."

"Shh. He'll hear you." Her friend Sarah Dawson closed the door.

"And another thing—for him to call me 'childish' showed a complete lack of professionalism. I know the inner workings of this place like the back of my hand. That newbie doesn't know a service plan from a coffee cup."

"I believe Matt referred to it as *infantile*."

"What? Oh. Semantics." Mel waved her hand. "For him to say something like that within earshot of the residents and my fellow co-workers was rude and ego-driven."

Sarah studied her for a second and smiled. "What is it that's really bothering you, Mel?"

Hmm. Where to begin? Mel plopped down at her desk and kicked off her heels. It didn't take long to come up with a list. "Everything about the man bothers me. His new ideas when there's nothing wrong with my old ones. His morale boosters. The new paint color he suggested for the activity room. The way he smirks when he thinks he's right. His choice of clothing. The truck he drives. That silly little gap between his two front teeth. The fact he could use a haircut. Should I continue?"

"No, not really. I get the picture." Sarah sat down in

the chair across from her desk and leaned forward. "But let me say—not as The Meadows' office manager, but as friend to friend—from what I've observed, Matt Enders seems to be a man of integrity. He really wants to help people, and most of the changes he's made have been good ones with the residents' best interests in mind. He's kind, compassionate, and easygoing. Everyone seems to like him except—"

"Me." Mel sighed. "I don't know, Sarah. I guess our personalities clash."

Her friend thought for a minute and nodded. "Could be. But you know, I think your personalities are similar. You're both go-getters, though perhaps, you're a tad more...um...spirited."

Yes, that's what her brothers said. In fact, her tenacity was what landed her the job here. She wasn't one to sit on the fence. She got things done.

"And that's always served me well. And Sunset Meadows too, of course."

"Look, Matt Enders isn't here to upset the apple cart. He's here for the same reasons you are." Sarah hesitated. "You guys may have your differences, but at the end of the day, you share similar goals. You shouldn't let a little diversity sideline your working relationship."

Mel laughed without mirth. "For heaven's sake, Sarah, in the six months Matt Enders has been here, our 'working relationship' has been strained at best."

Sarah cocked her head. "Why do you think that is?"

"Beats me." Enders grated on her nerves. She couldn't explain why.

"Well...could it be something you haven't considered?"

"Like what?"

"Like, maybe, you two have a thing for each other?"

Mel shot up from her chair and started to pace again. "You must be joking, Sarah."

"No. I'm not. When Andy and I first met, we couldn't stand each other. Remember?"

"But you two have been married four years!"

"Exactly. God's ways are wondrous to behold."

The knock at Mel's office door halted that train of thought. Grateful for the interruption, she ran a hand through her shoulder length auburn waves and slipped back into her heels. "I guess that's our cue to continue this later."

"I can't wait." Sarah rose to go. When she opened the door, she gasped. "Oh! Hello, Matt."

"Sarah." Then he directed his gaze toward Mel. "I'm sorry, Miss Brewer. I didn't realize you were in a meeting."

"Yes. Well, we're done now. Is there something you need?"

Matt Enders stepped aside to permit Sarah's graceful exit. "You could say that. Do you have a minute?"

As usual, his attire was the same—polo shirt and blue jeans—in an obvious effort to blend in around here. Casual and not too preppy. About right for the small, picturesque town of Ruby, Missouri and almost appropriate for his work place of the past several months.

His jet-black hair was neatly combed, though a little shaggy around the ears. The slight gap between his bright, white teeth wasn't as noticeable, probably due to recent orthodontic treatments. Mel hadn't meant to eavesdrop when Matt mentioned it to one of The Meadows' residents the other day…

She almost cringed when she recalled her harsh assessment of the man. Since when had she started to judge people by their appearance? It certainly wasn't a Christian thing to do, nor was it something she was proud of. It was a wonder Sarah hadn't taken her to task over it earlier. They might not agree on various work-related issues, but it was wrong to criticize Matt's physical characteristics. If he rated *her* on a personal beauty scale, he might notice she was about ten pounds overweight and had one too many freckles.

"Come in." Mel gestured toward her inner sanctum.

"Thanks. Mind if I shut the door?"

Why? What earth-shattering piece of news merited a closed door? Was there another change he wanted to discuss? She forced her features to remain neutral.

"Look, Miss Brewer—Melinda—I won't bite."

Said the spider to the fly.

"Be my guest." Mel brushed invisible lint from her navy slacks and slipped behind her desk as Matt closed the office door.

"Feel like you need a barrier, huh?"

"Careful, Mr. Enders. You're on my turf now."

Matt Enders sighed. Not necessarily a soft, polite, let's-work-this-out kind of sigh. No, it was more of an aggravated expulsion of air forced from one's lungs when he was at his wit's end. Matt's dark brown eyes fixated on Mel's blue ones. She didn't invite him to have a seat. Hopefully, this wouldn't take long.

"It's not like me to lose my temper, especially in a public setting. I apologize if I embarrassed you—hurt your feelings—earlier."

Mel's resolve weakened, but she wasn't about to make this easy for him. Feigning nonchalance, she shuffled papers on her desk. "Oh, Mr. Enders, you give yourself too much credit. It'll take more than a grown man pitching a temper tantrum to unnerve me."

Matt stepped closer. "*Who* pitched a temper tantrum? You've sulked ever since staff meeting this morning when I mentioned the idea of coordinating some of your weekly activities with mine."

He leaned forward, placing his palms on her desk. "Look, seventy-nine of the eighty resident surveys that were turned in yesterday indicated a desire for change—for group therapy to go hand in hand with other interests. Board games, exercise, and social outings are nice, but so is discussing life and the common threads that go with the aging process." His voice softened. "If we synchronize our work, we could enhance an already great thing Sunset Meadows has going. Wouldn't you agree that sometimes a team approach is more productive than a single-handed effort?"

"I guess it depends on how you define 'team approach'."

Matt gestured with his hand. "You know—you—me—working *together* rather than apart."

"Ahh, yes. Well, I suppose I should feel honored that you want *me* on your team. I mean, if you've got it all figured out after working here for a mere six months versus my five years then you definitely earned every bit of your degree."

His semi-attractive features registered surprise. "*Wow*. That's pretty harsh. Whatever got under your skin to make you so jaded?"

"Is there anything else, Mr. Enders? I need to leave on time today. I have a date." Mel dismissed his comment.

A muscle flinched in his cheek before his face turned to granite. "Poor guy. Give him my condolences."

With that he strode toward the door, opened it, and left Mel's office.

He grinned. To see pretty Melinda Brewer's mouth fall open and remain that way gave him great satisfaction. He'd rendered her speechless and he rather liked it.

I know, Lord. I shouldn't take pleasure in having the last word, but that woman drives me so—so—nuts! She always thinks she's right. It's either her way or the highway, and she views my ideas as opposition. She thinks I'm some sort of competition, for crying-out-loud!

Nothing could be further from the truth. He and Melinda were two separate department heads with very similar goals. How had this turned into a tug-of-war match?

Matt headed to his own office two doors down and attempted to quell his frustration with the pint-sized, freckle-faced package of TNT. For whatever reason, when his and Mel's paths crossed, there was always an instantaneous reaction. He didn't know why they couldn't agree. On anything.

With others, she seemed so sunny-dispositioned. In addition to scheduled activities, she mingled with the residents, joked with them and joined them for coffee. Mel took great pains to make sure that everyone who lived there was happy, comfortable, and as active as their health and age allowed. And she demonstrated compassion and sensitivity to everyone. Everyone *but* him.

Matt didn't get it. Since moving to Ruby last spring, most folks had bent over backward in welcoming him. The Brewer family even invited him to dinner one Sunday after church. Of course, Mel hadn't liked it.

He plucked at the sheaf of files stacked on his desk. He'd never forget that day. Jake and Billie Gail Brewer's gesture of kindness meant the world to him in the wake of a new move. They were the epitome of Christian hospitality. Their three sons, Gabe, Garrett, and Michael offered tips and pointers about life in Ruby—how *not* to wear dress shirts and ties if he wanted to fit in around here. How he should be the first customer in line on Saturday mornings at Pennies from Heaven if he wanted to sample delectable treats still warm from the oven. How *not* to leave leftovers on his plate down at the Come and Get It Diner, lest he offend the much-loved proprietress, Ida Mae Farrow—then, Ida Mae Hoscutt.

"And from now on, don't sit on the front pew at church," Gabe added. "Pastor Bill tends to spit when he gets wound up in the pulpit, and most likely, you'll be a good target. Sit about midway back and you'll be safe."

"Not from the Packards' kids though." Garrett clapped Matt on the back. "I suppose you may already know that since you bought Sam's place, but those little cuties will chit-chat you to death if you let 'em. Little Faith and Hope have really come out of their shells since Sam and Charla married. They have their new mama to thank for that."

"Yeah." Mike jumped in, grinning. "But keep in mind too, you don't want to plaster your rear end toward the back of the church either or else Erin Shaye will make cow eyes at you.”

Garrett Brewer jabbed his brother. “Mike, the only one Erin has eyes for is you, and you know it.”

Matt smiled, recalling the Brewer brothers’ pleasant exchange. Everyone around Billie Gail’s dinner table that Sunday afternoon had laughed and teased. Everyone but the youngest sibling and only sister. Melinda Brewer was reserved at best. In fact, she’d even gone home early under the guise of a headache.

“Oh, poor lamb.” Billie Gail Brewer hugged her daughter as she’d said good-bye. “You’ve been working too hard. All that painting and decorating at Doc Burnside’s old cottage is taking its toll, I think.”

“No, Mom. I’m fine. Everything’s almost done. I only have the fence row out back to clear—you know, all those crazy weeds and dormant vines—and Dad and the boys said they’d help me with that.”

“Well, indulge your mother, Sis.” Jake Brewer kissed his daughter’s forehead. “It’s Sunday. Go home and take an aspirin, kick back and relax. A little rest will do you good.”

Melinda’s ruse to get away was not lost on Matt. When her VW shot down the graveled drive, Garrett was the first to comment. “Mel sure was quiet. Must have been one booger of a headache.”

“Musta been.” Gabe grinned and turned toward Matt then. “Have you been giving our sister headaches?”

Matt immediately liked Mel’s brothers. “I certainly hope not.”

But now Matt knew. If he wasn’t sure then, he was sure now.

Yep. He could almost feel the invisible bull's eye on the center of his forehead. The one that screamed *giant migraine.*

For whatever reason, Mel Brewer disliked him. Be it her perception of his usurping her authority at Sunset Meadows or perhaps some other imaginary slight, the woman couldn't stand him. And it was really too bad, because despite the fire and ice treatment, he admired Mel's determination and commitment. She wanted the best for the residents and didn't want the new kid on the block messing with what her view of that was.

He supposed he ought to do the Christian thing and extend some brotherly love. *Hmm...*What to do?

"I've got it!" Matt snapped his fingers with the sudden revelation. After work today, he'd personally deliver a little present to her doorstep. It didn't matter whether she had a date or not. Mel should appreciate the interruption.

The absolute nerve of that man!

Mel slammed the front door to her abode so hard it almost rattled the living room window panes. Considering the amount of TLC she'd invested in this place over the past several months, it was something she would never do unless given good reason. And Matthew Enders was reason enough.

Tossing her keys on the coffee table, Mel shrugged out of her jacket and lobbed it at her comfy, new sofa. In an hour, Spencer Holms would be here, and she must shift gears. Matt Enders may have ruined her day, but he was not going to ruin her evening with Spencer.

Ahh. Spencer. Dependable, predictable, good ol'

Spencer. The twenty-nine-year-old science teacher she'd dated a couple of times in the past year. Mel fought the urge to yawn.

Attractive, well-mannered Spencer Holms had liked her for as long as she could remember. Like Mel, Spencer had grown up in Ruby and returned to the area after graduating college. He'd made no secret of his affection for Mel, and lately, he'd become bolder in his attempts to court her. He was a good-natured guy and eager to please. The only fly in the ointment was that Mel couldn't see herself moving past the platonic stage with a man she found so nice, yet *sooo* tedious.

Their dates were pleasant enough, though, and that was okay for now. Sharing the companionship of an attentive male at church socials and town functions was an added bonus. And besides, Mel had been frank with Spencer from the very beginning, so it wasn't like she was leading him on or anything. He was a friend. Nothing more.

"I'm not ready to pursue a full-time commitment, Spencer," she'd told him after their first three dates.

"That's all right, Mel." Honesty didn't dampen his resolve. "I'll grow on you. You'll see."

Like what? A wart?

Hadn't he realized how crazy-pitiful that sounded? She doubted it. He would have had to silence the fireworks first. The ones bouncing around in his brain every time they were together. It was an awkward situation and one that required discernment. Like with Matt—only for a different reason.

The man annoyed her. He reveled in his co-workers' kudos and pats on the back. It made Mel cringe every time she heard someone say, "Good to have you on board, Enders!" and "Way to go, Matt!" when he proposed yet another cutting-edge change.

How dare he swoop into town, enter her turf, and think he could suddenly shake things up at a place she'd worked *five years*!

Sunset Meadows was more than a senior citizen retirement complex. Like the small town of Ruby, the campus was a tight-knit community where residents were friends. It was also one of the most innovative senior housing facilities in the Ozarks, and its various programs had garnered multiple awards.

Sunset Meadows was unique. Its small-town appeal and intimate living concept made it special. Everyone— employees and residents alike—treated each other like family.

Mel poured her heart and soul into the place and wore many hats besides that of activity director, and she enjoyed it. At least she *had* until Matt came. Until Mister Fancy-Pants had decided to settle here and bring his fancy ideas with him.

She gave herself a mental shake and glanced around the tiny living room, her comfort zone. Far from elegant, her place held a certain cozy charm. All the furnishings were simple, yet tastefully done, with a nostalgic feel of yesteryear.

Built entirely of native stone, this historical nugget had captured Mel's heart as a child. On her walk to school each morning, she used to admire the quiet beauty that emanated from this cottage—Doc Burnside's home. One of its best features was the generous picture window where soft firelight glowed in the gloomier winter months and a Christmas tree twinkled during the holidays.

Mel dreamed the cottage would one day be hers, and when old Doc Burnside put the place up for sale, she prayed for God to open a financial door so she could purchase it.

"Tell you what, Miss Melinda," Doc drawled over coffee and gingersnaps. "We'll draw up an owner/buyer agreement. You come up with the initial down payment, and you just pay me what you can afford at the end of each month. How's that sound?"

Mel smiled, remembering.

"I...c...can't do that! That wouldn't be right. That's not fair to you, Doc."

"*Hmpf.* Fair-shmair. Let me decide what's fair, young lady. We'll make it all legal like." Doc clasped her hand and squeezed it. "In fact, I want you to have your mama and daddy take a look at the papers first. Heaven-to-Betsy, bring Jake and Billie Gail to our little closing party too. We'll all celebrate."

Sometimes, indeed, God's ways were not our ways. Before any papers were signed last year, old Doc Burnside died peacefully in his sleep one glorious, sun-dappled afternoon. Pastor Bill found him out back leaned against an old peach tree with an opened Bible sprawled across his lap and a clump of pink peonies still clutched within a cold, frail hand.

Mel mourned the loss of such a dear soul, but she was stunned at what came next. Doc Burnside, the beloved physician, with no family of his own and who'd been a fixture of Ruby forever, bequeathed Mel the cottage and the surrounding property, lock, stock, and barrel with no strings attached. At the reading of the will, Doc's attorney grinned and handed over the keys to the place. "Tend it and treasure it as he did over the years."

Doc Burnside defined the words *Christian love.* Such a sweet memory…

Mel snapped back to the present. *Help me demonstrate that charity toward Matt Enders, Father. I don't especially like the man, but I know he's one of your children too. Maybe we won't be friends, but help us to at least get along. And Father…thank you for all the blessings in my life…the ones I fail to remember to thank you for from time to time.*

Contemplating Christian love and blessings, Mel headed toward her bedroom humming.

She freshened up and changed into blue jeans and a pumpkin-colored sweater. Nothing fancy but perfect for a casual dinner and a movie. She hoped Spencer hadn't dressed up because she didn't want to give the man false hope. That wouldn't do at all.

Mel ran a brush through her shoulder-length hair and swiped a clear coat of lip gloss across her mouth. She was about to file a nail when three sound raps echoed from the living room. Why Doc Burnside never installed a doorbell in later years, she didn't know.

Typical. Spencer was early. His eagerness might appeal to some women, but she found his zeal trying. She didn't know why Spencer couldn't be on time just once. Oh, well. At least tardiness wasn't a problem.

Resigned, Mel sighed and went to receive her date. The front door, ancient and heavy, groaned as she opened it. *Yeah, that's the way I feel too.*

"I must say, your countenance seems sunnier than earlier today."

She'd never really noticed until now how good-looking Matt Enders was. With his dark, windblown waves, coffee-colored eyes, and that cocky full smile that played upon his well-defined profile, one might even think the guy was handsome.

Personally, she'd never found that sort of casual, rugged look appealing. Mel couldn't care less what her co-worker looked like. Though she had to admit, until this very moment his attractiveness hadn't fully registered.

"Mr. Enders?"

He grinned and held out a small orange gift bag.

"I don't understand."

"Open it. I think it's something you can use."

"Really, Mr. Enders—"

"*Matt*, please. Formalities are always so boring, don't you think?"

Was he serious? He seemed to be.

"I guess we have butted heads long enough to be on a first name basis." Mel stepped aside. "Come in."

Matt strolled past, his arm inadvertently brushing hers in the process. "Beautiful. This place, I mean. It suits you."

The male, woodsy scent of him filled the room and played upon her nostrils. He was too close. *Much* too close. She stepped back in an effort to reclaim her personal space. "Yes, I agree. When I was a little girl, I always dreamed that one day I'd live here."

"And your dream came true."

Mel nodded. "An answered prayer."

"That's the neat thing about God and dreams. He grants our hearts' desires when we least expect them."

Her face warmed. Didn't he find this awkward? They'd been at odds for months. What did he expect her to say? "Thanks for the gift, Matt. Now, if you'll excuse me, I really must—"

He held up a hand. "I know. Get ready for your date. But just open it, Mel. You don't even know what it is yet."

Well, it wasn't ticking, so it couldn't be something that would cause her bodily harm. Plus, the sooner she opened it, the sooner he'd leave. Okay. She'd bite. And then she'd usher him out quicker than he could blink and lock the door behind him.

With a perfunctory nod, Mel reached inside the gift bag until her fingers touched something small, round, and plastic. A bottle of some sort? She clutched the object within her palm and yanked it out. *Aspirin?*

"For the big headache I am to you."

She regretted the giggle the moment it flew past her lips. Professionals didn't giggle. Still, she couldn't help it. "I don't think I've ever received a more thoughtful present."

"I suspected you'd feel that way." Matt laughed too. "You could take two now and save the rest for our next staff meeting. Would you like me to get you a glass of water?"

"I'll pass on the water for now. But I appreciate your kindness."

Matt extended a hand. "Friends?"

Did he really expect them to shake on it? Mel stared at his outstretched palm. Her pulse galloped and her stomach churned. She wasn't raised to be unforgiving. It was un-Christian.

"Friends." The gallop became a race. When their hands connected, the warmth of his touch surprised her. His grip was tender, yet firm. They shook, pumping the handshake twice for good measure, their palms remaining linked longer than necessary.

"Excuse me. Am I interrupting?"

They directed their attention to the one who stood in the doorway. *Spencer Holms.*

For once, his timing was perfect. Maybe his early arrival would send the message *I'm not ready to pursue a full-time commitment* hadn't.